...ie is married and has

Further praise for *The Contract*:

'*The Contract* has such a fine sense of time and place it's hard to believe JM Gulvin didn't grow up in this day and age ... [Will] very much appeal to fans of James Lee Burke's Dave Robicheaux books ... The second in what I hope will be a very long and successful series.' *Crime Worm*

'A compelling read ... original and engaging.' *Never Imitate*

'John Quarrie is a great lead character – cool under pressure, a sharp shooter ... *The Contract* is written with perfect pacing and tone for the Deep South setting and the author has perfectly captured that feeling of 1960s life ... a wonderful tale with conspiracy, murder and corruption.' *Grab This Book*

'The landscape is deeply intertwined with the action and the setting is evoked with style and bullseye precision.' *Book Trail*

'A masterful thriller ... confident, complex, exquisitely written and expertly researched. The culture, the time, the people, and the history are impeccably drawn, and the superb plot gathers steam, driven by a nail-biting tension, to an explosive conclusion ...

'John Q is a brilliant construct, oozing masculinity and toughness in a highly self-contained way, and like the heroes of the American Western tradition, imbued with a rigid core of morality and decency that permeates his dealing with those that have sinned and are sinned against.' *Raven Crime Reads*

'I would recommend this slice of "Americana" to any reader of modern crime fiction … Combines elements of a conspiracy thriller with a pinch of police procedural … A quality thriller.' *Nudge*

'A noir thriller with some terrific descriptive prose that brings the vagaries of that time to vivid life … Addictive.' *Liz Loves Books*

'Ambitious … the characters are finely drawn, as is the underlying racial and social tension that was undoubtedly a feature in the American South in the 1960s and is never far from the surface of the narrative, giving a compelling, disturbing relevance to the story … Gulvin hits bullseye on plot, characters and style. His writing is pared-down yet atmospheric, with echoes of Elmore Leonard and even Cormac McCarthy.' *Thriller Books Journal*

---

also by JM Gulvin

THE LONG COUNT

The Contract

A John Q Thriller

JM GULVIN

FABER & FABER

First published in 2017
by Faber & Faber Ltd
Bloomsbury House
74–77 Great Russell Street
London WC1B 3DA
This paperback edition first published in 2018

Typeset by Faber & Faber Ltd
Printed and bound by CPI Group (UK) Ltd, Croydon CR0 4YY

A CIP record for this book
is available from the British Library

ISBN 978-0-571-32382-1

FSC
www.fsc.org
MIX
Paper from
responsible sources
FSC® C020471

2 4 6 8 10 9 7 5 3 1

For my wife, Kim

In memory of Gary Hirstius

1956–2012

'Always have, always will'

One

A dry heat drifting on a northern breeze, Franklin drove into town from the east. Cold blue eyes and cropped blond hair, he wore an open-necked shirt and slacks. Halfway along Main Street he saw the Oldsmobile parked outside the Dairy-Ette.

Inside the diner, Scott Henderson perched on a stool with a cup of coffee before him; he toyed with a sugar spoon. Floppy hair and red in the cheek, his gaze seemed to shift from the other patrons to the middle-aged waitress in a candy stripe outfit as she worked the counter with a dampened cloth. Wiley was watching TV. Long greased hair, he wore a combat jacket with the collar high. The TV was loud enough to hear Muhammad Ali tell the interviewer he didn't care if they stripped him of his title, he wasn't going to Vietnam.

'You done?' Henderson said.

Wiley got to his feet. 'He is. Sonofabitch don't want to fight for his country then he won't be fighting at all.'

Franklin watched from his car as they climbed into the Super 88. Wiley driving, they followed an old farm pickup till it turned into the TexGas Station where fuel was twenty-one cents a gallon and they doubled on Texas Gold.

'You ever buy anything with them stamps?' Wiley indicated the weak-looking neon sign.

Henderson shook his head. 'My mom used to collect them, still does most probably; used to have us the catalog and all.'

They drove almost the length of Main Street then slowed as they came to Hemmings gun store. Pulling into a parking space two doors down Wiley shut off the engine and stared at the window where a lackluster display of hunting jackets was beginning to fade.

The stub of a cigar in his mouth, old man Hemmings was halfway from the counter to the door when the two men stepped inside. Late sixties, he was heavy set with a grizzled mop of graying hair. 'Lunchtime, fellers, I'm about to close.'

Briefly Wiley looked at him then he dropped the dead bolt on the door. When he turned he had a thirty-eight in his hand and he cracked the old man over the head. Hemmings went down with a moan in his throat and his eyelids working like the wings of a butterfly. Breath harsh, the remains of his cigar lost to the sticky red blood that was beginning to form a pool.

'Fetch one of them duffels yonder.' Wiley pointed to a shelf holding a stack of heavy-duty canvas bags.

Leaving the old man where he lay they moved behind the counter and Wiley's gaze settled on a Garand M1C. Pressing the butt to his shoulder he worked the bolt action and dry-fired before dumping the rifle in the bag. Back at the rack he reached for a shotgun, stowed that then reached for another and shoved it in the bag as well. Using the butt of his pistol he smashed the glass cabinet where the handguns were displayed. A shadow at the window made Henderson look up and he saw someone pause on the sidewalk outside. The middle-aged waitress who had served them at the lunch counter was at the door with a hand cupped to her eyes. She saw the man on the floor. She saw the blood. Finally she spotted the two men and scurried across the road.

Stowing the last of the weapons Wiley grabbed two boxes of double-ought cartridges and picked up his thirty-eight. Stepping over the stricken storekeeper he unlocked the door and popped the trunk on the Olds. Grabbing one of the shotguns he threw the duffel inside.

Henderson was fumbling for keys as a state trooper's Plymouth turned onto Main Street coming from the north. Wiley stepped into the road with his eyes a little glassy and the shotgun held hip-high. The trooper slammed on his brakes, but the shot rang out and the front of the Plymouth just seemed to explode. The radiator popped and water spewed, the hood crumpling up with bits of metal tearing off and glass from the windshield littering the road. Wiley let go a second time and flames whooshed from spilled gasoline.

Fifty yards up the road Franklin saw it all unfold through the windshield of his car. He saw the cruiser go up and the long-haired man jump into the Olds. Walking the block he came to a drugstore and made his way to the phone booth in the back. 'I'm in Deacon's Mount,' he said when the call was answered. 'The gun store, I think we have a problem here.'

Two

Ten miles south Quarrie swung off the highway into Hank Miller's Diner, half-listening to a show on the radio where some old guy from New Orleans was talking about the number of young black men swapping the church for the Nation of Islam. Twisting the dial he switched stations to a discussion on how the drought was so severe right now ranchers and farmers had to slot coins at designated street pumps if they were to have any water at all.

Turning off the engine he had the window rolled down as a car hop came over and took his order for coffee with sugar and crème. She brought it on a tray she fixed to the door and a couple of minutes later the shortwave crackled with static.

'*Two-Eleven, Deacon's Mount. Officer down, repeat: officer down . . .*' The voice was breathless and panicked. Quarrie lifted the handset and pressed the transmit button.

'Trooper, this is Ranger Sergeant Quarrie. I'm outside Hank Miller's Diner on 287 about ten miles south of your position.'

'Car's on fire,' the man gasped. 'Glass from the windshield stuck in my shoulder, two suspects headed your way . . .' The voice tailed into static again and Quarrie changed channels. 'This is Ranger unit Zero-Six: dispatch, do you copy?'

'Roger that, Zero-Six, go ahead.'

'Did you get all that?'

'Yes, we did, I'll get an ambulance out there and have backup with you as soon as possible.'

Returning the transmitter to its hook Quarrie flipped the sun visor forward and reached to where his sunglasses were folded. Behind them was a photo of Mary-Clare taken twelve months before she died. For a moment he studied her picture then fired up the engine and pulled out onto the road. Minutes later he picked out a pale colored dot heading his way against two lanes of shimmering blacktop.

*

Henderson was driving. He looked sideways where Wiley lighted a cigarette, the shotgun upright between his knees.

'That went well,' Henderson said.

'Quit worrying, kid.' Wiley blew smoke. 'Couple of miles down the road we'll have us another set of wheels and they'll be looking for this here Olds.'

Henderson had both hands gripping the wheel; foot hard on the gas he was touching ninety miles an hour. Up ahead he saw a car coming the other way, the first they had passed since town. Gray, unmarked, a Buick Riviera with a clam shell grille. Henderson caught a glimpse of the driver as they flew by. Picking up the hunted expression in his eyes Wiley laid a hand on his shoulder. 'What is it?' he said. 'Do you know that guy?'

Peering in the mirror Henderson saw the car pull to the side of the road then spin all the way around.

'What's up, Scott?' Twisting where he sat Wiley glanced over his shoulder. 'Who the hell is that?'

Henderson let a breath creep audibly over his teeth. 'I think that's a Texas Ranger. The other car you talked about, we have to get this rig off the road.'

A hundred yards behind, Quarrie had the Riviera shifting through the gears. He was thinking about the landscape ahead, how they would pass Hank Miller's place again pretty soon and after that there were a couple of ranch roads but that was all. Flipping the switch for the red light he set the siren to howl. Stepping on the gas, the car surged forward as cold air was sucked through the intake and within seconds he was tailgating the Olds. If he had recognized him correctly that was Scott Henderson behind the wheel.

Backing off a fraction he pulled across the yellow line and then accelerated to come alongside. Jabbing with pointed fingers he indicated for Henderson to pull over and briefly the boy glanced his way. He did not slow down and the long-haired man in the passenger seat had the shotgun levelled at the window. Instinctively Quarrie lifted his foot off the gas and the Olds carried on for another hundred yards before Henderson braked sharply then swung across the opposing lane. All but on two wheels the car rattled between fence posts and leapt a cattle guard, dust flying as it hit the dirt road.

Reaching to the dashboard Quarrie lifted the radio handset. 'Dispatch, this is Zero-Six. Light green Olds exited 287 at Ranch to Market 835. Am in pursuit, have ambulance and wrecker standing by.'

Bringing the Buick around he swung across the blacktop and split the fence posts, staying far enough back from the Oldsmobile so as not to be blinded by dust. He knew this road, nothing much up here save an old wreck of a house that should long since have been torn down. It was possible this was part of their plan and they had another car ready to go. He thought about how the road cut through stands of oak and zig-zagged around the hill before carrying a trestle that forded the creek. There was another option rather than follow them and he considered the hunting rifle he had in the trunk. Just ahead the road forked, and instead of tailgating the Olds Quarrie took the other trail.

Pulling up to the side of the hill he got out of the car and unhooked the rifle where it was clipped to the underside of the trunk lid. He checked the pair of three-fifty-seven Blackhawks he wore western style on his hips then slung the rifle over his shoulder and started up the slope. Trees grew in patches, the trail a little scaly underfoot; in leather-soled boots it made the going slick. At the top of the rise he took off his hat and worked a palm through the sweat in his hair. It would take a moment for them to make it all the way around and from this vantage point he could see the old trestle built across the dried up creek. Beyond it was a battered-looking house. Using the rifle scope he picked a lean-to and a station wagon partially hidden by rusty-looking roofing tin.

The car came into view and Quarrie could see that Henderson was driving more slowly. Directly in front of where he was standing a boulder jutted and he secured his left foot then rested his elbow on his thigh. If memory served him right that boy had done two years in Ferguson and was barely out of pre-release now. Wrapping the shoulder strap around his left arm he sighted. Seven millimeter with the Mauser action; he paused long enough to allow his breathing to shallow then took out the near side front tire. The driver lost control, the car slewed to the right before slamming into a tree.

They were walking. As he came up on the incapacitated vehicle he could see its doors were open and the two men were hauling a canvas hold-all between them. They stopped when they heard the rumble of the Buick's engine and the wild-looking guy dropped his side of the bag.

Crossing the bridge Quarrie came on with the engine at barely more than an idle. He stopped thirty yards from where they stood and switched the motor off. Then he opened the door. Henderson looked at him and he looked back where the boy had an automatic trailing from his hand. He was wearing blue jeans and a denim jacket with a ten-dollar transistor radio protruding from the breast pocket. Henderson dropped the gun on the ground then placed both hands on top of his head while the other man stared wide-eyed.

'Wiley, we're done here,' he stated. 'There's but one road out and you can see how it's blocked. We're looking at assault with a deadly weapon, robbing a gun store and I'm still on parole.'

Quarrie stepped out from behind the door and Wiley's gaze drifted from his face to the pistols strapped on his hips.

Wiley racked a round into the shotgun's chamber and Quarrie stood his ground. Left hand hooked in his belt, his right hung loose at his side. 'You need to listen to your buddy,' he said. 'There's no way out. That other car, the one at the shack, you ain't going to make it that far.' Still he held Wiley's gaze. 'Things might not be as bad as you figure. I talked to the trooper on the radio just now and his car is wrecked all right but he ain't shot up so you got that much going for you.'

'We clubbed old man Hemmings, John Q,' Henderson piped up. 'Pistol whipped him, bleeding when we left out he was.'

Quarrie did not look at him. He kept his eyes on Wiley. 'Hemmings is a tough old bird. He can survive a pistol whipping.' He spoke to Wiley again. 'You want to shoot at me you can do that. I die and it'll be the chair you got to look forward to, but the odds are I put you down.'

Wiley did not speak and he did not look at Henderson. His gaze was fixed on Quarrie and he stood with a hip thrust out where he rested the butt of the shotgun. For a second he seemed to waver and Quarrie thought he might just do as he said. But then he saw the way his shoulders hunched, how his eyes dulled and the corner of his lip seemed to pucker just a fraction. He saw the twitch of his knuckle in the trigger guard but before Wiley could squeeze he drew a pistol and covered the hammer.

Wiley lay face down on the ground with his hair scattered across the dust and blood snaking a crimson trail. Henderson stood a couple of paces away with no color in his face and Quarrie stared at the dead man conscious of the metallic taste in his mouth. 'Are we done here, Scott?' he said.

'Yes, sir.' Henderson's voice was barely more than a murmur. 'Been that way since I put the piece down.'

The duffel lay on the ground a little way from where Wiley sprawled. Quarrie holstered his gun and settled the hammer clip. Unhooking a pair of handcuffs from his belt he tossed them over to Henderson. 'Fix yourself up in front then set on that rock where I can see you yonder.'

Henderson did as he was told and Quarrie dropped to his haunches to check the contents of the duffel: shotguns and handguns. His eyes narrowed as he saw the rifle.

'So talk to me,' he said. 'I know how you only just got done with prison already. What the hell were you thinking?'

Henderson did not say anything.

Feeling in his shirt pocket for cigarettes Quarrie shook two out and lit them both then passed one across to Henderson. 'So who is this guy and what's with all the hardware?'

Henderson released a breath. 'Wasn't my idea, John Q, I only met him after I got done with pre-release. I guess we split us a pitcher. He's a Veteran, been in country for a couple of tours. All he told me was how he needed to get hold of a rifle. Never said nothing about no other guns and I figure he fixed on taking all he could carry.'

'What did he want with the rifle?'

'Beats me, weren't any kind of talker and I know how not to be asking.'

'So why hook up with him in the first place? What did he promise you?'

'Five hundred dollars.' Henderson sucked on his cigarette. 'Asked me if I knew a gun store where the pickings were easy and promised me five hundred bucks.'

Crushing his cigarette carefully in the dirt Quarrie went back to the dead man and rolled him over. In the distance he could hear the wail of a siren. Wiley had taken two bullets about an inch apart and his shirt was coated with blood and dust. Quarrie went through his pockets and found thirty dollars in cash, a driver's license and a card from the Veterans' Association. In his wallet was a slip of paper with the word *Jacinto* scribbled on it.

'What's this?' He showed the paper to Henderson. 'Out of San Jacinto County is he or are we talking Dallas?'

'I don't know, sir. I got no idea.'

Stuffing the paper inside his own wallet Quarrie fetched a piece of tarp from the trunk of his car and laid it over the dead man. Picking up the fallen shotgun he took both Henderson's pistol and the one from Wiley and wrapped them in a sheet of see-through plastic. Stowing that and the duffel in the trunk he drove Henderson back to the wrecked Oldsmobile. Settling him in the driver's seat he unhooked one of the handcuffs before securing it again through the steering wheel.

Three

Leaving the highway patrol to deal with Henderson he drove to Deacon's Mount and pulled over by the state trooper's wrecked vehicle. A couple of city cops were looking on but most of the rubberneckers had been and gone. Squaring his hat on his head Quarrie took a good look at the vehicle.

'Just a hell of a mess, Sergeant, ain't it?' The younger of the two cops had sweat staining his shirt at the armpits.

'How's old man Hemmings?' Quarrie said.

'Took him a whack on the head but he was conscious when they loaded him into the ambulance.'

Walking down to the gun store Quarrie nodded to a third officer as he ducked under the 'Do Not Cross' tape. The floor was covered in glass where the handgun cabinet had been smashed and he was careful to avoid blood where it stained the linoleum. On the wall behind the counter a few rifles still hung on hooks as well as a couple of shotguns. Quarrie thought about the M1C he had found in the bag. There was nothing else to see in the store so he went back outside and shook a Camel from his pack. Offering one to the city cop he asked him where he'd find the woman who called this in. The cop directed him up the road to the Dairy-Ette.

There weren't many people eating, plenty of stools free at the counter. He took off his hat and laid it down as the middle-aged waitress came over with a pot of coffee. A little lined in the face, she wore her hair in a single plait that fed from under her cap.

'Sergeant,' she said. 'What can I get you?'

'Just some coffee, mam: thank you.'

She poured him a cup and set the pot back on the warmer then rested on her forearms as he reached for sugar and crème. 'You're here about the shooting,' she said.

'That's right. Were you the one who spotted them?'

'Yes, I was.' A little pride in her voice, she stood straight. 'They were in here first off and the one guy with long hair, he was cussing in front of the customers. I can't have decent folks putting up with that so I had to say something to him.' Lips pursed she shook her head. 'He didn't like it. He didn't like that at all.'

Quarrie nodded. 'I guess they were talking some, the two of them. Did you pick up on anything? They stole a whole bunch of guns from Mr Hemmings's place, one of them a military rifle.'

'I know they did,' she said. 'I saw them through the window. Mr Hemmings on the floor all bloody about his head.' She shuddered. 'No, sir, they didn't say anything I really picked up on. The one guy was looking at the TV all foul-mouthed like I said. The other one, the younger one, he just looked plum nervous.'

Quarrie took a sip of coffee.

'The way he was and all, it's what got me thinking about what they might be doing so when they left out I went outside myself and stood on the sidewalk.' She pointed through the window. 'Watched that Olds drive down the street aways then I saw it pull over. I knew something wasn't right and I walked on down and that's when I ran for the council office.'

That was all she could tell him and Quarrie drove north once more and left the highway at the exit for Wichita Falls. Passing the Triple D Motel he could see a bunch of kids splashing around in the swimming pool where it was separated from the parking lot by a six-foot steel mesh fence. The old Tejano caretaker was keeping half an eye on them from where he painted a wall in the back. Hot today, it had been that way all year. With so much dust in the air the drought was taking its toll.

As he turned onto Indiana he could see a coroner's ambulance parked outside the Roosevelt Hotel. A couple of blocks beyond the First National Bank, the lights were going and the back door standing open. A mass of people were gathered on the steps and they moved aside as he flipped the switch for the siren briefly, before pulling up to the curb.

Inside the hotel he crossed to the desk where a young clerk glanced at the badge on his chest.

'What's going on here?' Quarrie asked.

'One of the guests passed away in the night. Room 404,' the young man indicated, 'coroner's crew just went up.'

Quarrie climbed to the fourth-floor landing where a Tejano maid was in tears as she gave a statement to a uniformed cop. The door to the bedroom was open and the crew from the ambulance inside. The dead man was lying in bed with one arm hanging over the side and the two men in white shirts and black ties were about to lift the body onto a gurney.

'Hold your fire there a minute, boys, would you?' They looked round and Quarrie indicated the body. 'Ranger, I need you to hold off for a second, OK?'

They left him alone and he stood in the doorway, a regular room with the bathroom to his right and a king-size bed. He approached where the man was half on his side and half on his front, the skin of his face marked by the pattern from a rumpled pillow. His eyes were closed and his mouth open, with the tongue protruding slightly. The bed sheet only partially covered his torso and Quarrie took a minute to study the upper body but could find no sign of trauma. There were no cuts or bruising that he could see and no indication of blood settling in places that would suggest the body had been moved after the man was dead. Stepping closer he considered the hand where it flopped to the side of the bed. He took off his hat and bent to his haunches. Carefully he lifted the hand and it was chill to the touch but not stiffened by rigor mortis. He inspected each nail in turn then let the hand drop and went around to the other side. Nothing under the nails. He looked closely at the man's features and figured him for being around thirty. His lips were drawn back over his teeth and Quarrie noted the yellow film on his tongue. He sniffed his mouth. Maybe there was the tang of something; he could not say for certain.

He turned his attention to a small overnight bag lying on the floor underneath the desk. Inside he found a T shirt and underwear. No paperwork or documents. A set of clothes were laid on the chair but he could find no wallet or billfold among them. There was nothing that identified the dead man. He checked the nightstand drawer and the wall closet but did not come up with anything. In the bathroom there was a wash-kit and razor, some shaving soap and a hairbrush, but no sign of any ID.

'Don't make a whole lot of sense,' he muttered. 'What kind of man is it checks into The Roosevelt without a credit card or driver's license?' Looking round he saw one of the coroner's men watching him. 'Any idea what killed him?'

'Looks like a seizure of some kind,' the man said, 'heart attack maybe, we won't know until the autopsy.'

They carried the body down in the elevator and Quarrie

watched from the balcony overlooking the width of the lobby. Then he went back to the dead man's room and studied every aspect of it over again. Standing in the middle of the floor he considered the desk and drawers once more then bent to the garbage can where he found a sheet of screwed-up hotel notepaper. Taking a kerchief from his back pocket he flapped it out and used it to pinch the edge of the paper. The word *Liberty* was scribbled with a ballpoint pen. For a moment he studied that then folded the paper carefully again before slipping it into an envelope he took from the desk.

Downstairs, he spoke to the clerk who told him the man had checked in under the name Williams. He had paid in cash. They had no credit card details, no forwarding address and no license number for any vehicle. Quarrie asked to see the register and noted where Williams had scrawled his name. On a hunch he cast his eye across the rest of the page and paused when he came to Room 210. 'It's almost noon,' he said. 'Are they all done with the housekeeping?'

The clerk checked to see if that room had been cleaned yet and was told it hadn't. He found the pass key and gave it to Quarrie who climbed the stairs to the second floor and fit it in the lock. Dark inside, with the drapes drawn across the window the room was all but black. He felt on the wall for the light switch and a couple of lamps came on as well as the one overhead. He stared at the pair of unmade beds.

Just as he had in 404, he studied every aspect of the room collectively then separated it into sections. A short corridor with a wood-panelled closet led beyond the bathroom to where the beds were set. He took a look in the bathroom but it was empty save a metal garbage can with a few spent matches in the bottom. Looking more closely he could see that one wall was lightly coated with soot and he considered that for a moment before his gaze was drawn to the toilet. Lifting the lid he saw a small wodge of ashes floating in the water.

He went through to the bedroom again, found a ballpoint pen in a drawer and used it to pry what he could from the toilet bowl. Most of what he salvaged was so sodden it broke up as soon as he touched it. He placed the residue on a bath towel which he laid on the floor. There were a couple of slightly larger pieces; one corner was almost intact and he thought the paper thick enough to have been a photograph maybe.

Back in the bedroom he checked the trash under the desk where he found a few more screwed-up pieces of hotel note-paper. Right at the bottom was a small brown bottle that had contained prescription drugs. The top was missing and the bottle empty. Quarrie inserted the pen in the neck. 'Proloid': he had no idea what that was, but there was an address for the pharmacist in New Orleans together with the patient's surname. From the bathroom he collected a couple of sheets of toilet paper and wrapped the bottle in that. Turning for the door once more he paused at the table where a few grains of white powder seemed to brush the surface.

Half an hour later he parked his car outside the sheriff's department and grabbed the weapons from the trunk. He walked the corridor to the mensroom and splashed cold water over the back of his neck. In the squad room he laid the duffel on an empty desk along with the shotgun and Henderson's automatic. Dayton was on the phone; fifty years old, he was full in the belly and fleshy about the head. In the alcove outside his office, his secretary worked the keys of an LC Smith typewriter.

'How you doing, John Q?' The same age as the sheriff with red hair and pale skin, she looked up at him a little cautiously.

'I'm fine.' Quarrie glanced across the parking lot to the jailhouse. 'Did the trooper bring Henderson in?'

'Yes, sir, they just got here.'

'Has anybody called his mom?'

'Not as far as I know.'

'Best go ahead and get her done. With him just getting out and all she ain't going to be very happy.' He indicated the duffel on the desk. 'I need somebody to bag those weapons for the lab. Tell them we're looking for any kind of powder residue that might be there as well as prints.' He glanced through the office door where the sheriff had put down the phone. 'The one guy – Wiley – threw down on me with a twelve-gauge pump.'

'Yeah, that's what Henderson said.' Dayton beckoned him in. 'Spoke to him just now and he told me how it was that feller pistol whipped the old boy and him who shot up the cruiser. Told me how he tried to talk him out of fixing to shoot you.'

'Yes, he did.'

The sheriff made a face. 'Well, we can tell his mother that's something in his corner I reckon.'

Quarrie leaned against the doorjamb with one hand in a pocket. 'When I talked to him he said the whole thing was Wiley's idea and it was an M1C he was after.'

Dayton arched one eyebrow. 'What'd he want with a piece like that?'

Quarrie shrugged. 'First off I figured on him for having a buyer lined up, but now I'm not so sure.' Stepping into the office he took a seat across the desk and plucked the empty bottle he'd wrapped in toilet paper from his shirt pocket. 'I just came from The Roosevelt, Sam: one of the cleaners found a guest lying dead in their bedroom.'

'Yeah, I heard about that.'

'Young guy, no marks on him. Some kind of seizure. They reckon he died in his sleep.' Quarrie placed the bottle on the desk. 'I checked the room but couldn't find any ID. The guy had no driver's license or credit card, no check book or anything like that and it kind of struck me as odd so I took a look in the register.' He lifted a hand. 'The feller I killed on that dirt road, he spent last night in Room 210.'

The sheriff sat back in his chair.

'Him with the shotgun,' Quarrie went on. 'He signed the register and paid in cash but the room had two beds and both of them had been slept in.'

'Which means Henderson was there as well. That what you're telling me?'

'Sure looks that way. Only he neglected to mention it.' Quarrie was silent for a second then. 'They'd been burning some kind of papers, Sam. I found ashes they tried to flush down the john.'

'You want to talk to the kid right now?' Dayton glanced towards the jailhouse.

'No, sir.' Quarrie shook his head. 'They won't be done processing him yet. I'll give him the night to think on it and sit him down first thing.'

Reaching for the pill bottle he peeled the toilet paper away. 'This was in the trash can,' he said. 'Pharmacist out of New Orleans dispensed the drugs and we have the patient's surname.' Quiet for a moment he added, 'Sam, something ain't adding up here. I got those rooms taped off and I want a team down there to dust them.'

Four

Gigi woke to cramping muscles and the sound of a road crew working a pneumatic drill. Throwing off the sheet she had to grab the end of the bed for support and stood for a moment working palms up and down her legs. Through in the bathroom she caught a glimpse of her reflection in the mirror as she searched the cabinet for her medication. Dark eyes and ebony skin, her hair cut so short it formed a dusky cap on her head.

She could not find her meds. Cursing softly she grabbed a robe, went downstairs and picked up the phone.

'Earl,' she said, when he answered. 'You were here the other night and I got a question for you. The cabinet in my bathroom, I had meds back there and I can't seem to find them and those meds are for my thyroid. That's the second time a bottle's gone missing and . . .'

'For Christ's sake,' he said. 'I don't know anything about any meds and you can't call here. Not anymore.'

'What do you mean?'

'Things have changed. I don't want you on this phone. I'll call you from now on, OK?'

Hanging up the phone Earl stared at the green painted walls of his study. A tiny space at the back of the house, the room seemed to close about the desk as he slumped in the chair. Through in the hallway he could hear his wife talking to one of the children and he stared at the wedding band on his finger with sweat soaking his light brown hair. He jumped as his wife knocked on the door. 'Earl,' she said. 'Honey, did you call Mr Gervais back?'

'Not yet.'

'He called a while back trying to get hold of you. Aren't you supposed to be in the office already?'

'No, he knows I'm working from home.'

'Well, he said he was trying to get hold of you. I think you should give him a call.'

Again Earl stared at the phone. He picked it up and started to dial but seemed to change his mind and put the receiver back in the cradle. He sat with the palms of his hands pressed together then picked the phone up again and dialled. When the call was answered his words came harsh and hurried. 'I've just had Gigi on the phone.'

'So?'

'She was asking if I took her meds. That's twice now. I got away with it the first time. What the hell am I supposed to tell her?'

'You don't tell her anything.' The voice was chill in his ear. 'Maybe you misunderstand the nature of our relationship. You don't ask questions. You don't make demands. You do exactly as you're told. Earl, you need to think about what we know about you and the fact we're paying for your education. You need to understand that everything you've done, everything you've given us implicates nobody but you. Probably it's best that you don't call me again. I think you should stay off the phone.'

'And supposing I don't want to do that,' Moore said. 'Supposing I decide this just isn't worth it?'

'You won't do that.' The voice had dropped to a whisper. 'You're not that foolish. Remember that blond-haired guy back in February? His idea of a good time is to wait till you're out then drive to your house and visit with your family.'

*

On the other side of town Rosslyn F Tobie sat in the leather swivel chair with the telephone to his ear. In his seventies, a mane of silver hair seemed to climb from his forehead; he was deeply tanned in the face. 'No, my wife is sick,' he said. 'She has a temperature and won't be able to make it tonight, which is a shame. But everyone else will be there.' He nodded. 'Yes, yes, the governor will be at the top table. His office already confirmed.' With that he hung up the phone.

The French windows opened onto the patio and he could smell diesel where it lifted from the surface of the Mississippi. No cloud in the sky, the city seemed choked with the weight of the air. There was a knock on the door. He turned to see the sweating face of his butler. 'Sorry to disturb you, sir, but there's someone else on the phone. I said you were talking to the mayor, but I see you're done with that. Downtown, sir, are you available for another call?'

With a nod Tobie waved him away. He did not take the call right away; instead he poured coffee from the china pot and replaced the pot on the tray. After that he picked up the phone. 'What do you want?' he said. 'I'm busy this morning. There's still a lot to arrange.'

'I need to talk to you, Rosslyn,' the voice said. 'I just listened to that program you recorded on the radio. Apparently it's been broadcast all across the south.'

'So they tell me,' the old man said.

'Well, that's got to be good publicity for the foundation and the timing couldn't be better right now what with the fund-raiser at City Hall.'

'A sentiment echoed by the mayor. Is that the reason you called?'

'No, it's not. Franklin, he's in Deacon's Mount, Texas; the gun store. It didn't go well over there.'

Pausing with his coffee cup halfway to his mouth Tobie stared where a starling pecked at the lawn.

'Wichita Falls,' the other man went on. 'The mark wouldn't give up his real name. It's Franklin's fault, his idea to use that guy for both jobs. I never agreed with it. You know that. I voiced my opposition at the time.'

'He made a case for it,' the old man said, 'kill two birds with one stone. So he wouldn't give us his real name. Apart from that, did it go as planned?'

'I think so. Franklin said everything should appear just as you said it had to. There is one thing though; the mark did give up an address but it was Louisiana Avenue Parkway.'

Placing his cup back on its saucer Tobie shifted the phone to his other hand. 'Did he?' he said. 'That sounds like he knew more than he was telling us. It sounds like he was playing games.'

'That's what I thought. I'm checking into it now. There's another thing, I just had Earl Moore on the phone. He's getting a little ahead of himself. He . . .'

'Deal with him,' Tobie said. 'Right now he remains important.'

'It's OK. I took care of it. What about Texas, do you want me to make any calls?'

'No. Franklin's supposed to be phoning me. I'll talk to him and we'll go from there.'

When he put the phone down the old man's gaze pitched from the yard outside to his snake's head walking cane. He reached for it. Almost tenderly he held it, cupping the silver handle where the serpent's tongue protruded slightly. Switching his grip from the handle to the shaft he buried the tongue in the coffee table.

*

Early evening and Franklin picked up the cab he'd left at Moisant Field, a '65 Impala Sedan with a neon sign on the roof. Behind the wheel he tossed his jacket over the back seat and drove into New Orleans. Twenty minutes later he stopped outside a three-story red-brick apartment building on Washington Avenue.

Minimalist and modern; an oak floor and white painted walls dominated by a single pen and ink painting. Hanging his jacket on a chrome stand he crossed to a similarly styled bureau. He pumped the air from his cheeks as he grabbed a whiskey tumbler and scooped ice. Glass in hand, he perched on a Toledo chair, one of four that furnished the room. He considered the phone where it hung on the wall.

Tobie was in the office on Baronne Street when the call came through from the desk. The girl had already left for the day and he let the phone ring a couple of times before he picked up.

When he spoke his voice had an edge to it. 'Franklin, I've been waiting for you to call. I know about the debacle at the gun store and I know about the failed attempt to get what we wanted in Wichita Falls.'

'He recovered the photograph,' Franklin said. 'He got an address here in New Orleans.'

'Yes, he did, and we know whose address it was. If he knew about that then maybe it wasn't just the photo he had, perhaps there was something else.'

'Like what exactly?'

'I don't know. You tell me.'

'Look,' Franklin said. 'You told me we couldn't beat him up and I chose Wiley because he's a Veteran. I figured the army would've taught him how to get information without leaving any sign and he was in Texas for the gun store anyway.'

'Yes, that's what you told me and like a fool I listened. But he had no such interrogation skills and now we're left with a problem.' Tobie stared at the wall, listening to the weight of Franklin's breathing. 'I know there's something else,' he said. 'You didn't call me from Texas as instructed. Why was that? What is it you're afraid to tell me?'

Franklin sighed. 'The 28th, I think we're going to have to speak to the client.'

'What do you mean?'

'I think we should postpone.'

'Are you mad? This organization hasn't postponed an engagement in a hundred years. We're not about to start now. What exactly is it you're struggling to tell me?'

'Wiley's dead,' Franklin said. 'After he screwed up at the gun store he was killed by a Texas Ranger.'

*

Earl was at his desk in the office on Tulane Avenue, staring at the clock on the wall. After seven already, he had a stack of paper files in front of him and perspiration coated his palms.

'Are you still here?' The voice came from the open doorway and he looked round to see Pershing Gervais, the chief investigator, in tuxedo and black bow tie.

'I was catching up on some reading.'

'Anything I need to know?'

'No, I don't think so.'

'Who was that just now on the phone?'

'Just some girl chasing a bunch of paperwork.'

Gervais regarded him with his head to one side. 'Well, I'm out of here,' he said. 'I have a fundraiser to go to. You should get going too. Isn't it time you were home with your family?'

When he was gone Earl slipped on his jacket and walked the corridor past the empty offices and out to the landing. Plucking a paper cup from the dispenser on the side of the cooler he downed a long draught of ice cold water.

He took the back stairs making his way to the basement then across the underground parking garage before climbing another set of stairs to the coroner's office. He nodded to the security guard who was settling down at his post, then headed for the back of the building. He stopped when he came to a room at the end of an empty corridor. Inside he found a Telecopier on top of a file cabinet and a telephone on the desk. Throwing a quick glance back the way he had come he closed the door then lifted the copier down. He checked to make sure the phone was working then unravelled the cable, located an outlet and hooked the copier up. There was no paper on the reel and he searched the drawers of the file cabinet. Palms moist, he set the paper in place then attached the phone to the copier.

Behind him the door swung open and a young woman stood there. With short-cut hair and eye glasses, she wore a pencil skirt and cotton blouse. 'Kind of late for you to be back here, isn't it?' she said. 'I didn't think we were using that machine anymore.'

Earl was a little red in the face. 'I'm from across the way,' he stuttered. 'Our copier is down right now and I figured nobody would mind.'

'Nobody does. But if you're looking for a reply I don't know as anyone will be back this way to get it for you.'

'No problem.' He tried to smile. 'There's no need to bother anybody. I'll swing by and fetch it myself.'

*

After he put down the phone to Franklin, the old man left the office with his overcoat draped around his shoulders and went down to the ground floor. The concierge opened the doors, and outside his chauffeur was waiting as he crossed to the Lincoln.

'City Hall, Mr Tobie?' He opened the forward-facing rear door.

With a brief nod Tobie glanced at him.

'I imagine events like this might sometimes be seen as a bit of a chore,' the chauffeur suggested, 'but the fact is you do a lot of good.' He nodded to the canopied doors. 'A lot of folks rely on what you do with that foundation and I know how grateful they are.'

They drove across town to New City Hall, pulling up to the steps where half a dozen camera crews were gathered and the car was surrounded by reporters from local newspapers. Another concierge was there to open the door and Tobie leaned on his cane. He allowed a couple of pictures to be taken and answered questions as to why he was alone, telling the reporters his wife had a fever and had to remain at home. After that he went inside and checked his coat then made his way to the banqueting hall.

On the far side of the room, Pershing Gervais rested with his back to the rosewood bar. Alongside him Lieutenant Colback from the NOPD's organized crime squad stood with a glass in his hand.

'Rosslyn F Tobie.' Gervais looked on as the old man was escorted to the top table. 'He finally got here then and only a half hour late.'

'Call it fashionable, don't they.' Colback watched Governor McKeithen shake Tobie's hand.

'I suppose they do and it's a hell of a welcome right there.' Gervais picked up his own glass. 'They're all here, the governor, Supreme Court Justice Hawthorne, Chief Justice Fournet, not to mention the attorney general. He and Tobie went to law school together.'

'Yeah, I heard that. It's a story he likes to tell.' Colback worked a palm across his scalp.

Gervais indicated another table. 'I see Mary Parker's running for state treasurer.'

'Democrat or GOP?'

'Democrat, she's up against Allison Kolb and she's sitting right over there.' Gervais clicked his tongue. 'I swear there's more money in this room right now than the whole of the rest of New Orleans.'

'So how is it you were invited?'

Gervais smiled. 'For every rule they say there's an exception. I'm here because the DA couldn't make it. And talking of which,

I see Shaw's here tonight. That guy with him is Ferenc Nagy.'

'Who's he?' Colback followed where he indicated.

'Before the Russians rolled into Budapest he was the Prime Minister of Hungary. These days he's not really anybody but he's a man with contacts and he's happily settled in Dallas.' He turned his attention to another table. 'There's old HL Hunt holding court. You know him of course, don't you?'

'Sure,' the lieutenant said. 'Billionaire oilman. I heard how he was running a cotton plantation back in the day but it got flooded. Word is he brought his last hundred dollars down here to New Orleans.'

'I heard the story.' Gervais set his glass down on the bar. 'Hit the card clubs pretty good and it wasn't long before that hundred became a hundred thousand.'

'The great and the good,' Colback said. 'More limos outside than you could shake a stick at and every man-Jack of them here to support that old man and his foundation.'

It was eleven o'clock when Tobie left the fundraiser and walked outside to where Franklin was waiting behind the wheel of his taxi. He didn't get out, he just watched in the rear view mirror as Tobie settled in the back. 'Where'd you want to go, Rosslyn?' he said.

For a moment Tobie did not reply. He peered out the window as the governor was escorted to his limousine.

'How come you summoned me?' Franklin looked round. 'What's wrong with the Lincoln?'

'I gave Johnson the rest of the night off.' Tobie spoke without looking at him. 'Take me to Orleans Street. There's someone I need to talk to.'

Franklin pulled away from the curb and headed for the

French Quarter. The traffic still heavy he drove with one hand on the wheel and the other on the armrest.

'So Wiley is dead.' Tobie seemed to air his thoughts from behind him.

'It's why I said what I did. I wouldn't have suggested it otherwise.'

'I know why you suggested it but we don't postpone, it's something we just don't do.'

'What *are* we going to do then?' Pulling across the lanes Franklin glanced over his shoulder. 'There's no time to find a replacement. I don't see we have any choice.'

'He's dead because of you,' Tobie stated. 'Don't forget that, boy. It's down to you we had this problem in the first place.'

Franklin curled his lip. 'It was one photo, and according to Moore, it wasn't me he recognized at all.'

'You or him, it was a slip up and we don't do that.' The old man's eyes were tight where he sought Franklin's gaze in the mirror.

'So, who is it you're visiting on Orleans Street?' Franklin asked as he turned onto North Rampart.

'Just someone I haven't seen in a while.'

'Do you want me to wait?'

'No. I want you to start thinking about the 28th and what we're going to do without our man. The client was very specific. They want maximum resonance and it's resonance we're going to give them.'

Franklin turned back towards the river and the old man indicated where he should pull up. 'If I want you later I'll call,' he stated. 'And Franklin, mention the word "postpone" to me ever again I'll peel the flesh from your bones.'

The rain had stopped and he stood on the sidewalk as the

cab pulled away with a squeal from the tires. Gazing above a set of solid steel gates he considered the balcony of an old carriage house that had long since been converted into apartments. He could pick out the glow of a lamp from the living room as he searched his pockets for a key. To the side of the gates was a smaller one and he stepped into a courtyard laid with Italian floor tiles. A flight of steps at the back led to a narrow open landing. As he crossed he heard the door open. Light flooded the landing and he saw the willowy figure of an elderly black woman with close-cut, snow-colored hair.

'Nana,' he said. 'This will always be my apartment. You can put that pistol away.'

He made his way up the stairs to where she stood with a snub-nose thirty-eight in her hand. 'I know you too well,' he said. 'I always did.' Stepping past her he went into the apartment and hung up his coat.

'What're you doing here, Rosslyn?' the old woman said.

He did not reply. He watched her put the gun away in a drawer then fetch a pitcher of mint julep from the kitchen and place it on the coffee table in the living room. The balcony doors were open and a breeze seemed to pluck at the drapes. A little way down towards the river lights in the walls illuminated the triple spires of the St Louis Cathedral.

'I see you still carry that cane.' Nana's voice had an edge to it.

The old man closed his fingers around the snake's head handle. 'One never knows when one might have use for it.' He looked at her then with his head to one side and Nana avoided his eye.

'You've still got it,' he told her. 'Whatever it was that brought you to me all those years ago, it might not quite have

31

the luster it did, but it's there all right. You haven't lost it.'

Still she avoided his eye.

Reaching for his drink Tobie worked the tall glass against his palm. 'It's a funny thing,' he said. 'I never did much care for mint julep. It was never a drink of choice, not unless it was you doing the pouring.' Taking a sip he smiled but it didn't quite reach his eyes.

'You're all dressed up,' Nana said. 'Where you been tonight, Rosslyn? What brings you all the way over here?'

Getting to his feet Tobie placed the glass on the table and took a moment to consider his surroundings. 'I like what you've done with the place,' he said. 'The Queen Anne stuff, it's well appointed.'

'Rosslyn, it's got to be twenty years. What brings you over here now?'

He paced the hallway and flicked on the light in one of the bedrooms. 'It's nothing like it used to be, though you've still got the bed I see.' He indicated the cast iron spheres on each corner embossed with a coiled snake that echoed his cane. He stood still for a moment as if he was rapt by memory. 'We had us some fine old times in this apartment. When was it I bought the place, '26 or '27? I can never remember exactly.'

'It was 1927. You didn't come around again till '35 and you haven't been back hardly since.' Nana considered the tip of the serpent's tongue where it formed a sharpened point. 'Rosslyn, it's late. What is it you want with me?'

He looked at her then, a light in her eyes that seemed to mirror his. 'You're not afraid of me are you?'

Still the old woman peered at him. 'I used to be. Looking at you now after all these years, are you telling me I should be?'

Five

From the sheriff's office Quarrie headed home by way of the farm supplies store. A couple of weeks back he'd promised his son he would show him how to read footprints made by men in the same way he was learning about the tracks of different animals. With that in mind he picked up a wooden sandbox so James could practice making his own.

Three miles into the hills the ranch looked like some old-world hacienda. Flat-roofed and cut in whitewashed adobe, the big house was set on a low bluff with steps leading up from the horse barns and corrals, the bunkhouse and three small cottages. As Quarrie pulled up outside his place the screen door flapped and his son appeared wearing a pair of blue jeans and a plaid shirt. Lean-looking like his father, James was tanned in the face and that accentuated the gray of his eyes and corn-colored hair he'd inherited from his mother.

'Hey, kiddo,' Quarrie said, 'what're you doing?'

'Waiting on you, Dad, did you get the sandbox?'

'Sure did. Just give me a minute here and we'll get to her.'

Inside the house Quarrie hung up his hat and gunbelt. James had some homework to finish and he did that while his father fetched the sandbox from the trunk of the car and shovelled dirt as he'd promised. After that he took a shower and then it was time to go over to the bunkhouse for supper. Before they crossed the yard, however, he sat his son down on the stoop out front, the sun long gone and the air thick with singing cicadas.

'James,' he said. 'There's something I have to tell you; something you need to hear from me before you hear it from anybody else.'

The boy looked up with a solemn expression on his face.

'I killed a man today,' Quarrie told him. 'Shot him dead after he tried to kill me with a shotgun. Fact is he robbed a store and shot up a state trooper's vehicle. It's going to be in the newspaper and on the radio and your buddies will hear all about it. It ain't anything to be proud of and it sure ain't something anyone would want to brag on. Sometimes it goes with the job is all, and better it's me who tells you rather than somebody else.'

Slowly James nodded.

'That's all I got to tell you except the man's name was Wiley. He fought in Vietnam and I guess he got back from over there not quite the same as when he left out.' Pausing for a moment he added, 'Do you understand what I'm telling you?'

'I don't know, Dad.' James's brow was deeply furrowed. 'I'm not sure I do. I'll have to think on it some I reckon.'

'You do that.' Quarrie helped him to his feet. 'You think on it as long as you want and if you need to ask me anything then go ahead. It ain't the kind of thing anybody likes to be doing, but we got our fair share of screwed up folks in Texas and if you're any kind of cop it's a fact you're going to run across them.'

Together they walked to the bunkhouse where the hands were gathered around the long table and Mama Sox, Pious's mother, was serving prime rib. Quarrie had known her since he was a boy and he still didn't know her given name. She had always been Mama Sox because no matter what else she might be wearing she always wore a pair of cotton socks. Pious was sitting at the end of the table, his job to fix the trucks and pilot the ranch plane. Quarrie hunched on the bench with his son alongside and James picked at his food as if contemplating all that his father had said. He brightened when the meal was over though, and Nolo asked him to help lunge a colt that wasn't yet ready for the saddle.

Quarrie went back to his cottage and sat on the stoop smoking a Camel regular. After a while Pious wandered over with a couple of ice cold bottles of Falstaff. 'So what's eating you?' he said. 'You were kind of quiet over dinner. That firefight bugging you, is it?'

'Wasn't so much of a firefight, Pious: man threw down on me when his buddy had already folded.'

'And now he's dead. Better him than you, don't let it bother you.'

'It don't.' Quarrie gestured. 'One thing my godfather taught me about this job is to understand why a thing goes down and don't be raking over it again. I told James just now is all and it's him I'm thinking about.'

Pious took a pull at his beer. 'Well, he ain't going to hear anything from anybody at school that he didn't already hear from you. All you can do, John Q.' He looked askance at him then. 'That the only thing on your mind, is it?'

*

The following morning Quarrie was up at six and it was seven when the captain rang.

'John Q,' he said, 'I need you in Amarillo.'

'What's up?'

'SAC Patterson is on his way up.'

'From Dallas, what does he want?'

'He wants the lowdown on what happened yesterday. He was at pains to tell me how the world's changing. It ain't what it used to be.'

'In Dallas maybe, that ain't how it is up here.'

'That's what I told him. Said how the man threw down on you and you defended yourself. He wants to talk to you just the same.'

Quarrie pressed air from between his lips. 'All right,' he said. 'I got some errands to run. I'll be there as soon as I can.'

When he left the ranch he drove south to Wichita Falls and stopped at the hospital on 8th and Brook Street. There was no sign of any clerk at the desk in the morgue so he went through the automatic doors into the examination room. Four porcelain tables were set side by side with stainless steel sluices at the base. The red light on the ceiling was on and Tom Dakin, the medical examiner, was working the farthest table assisted by a nurse while he spoke into the microphone clipped round his neck. Quarrie approached as quietly as he could but the nurse looked up and the medical examiner switched the microphone off.

'Speak of the devil,' he said. 'We just had one of yours in here with two in the chest at a half-inch spread. You know I heard somewhere how in the last round of state shooting exams you'd gotten your time below a quarter of a second. That was to draw, fire twice and re-holster. Did I read that right?'

Quarrie nodded.

Dakin indicated where the dead man from the hotel lay on

the slab. 'Well anyway, I guess you'll want to hear how this guy made the pass by himself.' Setting aside the scalpel he was holding he wiped his hands on a cloth. 'Blood vessel burst in his brain. Aneurism he probably never knew he had, seizure would've killed him like that.' He snapped his fingers. 'Kind of young for it maybe, I figure he's only about thirty, but then anomalies like that never did make allowances for age.'

Quarrie considered the marbled skin of the cadaver. 'The ambulance crew said they thought it might've been a heart attack.'

'I can see how they'd come to that conclusion because there is a bluish tint to his lips and that can happen with an aortal aneurism. Only this one was in his brain.' Taking off his glasses Dakin wiped them on his house coat then sipped from a cup of coffee. 'Could be it only occurred quite recently, then again he might've had it all his life.'

'But it's natural?' Quarrie said.

'Sure is. No sign, no real symptoms to give the sucker away. It just creeps up on you is what it does. Do we know who this feller was?'

Quarrie shrugged. 'Checked into The Roosevelt under the name Williams; can't tell you any more than that.'

'So I guess you'll be wanting this then.' The nurse offered him a piece of white card where she had pasted the dead man's fingerprints. 'I already made one for the coroner and allowed that you probably would.'

Quarrie slipped the card inside his jacket and turned to Dakin again. 'Did you come up with anything else?'

'No, sir, nothing but a trace of blue ink on the skin of his right forefinger.'

Quarrie nodded. 'I got a question for you, Tom. What does Proloid do?'

'The drug, you mean?' Dakin made a face. 'Usually a doctor will prescribe it to somebody whose metabolism is running slow. Thyroid playing up, stuff like that; kind of redresses the balance when things aren't working quite as they should be. Why'd you want to know?'

'I found an empty bottle in Wiley's hotel bedroom.'

Dakin looked puzzled.

'The feller you had in here with two at a half-inch spread. There was some powder on the table and I got a hunch he was grinding tablets with the butt of his handgun.'

Dakin glanced at the nurse.

'So, I was wondering,' Quarrie said, 'what would happen if somebody took Proloid when their metabolism wasn't running slow?'

'It would depend on how much they took.'

'How about they swallowed the whole bottle?'

'Then they'd be toast.' Dakin jutted his chin at the corpse. 'Either from a heart storm or burst blood vessel in the brain like him.'

Quarrie followed his gaze. 'Is there any way you can tell?'

'Overdose of Proloid, if you're looking for it, sure there is.' Stepping around the table Dakin took another swallow of coffee. 'You'd need to run some extra tests, more blood maybe, spinal fluid; one sure sign is an overabundance of iodine.'

'Test for it would you?' Quarrie said.

He drove from the hospital to Amarillo and pulled into the Department of Safety building where Captain Van Hanigan was based. Outside in the parking lot he spotted a government issue Ford and figured the FBI agents had arrived. They were waiting for him, two men in dark suits and narrow ties. One had a trilby with a feather in the band resting on his lap. Quarrie caught Van Hanigan's eye from the corridor then made his way to the ID Bureau and asked them to send the fingerprint card to both Ranger HQ in Austin and the National Crime Information Center to see if they could come up with a match.

Back in the office Van Hanigan got to his feet. The two men seated before his desk remained where they were and the captain introduced the older one as the Special Agent in Charge. His name was Patterson, hair the color of iron filings; he looked to be in his mid-forties. Quarrie considered him briefly then the other agent who was smaller, squatter and balding.

'This is Sergeant Quarrie,' the captain said.

Patterson looked up from where he sat. 'Yes, we know who he is.' Half a smile on his face, he gestured. 'Yesterday, Sergeant: the shooting off 287.'

'What about it?' Quarrie said.

'I'd like to know what went down. I guess you'll be talking to the district attorney at some point and I'm going to need a copy of his report.'

'Has somebody made a complaint?'

'Not as far as I know.'

'So why do you want the report?'

'I want to be abreast of the situation.'

'There's no need.' Quarrie looked from him to the other agent. 'A couple of sleazeballs rob a gun store and club old man Hemmings over the head. When I come up on them one puts his piece down and the other one doesn't. There ain't anything more to it than that.'

'Old school, aren't you?' It was the balding agent who spoke. 'It doesn't really fit with the times.'

Quarrie turned to him. 'And what times are those exactly?'

'These times,' Patterson cut in. '1967. The old days are gone in case the news never made it up here to the panhandle.' He spread his palms. 'Look, I know all about your Uncle Frank and Lone Wolf Manuel T. I know about Dick Crowder and how they made sure Mickey Cohen was on a plane back to LA. I know about how it used to be but the days of the old-school Ranger are gone.' A little condescendingly he shook his head. 'Law enforcement is accountable now in a way it's never been. The world's not like it was, there's a war on TV every night and folks see how it really is. Sergeant, you shoot a suspect dead, we need to know what happened, that's just the way it is.'

Quarrie glanced from him to Van Hanigan and back.

'Think about it,' Patterson went on. 'We've got coloreds wanting to be treated like white folks and students on the streets protesting about Vietnam. We got hippies living in communes along the Red River. God knows it'll be the Mexicans next.'

'So what-all you're telling me,' Quarrie said. 'Two of them and one of me, next time I should ask if they'd be so kind as to set their piece down?' He looked a little weary. 'And what if they don't want to do that? I defended myself. That's the front and back of it.'

Patterson sat back. 'Sergeant, nobody's saying you can't defend yourself. It's—'

'It's a fact that some things don't ever change.' Quarrie peered at the other agent. 'If a man's pointing a gun at you it don't matter whether it's 1967 or 1867, things are the way they've always been.'

Nobody spoke for a moment and Van Hanigan shifted his weight. Patterson glanced at him then he looked back at Quarrie. 'Even so, I will want a copy of the report. Look, we're on the same side here and the last thing I want is to sound off to a fellow cop, but a man is dead and I need to understand what happened.'

Quarrie studied him for a moment. 'All right, Special Agent, when I'm done with the district attorney I'll have him send you a copy.'

'That's all I ask,' Patterson said.

Taking off his hat Quarrie passed the brim between the tips of his fingers. 'By the way,' he said, 'he wasn't my uncle, he was my godfather.'

'Excuse me?' Patterson lifted an eyebrow.

'Captain Hamer. He wasn't my uncle, he was my godfather.'

Patterson got to his feet. 'Before we go, this other business in Wichita Falls, the dead guy at The Roosevelt, is there anything we should know?'

'Nope,' Quarrie said. 'Right now I'm checking his ID.'

When they were gone Quarrie gazed the length of the corridor. 'Captain,' he said, 'what was all that about?'

'Beats me,' Van Hanigan said. 'With Hoover on their case all the time I guess they like to be seen to be flexing their muscles.' He flapped a hand. 'So anyway: The Roosevelt, this guy with no credit card or driver's license. After what you told me yesterday I spoke to a cop in New Orleans name of Colback to see if there's anything he could tell us.' He made a face. 'Said to me how there's a couple of crews he's looking at down there but no one with links to Texas.'

Quarrie nodded. 'Right now I got Tom Dakin running tests

on the body and if I hadn't had to come up here this morning I'd be finding out what-all Henderson forgot to tell me.' He was quiet then for a moment. 'Colback, you said that cop you talked to's name was?'

'That's right; he's a lieutenant with the organized crime squad.' Sitting back in his chair Van Hanigan broke out a cigar.

'Captain,' Quarrie said, 'I got a hunch the lab's going to come up with Proloid residue both on that table in the hotel room and the butt of Henderson's handgun. That means those meds were ground into powder so they could be mixed with water. That might work if it's Wiley with a thyroid problem, but I ain't going to hold my breath.' He adjusted the leg ties on his gunbelt. 'Colback,' he muttered. 'I don't know where it was, but I heard that name someplace already.'

Back in Wichita Falls he stopped by the sheriff's office and grabbed a cup of coffee then picked up the phone to the district attorney. He told him about his meeting with the SAC and asked him to send a copy of the report to the field office in Dallas. When he put the phone down again dispatch buzzed through with a message to call the morgue.

'Tom,' he said when the medical examiner answered. 'This is John Q.'

'What we talked about,' Dakin said, 'cerebrospinal fluid. I performed a spinal tap and there's more iodine back there than fluid. Good job you mentioned that bottle otherwise I'd never have thought to check.'

Perched on the edge of the desk, Quarrie narrowed his eyes. 'So what you're telling me here, that feller didn't die of natural causes, he was killed by prescription drugs?'

'Yes, sir, that's what I'm telling you.'

When he put down the phone for the second time Quarrie was thinking about yesterday on the dirt road and what Henderson hadn't said. Unbuckling his gunbelt he opened the large drawer in his desk, stowed the weapons then locked the drawer and pocketed the key. Leaving the office he crossed the parking lot to the jailhouse, a newly built brick building with a single line of cells. At the desk he asked the deputy for a copy of Henderson's fingerprint card.

Two minutes later he locked the door to an interview room with no windows save the one that overlooked the hallway. He closed the blinds so nobody could see in then turned to where Henderson was sitting on the other side of the table with one hand cuffed to a fixed metal ring. Quarrie did not say anything. He leaned against the wall with his arms folded and studied Henderson. There was nothing in the room except the table, two chairs and an ashtray made from aluminum foil. Shaking a cigarette from his pack Quarrie rolled the wheel on the Zippo he'd been issued in Korea. Still he didn't speak; he just cast a glance from Henderson to the fingerprint card and back.

'What's up, John Q?' Henderson said.

'Did you talk to your mom yet?'

Henderson seemed to hunch where he sat on the chair. 'Yes, I did, and she bawled me out some, I can tell you.'

'What did you expect? You just got done with pre-release. What the hell were you thinking?'

'I don't know what I was thinking, probably five hundred dollars.'

'And did you get it?'

Henderson squinted at him.

'The money: did Wiley pay you?'

43

'Well, if he did it don't matter now.' Henderson let go a sigh. 'Matter of fact he didn't get around to it, no.'

'And you're set there having only just got out of Ferguson the first time.'

Henderson looked away. 'I'm hoping the way I surrendered to you will help some. What-all I said to Wiley about giving it up. How much more time d'you figure they're going to give me?'

Quarrie sat down in the opposing chair and tipped ash from his cigarette. 'We ain't talking jail time, Scott. Right about now I figure you'll be lucky if you don't get to ride the lightning.'

Henderson stared at him wide-eyed.

'If what you'd told me yesterday was all there was then the way you hung up your gun and put your hands on your head, what-all you said to your buddy, that might've meant something.'

'What're you talking about?'

'I'm talking about the Roosevelt Hotel. A room booked out to Wiley with two beds and both of them had been slept in.' He stared at Henderson then. 'It don't matter that you told Wiley to put his piece down, not after what you did.'

'I don't understand.' Henderson tried to spread a palm but the handcuff held it.

'Sure you do,' Quarrie said. 'It don't matter what you told me yesterday. You kill a man in Texas you're going to the chair, ain't no two ways about it.'

Henderson's face was the color of chalk. 'Mr Hemmings you mean? He ain't dead, is he? That whack on the head, it was Wiley done it, not me.'

'Will you quit jerking my damn chain?' Quarrie leaned

across the table. 'I ain't talking about old man Hemmings. I'm talking about the feller in the Roosevelt Hotel.'

Henderson tried to hold his eye but he had to look away. Quarrie stubbed out his cigarette and then he walked around behind Henderson and bent with his mouth to his ear. 'There ain't a whole lot I like less in life than somebody lying to me. The fact is you didn't just hook up with that asshole and split a pitcher like you told me, you took a room at the Roosevelt Hotel.'

Henderson stared at the table top.

'So what happened, the truth this time? I don't want any more bullshit.'

'It wasn't me.' Henderson shook his head. 'I didn't do anything. I—'

'Sure you did.' Quarrie pointed to the fingerprint card. 'Those are your dabs right there and I found a set in the room where a man was killed and another bunch in 210. I ain't talking about the door handle or TV remote, I'm talking powder residue we recovered from the desk.'

He paced around the table again and Henderson was trembling. 'Where did the pills come from? *G Matisse*, the name of the patient on the bottle, Scott. Who is that? I know we're talking New Orleans on account of the pharmacist, but who were those drugs for, huh?' He slapped a palm on the table and Henderson jumped. 'Wiley's dead so that leaves you and me. It might be you read somewhere how there's a moratorium on the chair right now, but this is Texas and I got strings I can pull if I want to.'

When he went back to the office he unlocked the drawer in his desk, took out his gunbelt and buckled it on. As he fastened the leg ties he was thinking about the dead man and an address in New Orleans. *Louisiana something*, Henderson had told him; he couldn't remember the rest. Quarrie was thinking about the photograph they had found hidden in the trouser press. Henderson swore he never got to see what it was because Wiley burned it as soon as they were back in their own room.

He looked up as a helicopter passed overhead. It was making for Andrews Airforce Base and as he listened to the distinctive sound of the rotor blades he was reminded of the time he'd been medi-vaced off a freezing mountain in Korea. He'd taken a bullet in the stomach and Pious had dragged him into a foxhole before carrying him down to where a Huey flew him to the MASH unit. The memory was as clear as if it was yesterday and as he turned from the window he knew where he'd heard Colback's name.

Picking up the phone he asked the operator to connect him with the organized crime squad in New Orleans. The line went quiet and a minute later a gruff voice spoke in his ear.

'Lieutenant Colback?' Quarrie said. 'My name's Quarrie, Ranger Sergeant out of Wichita Falls. Yesterday you talked to my captain.'

'Did I? What about it?'

'Your name, Lieutenant: it's familiar. Korea I'm thinking, 1951, hill 500, I was fighting with 4th Company and we had us a trigger sumbitch who was far too sharp with a long barrel. The way I remember it a sergeant out of 2nd Company called down asking for a sniper. The guy they flew in, I'm sure his name was Colback. Does that mean anything to you?'

'Could've been me,' Colback said. 'I was over there for a spell and I was a rifleman, yes. Shot a lot of gooks in my time though, and given it was at six hundred yards mostly, I don't remember them all.'

'Well, sir, you might remember this. 2nd Company was an all black unit and that sergeant's name was Noon.'

He heard Colback take a breath. 'Yeah, I remember all right. They court-martialled him for cowardice.'

'Only he wasn't a coward, was he?'

'Not according to you. I remember you now, Quarrie: you're the one wrote the president about him. The letter was in the newspapers and all kinds of hell cut loose; cost you a career in the army.'

'If I'd wanted one, yes it did.'

'But it worked though, that newspaper article.'

'*New York Times*,' Quarrie said. 'Reporter name of Moretti who used to hang around the hospital in Osaka hitting on all the nurses. I was in there on account of being gut shot and it was Noon who brought me off that hill.'

'And they printed your letter and he got off because of it.'

'He didn't get off exactly,' Quarrie said. 'The death sentence was commuted to life in prison but in the end he only served five years.'

'Right, right: I remember now and all because we never declared war in Korea.' Colback clicked his tongue. 'So then, now we've swapped a couple of war stories what is it you want?'

Six

Tobie ate lunch at his usual table in Broussards. The walls half mirror and half veined marble, he looked up as Franklin opened the door. He didn't come straight to the table. He waited a moment as the waiter brought Tobie a Martini.

'What is it?' Tobie said as Franklin sat down. 'I like peace and quiet while I eat my lunch and I like to eat alone.'

Franklin stared at him with his lips hollowed into an oval.

Breaking pieces of bread Tobie stirred them into his soup. 'One of these days you might be in a position to look at me like that,' he said, 'but that time is not now. In case any of what's happened over the last couple of weeks has escaped your notice the 28th is just a few days' time.'

Franklin didn't say anything.

'Let's assess where we are for a moment.' Tobie's voice had dropped to a whisper. 'In your wisdom you chose to use the man we'd selected for the 28th to take on another job and one too delicate for him. Instead of working alone he decided to recruit some kid we knew nothing about and between them they shot up a state trooper's cruiser. Right now that kid is sitting in jail having been interrogated by a Texas Ranger.' His gaze grew a little bitter. 'Our man is dead and before he was killed he was careless enough to toss an empty bottle in the trash. The label on that bottle not only identifies the pharmacist as being from New Orleans, it gives up the patient's name.'

'Let me deal with the Ranger,' Franklin said. 'As you keep reminding me, it's my mistake. I should be the one to take care of it.'

Tobie laughed out loud. 'Franklin,' he said, 'have you any idea how ridiculous you sound when you suggest something like that?'

'I can take care of him,' Franklin hissed. 'So he's a cop, so what?'

As if he'd lost his appetite suddenly the old man pushed his bowl away. 'Didn't you hear what I said? There's a witness in the jailhouse. You can't kill anybody, not unless you want every Ranger in Texas down here sniffing around.'

'That kid doesn't know anything. Wiley just needed the heads up on a gun store so he could get hold of the M1C.'

'Right.' Tobie's tone was derisory. 'The heads up. That's all he needed then he decided to take him to Wichita Falls, have him hold a gun on Williams while he made him drink a cocktail of prescription drugs.'

'Henderson didn't see anything. He doesn't know anything. Wiley couldn't have told him anything because Wiley didn't know anything. Jesus, how stupid do you think I am?'

The old man did not answer.

'Look,' Franklin said. 'The photograph was hidden in the trouser press. Wiley burned it. There's nothing that kid can tell the Ranger. I can deal with him and I will.'

For a short moment Tobie toyed with his napkin. 'No, you can't and you won't. You will leave whatever comes of this to me. Kill a Texas Ranger with a witness in jail and you'll bring the rest of them down here and they won't give a shit about jurisdiction. Do your homework, Franklin. They're more like soldiers than cops. The way they are, what they've become, they've been shaped by the enemies they've fought.' He gestured with the flat of his hand. 'I'm talking about Comanche and Kiowa, not to mention the comanchero bandits from Mexico and every mother's son ever since. Think about who those Rangers have been. John "Coffee" Hays, Ben McCulloch, Frank Atlee, not to mention Frank Hamer and Lone Wolf Manuel T.' He paused to dab flecks of spittle from his lips. 'Why do you think there's never been any mafia activity in Texas? Because the Rangers won't allow it, that's why. They believe in prevention not cure and as soon as any wise guy shows up in Houston or Dallas they're loaded onto a plane.' He drew his soup bowl towards him again. 'The Mexicans used to call them *Tejanos Diablos*. They never forget and they never quit. They might be the state police force now but that's not how they began and the history of where they've come from is ingrained in every one. Hamer was Quarrie's godfather, the guy they brought out of retirement because nobody else could track down Bonnie and Clyde.' Pausing for a moment he said, 'Does the "Sherman Riot" mean anything to you?'

Franklin looked blank.

'1930: George Hughes, a field hand who raped his boss's wife. A white woman, Franklin: when the people of Sherman tried to lynch the sonofabitch they were repelled by Captain Hamer. Shotgun and tear gas. He was there to make sure Hughes was tried in a court of law. Think about that for a moment, one Ranger protecting the life of a rapist against a rioting mob and that rapist was a nigger. We're talking the time when the Klan was at the height of its power. Black lives were worth less than they are even now and no county sheriff could give a damn. Most were either Klan members themselves, or agreed with the lynchings anyway. Black prisoners didn't make it to trial. They were burned and hanged from a tree. That's why they brought in

Rangers. To them the law is the law and a man is entitled to its protection no matter his color or creed. If that's how they deal with a nigger, how will they react when it's one of their own?'

Franklin was smarting. 'All right, you've made your point. So what do you want me to do?'

Tobie signalled for the waiter to bring him another drink. 'When does he arrive?'

'He's flying in tomorrow I think.'

'Moisant Field or the Lakefront?'

'I don't know.'

'Well, find out. When he gets in make sure you're there to meet him. That's what I want you to do.'

'What do you mean?' Franklin furrowed his brow.

Wearily the old man sighed. 'You drive a taxi, remember? It enables you to go anywhere in the city without drawing undue attention. Who's he meeting with – Colback?'

Franklin nodded.

'All right then.' Tobie emptied his glass. 'Your job is to keep tabs on him right from the get-go. Now,' he said, 'I want to enjoy the rest of my lunch so go ahead and leave me in peace.'

*

James sat on the chair in his father's bedroom as Quarrie laid out clean clothes. He selected a canvas Carhartt jacket with ribbing at the waist, and a couple of press-stud shirts. James watched him place them on the bed and then he packed them into his bag.

'Bud,' Quarrie said, 'Eunice and Mama will look out for you while I'm away and when I get home we'll see if we can't side-line that colt Nolo picked out and try to get a saddle on him.'

His son looked a little happier. 'Where're you going though, Dad?'

'I told you already, New Orleans.'

'And I can't come?'

'Not this time. It's business but we'll go another time, I promise. They've got one heck of a zoo down there and—'

'Audubon,' James interrupted.

'That's right, Audubon Zoo. Where'd you hear about that?'

'In school I guess, I don't remember.'

Quarrie ruffled the young boy's hair. 'And how is school? How's Miss Munro?'

'She's all right; yesterday she was teaching us something called ana . . . ana . . .'

'Anagrams,' Quarrie finished. 'Is that what-all she said?'

'Yes, sir.' James nodded. 'I think so. Making words out of letters mixed up from other words. She told me I was doing OK.'

Strapping on his twin-rig shoulder holsters Quarrie led the way out to the yard where Pious was sitting in a Jeep waiting to drive him up to the plane.

'You hang tough while I'm away,' he said as James loitered at the kitchen door. 'Spend some time leaving different footprints in that sandbox and make drawings of what you see. We'll talk about how to read them just as soon as I get back.'

Fifteen minutes later Pious had the nose up and they were making a sweep over shallow mesquite hills that surrounded the Feeley property. As they banked shafts of sunlight caught on a string of pump-jacks that cut through a low-walled canyon.

'Place has changed some since Pick passed,' Quarrie commented.

'Sure has,' Pious's voice crackled through his headphones.

'So this cop you're hooking up with, it's the same guy we had deal with the Chinaman that time back in Korea?'

'Hill 500, yes it is. Name's Colback, do you remember him?'

'Not really, alls I recall is asking the CP for a shooter that day because we were getting pretty beat up and couldn't get a bead on who-all it was doing the killing. Probably I wrote it up in my diary like I used to but I kind of had my hands full after.' He stared into clouds where they massed straight ahead. 'Last time I landed at the Lakefront was when I flew Mrs Feeley in for Mardi Gras. She sure likes to party now, doesn't she?'

'That she does,' Quarrie said, 'at least since Pick passed anyway.'

Late that afternoon they flew over the causeway that spanned Lake Pontchartrain and a few minutes after that they were on the ground.

Quarrie reached for his bag. 'Pious,' he said, 'why don't you tie this rig down and stick around for a night or two?'

'No can do I'm afraid. Much as I'd like to set on a stool someplace and listen to the blues with you, Mrs Feeley wants to go to Houston tomorrow and she wants to go in her airplane.'

*

Franklin sat at the wheel of his taxi with the 'For Hire' sign switched on and the vehicle at the head of the line. He saw the small plane sweep in from the lake and opened the glove box to inspect his short-barrelled Beretta. Checking the magazine he put it away again and ten minutes later he saw the terminal doors open and Quarrie step onto the sidewalk wearing tan-colored pants and a pale gray cowboy hat.

Damp air seemed to cling as Quarrie signalled the '65 Impala. The humidity felt far more acute than it had in Texas and his shirt was sticking to his back. Tossing his bag ahead of him he climbed in.

'Just arrived?' Franklin looked over the seat.

Quarrie nodded.

'First time in New Orleans?'

'Yes, it is.'

'So where is it you want me to take you?'

Quarrie regarded the young man with cropped blond hair. 'Hotel I guess, I got a meeting in the morning near the International Trade Mart building.'

'That's on Camp and Common,' Franklin said. 'There aren't too many hotels over that way but I can take you to a place on Canal Street.'

They drove across town in silence and when they got to Canal Street Franklin pulled into a bay in front of the American Bank. Rolling down the window he pointed across four lanes of heavy traffic to a courtyard next door to a sign advertising the Central Savings & Loan.

'Hotel Magnolia,' he said. 'It's not the best in the world, but it's pretty central and it's not the most expensive around here either. Handy for where you want to go in the morning.' Reaching into a pocket he took out a business card and passed it to Quarrie. 'You need to think about whose cab it is you're getting in. There're plenty of folk driving taxis in this city who aren't quite what they seem. I run this outfit myself, so if you want a ride you can trust, all you got to do is call.'

'How far is it to walk?' Quarrie asked him.

'To the Trade Mart? Not far I guess, about a half dozen blocks.'

Grabbing his bag Quarrie crossed the street at the light and passed under the arch into a small courtyard where the doors to the hotel lobby stood open. Inside he found a desk shaped like a horseshoe with a wooden stool behind and a dozen hooks bearing room keys fixed on the wall. Above the hooks were various old photos of black musicians and he could hear jazz music lifting from somewhere in the back. There was no sign of anybody serving so he pressed the bell on the counter. A moment later a middle-aged black woman came through and smiled at him. She told him her name was Yvonne and showed him up the stairs to a cast iron walkway. 'Looks like it's fixing to get wet,' she said, nodding to the reef of low-slung clouds, 'got us some rain blowing in.'

'That's just fine with me, mam. Where I come from we ain't seen a drop since fall.'

The room was pretty spartan, a window in the front with a pair of thin drapes that hung limply on either side. A double bed seemed to hunch against one wall where the paper was beginning to peel. Other than that the only furnishings were a small table and a high-backed chair. In the back was a bathroom with no shower, just a claw-foot, free standing tub. On the wall to the side of the bed there was a wooden closet where the doors did not shut quite properly. Unhooking his pistols, Quarrie folded the leather shoulder holster and placed it in the closet with his guns in the nightstand drawer.

In the morning he woke early and shaved to the sound of the rain Yvonne had promised rattling the roof above his head.

Sweeping in from the gulf the wind brought a chill with it and he put on his hat and coat. Yvonne was at the desk downstairs with a pot of coffee going on a single-ring stove. Pouring a cup for Quarrie she said that if he wanted breakfast the best place was the A&G. Quarrie considered the photographs on the wall above the hooks where the keys to the rooms were hanging. Jelly Roll Morton and Barney Bigard; there was one signed by Lizzie Miles.

'All of them from the 7th Ward,' Yvonne informed him with pride. 'Back of town we call it. That's where I'm from myself.'

Quarrie decided to walk to his meeting with Lieutenant Colback, it wasn't far and after so long with nothing but dust in the throat he enjoyed the fall of the rain. Walking a block on Magazine he came to Common Street and spotted the pink painted building Colback had told him about on the phone. The lot next door was being run as a parking garage by two young guys from a wooden kiosk and alongside that was the Trade Mart Café.

When he went in he spotted a man of about fifty with razored hair seated at a window table. He wore a business suit and a fedora lay upturned at his elbow. Quarrie did not recognize him. He had seen him only once and that was just briefly after Pious called the command post sixteen years before. Shaking the rain from his shoulders he took off his hat and crossed to the table. 'Lieutenant Colback?' he said.

'You got to be the Ranger.' Colback took a moment to look him up and down. 'I don't get over to Texas so much. How many of you guys are there?'

'Not a whole lot, we got a lot of country to cover.'

'Only that country doesn't stretch to Louisiana.' He

motioned for Quarrie to sit down. 'So, on the phone you said you got a murder made to look like natural causes?'

'That's right.'

'A bottle of prescription meds that brings you all the way down to New Orleans. Well.' Colback looked him hard in the eye. 'Your jurisdiction ended in Texas. You want to talk to anyone in this town you're going to have to do it through me.'

Seven

On the other side of the road Franklin sat behind the wheel of his taxi. Tobie was in the back, he watched as Quarrie emerged from the café.

'So that's him?' the old man said.

'That's him.'

For a moment Tobie stared. 'All right, I want you to go and wait outside his hotel.'

Resting his arm on the back of the seat Franklin looked round.

'Take him wherever he wants to go.' Still watching, Tobie chewed his lip. 'You've spoken to Earl Moore, told him what I said?'

Franklin nodded.

'He's the only one I'm concerned about. Right now the client still has need of him and we did a lot of work back in February. For the time being at least he has to remain alive.' Still staring the length of the street he watched till Quarrie disappeared at the corner. 'Tell him to talk to the girl. Tell him to make sure she stays away from anyone who wants to speak to her.'

'And if she doesn't?' Again Franklin looked back at him.

'Then believe me, she'll wish she had.'

'What about Williams? His real ID, I mean. We could talk to the supplier; ask him to make a call?'

Tobie shook his head. 'We use the supplier for one purpose and one only. If that Ranger's asking questions there's a way we can find out what we want to know without anyone being aware.'

Franklin looked puzzled.

'Franklin, just do what I tell you. Quarrie's first port of call will be the pharmacist on St Ann Street. I doubt Matthews will tell him anything, but we'll deal with him just in case.'

'You want *me* to do that?' Franklin said.

Tobie shook his head. 'No, Matthews is a black man. We don't need that kind of attention.' He thought for a moment then he said, 'Go and see Soulja Blue. Have his crew pick up Matthews and take him back to the club. Tell them to hold him. Tell them to wait for me there.'

'Why would that pimp do anything for us?'

Tobie smiled. 'There's an unpaid debt on his books. Tell him we'll pay what's due.'

*

When Quarrie got back to his hotel the rain had stopped and he spotted the taxi parked outside the American Bank building. He lifted a hand and Franklin drove the block to the light then swung around to pull over.

'So you decided to walk in the rain and you want a cab now that it's stopped?' He smiled as Quarrie got in. 'Mister, that doesn't make a whole lot of sense.'

'It does where I come from,' Quarrie said.

'So where is that, Oklahoma, Texas maybe?'

'Texas.' Quarrie felt in his pocket for the bottle. 'There's a pharmacist I need to go visit, North Rampart and St Ann.'

They drove towards the railroad station where a Trailways bus was parked and porters were loading luggage onto hand-carts.

'Listen,' Franklin said. 'I know this city so if you want to go anyplace special I can almost certainly take you.' A light in his eye, he glanced in the rear view mirror. 'I'm talking about anything you might want to do when you're not working, com-pany, that kind of thing. I can bring you places and I'm not talking about The Storyville.'

'I'll bear that in mind.' Quarrie squinted at him. 'Kind of young for this job, ain't you?'

'That's what everybody says.' Franklin lifted a hand. 'The fact is I'm in college right now on a football scholarship. I only do this to make up the extra.'

'Football scholarship, huh, so what are you – running back, wide receiver?'

'No, sir, I'm the quarterback. It's my job to set up the play.'

A few minutes later they pulled up outside a small, glass-fronted pharmacy on North Rampart and St Ann. 'Do you want me to wait for you?' Franklin said.

Handing him a couple of dollars Quarrie shook his head.

From the sidewalk he watched as the cab pulled away then thumbed back his hat where his forehead was sweating at the band. He was between the French Quarter and the 7th Ward here with the buildings clustered tightly together and a haze in the air where St Ann Street led to the river. Matthews Pharmacy occu-pied the corner, the glass door set on the angle facing across the four lanes of North Rampart. A red Spanish-style window dom-inated the sidewalk and a wrought iron gate secured the doorway.

Inside two black women with their names stitched into knee-length housecoats were serving. In another section stools pressed a counter with coffee, cookies and jars of hard-tack candy.

Quarrie approached the woman at the cash register. 'I'm looking for Mr Matthews,' he said.

'Are you here for a prescription?'

'In a manner of speaking I guess. Is he back there?' He nodded to the screen that shielded the dispensary.

'Hold on,' the woman said. 'I'll see if he's available.'

*

Franklin drove North Rampart Street as far as the junction with Governor Nicholls then turned towards the river again. Cruising as far as Bourbon Street he parked. A drugstore occupied the corner and he went inside where a young woman was behind the counter. With a nod in her direction he crossed to a doorway hidden behind a metal ring curtain. The girl pressed a buzzer and Franklin waited. A couple of minutes later the door opened and a heavily built black man of about forty filled the gap. His head was shaved to a polished sheen, muscles worked the sleeves of his Nehru jacket and his eyes glinted with the light of steroids.

'Soulja,' Franklin said. 'The old man's got a job for you but first you need to make a phone call.'

*

Quarrie laid his hat on a stool at the coffee bar and a young black man appeared wearing a short, white housecoat. He

61

looked at the hat then at Quarrie and smiled. 'Sir, I guess you're not from around here, are you?'

'You figured, huh? There goes my incognito.'

'Do what now?'

'Never mind, pour me a cup of that coffee.'

A couple of minutes later the pharmacist came through from the dispensary, middle-aged with tortoiseshell glasses and curling gray hair. He wore a similar coat to the one the young man was wearing only his did not carry a name tag. 'Can I help you?' he said.

Quarrie looked up from his coffee. 'Mr Matthews, yes, sir, I hope you can.' Taking the empty bottle he'd recovered from the hotel room he placed it on the counter. 'I'm reaching out here, I . . .'

Matthews looked a little puzzled. 'You'll have to forgive me, but who are you?'

'My name's Quarrie. I'm a Texas Ranger.' Taking his badge from his pocket Quarrie laid it down next to the bottle.

A star in a wheel cut from a silver five-peso piece; Matthews took a moment to study it. 'A little out of your jurisdiction aren't you, all the way down here in New Orleans?'

'I'm working a murder investigation and I need to talk to this patient.'

'Well, I'm afraid I can't help you. I'm sorry, but drugs are prescribed by a doctor and a doctor's relationship with his patient is confidential. When a pharmacist dispenses those drugs on behalf of the doctor he becomes part of that confidence.' Sliding onto a seat next to Quarrie, Matthews waved the boy away. Hands clasped, he looked at Quarrie. 'I can't talk to you,' he said. 'I can't break a confidence.'

Quarrie studied him with his eyes hooded. 'How about I tell you the drugs were ground into powder, mixed with water and tipped down some poor guy's throat? Thirty years old, Mr Matthews. He died in a hotel bedroom knowing he was going to.'

'I'm sorry about that.' The pharmacist shook his head. 'But it really doesn't make any difference.'

'Sure it does. You dispensed the medication and it ended up being used in a murder.'

'Sergeant, really, that is nothing to do with me.'

'You don't think so, huh?' Quarrie cocked his head to one side. 'If this was another pharmacist the patient's address might well be on the label.'

'But it's not.' Matthews's tone had sharpened. 'We don't do that here. Now, I'm sorry but I've already explained my position so if you'll excuse me I have to get back to work.'

*

Gigi was in the living room when she saw the Ford pull up outside. She was rooting around in her purse for keys as Earl got out and glanced both ways up and down the street.

Gigi had the door open as he came up the steps. 'What're you doing here, Earl? You never called. I was on my way out. I . . .'

'I need to talk to you. It won't take a minute.'

She gazed at him as if from a distance then ushered him into the living room. 'When you told me not to call I thought that was us over with. What's going on? For two months I can call that number then I can't be calling anymore.'

'The number's been disconnected,' Earl told her. 'It's for the best.'

Gigi glanced at his wedding finger where there was no ring. 'You know, in all this time you never told me your last name or what you did for a living. I know you're married. It don't matter that you don't wear a ring. I smell your wife's perfume on you every time we meet. Women notice that kind of thing.'

'I'm not married,' he said without conviction.

'Then how come I can't call?' She studied him with her arms across her chest. 'Look at you, like a rat got trapped in the corner. What's up, Earl? What's going on?'

'Nothing,' he said. 'Nothing's going on. I just came to tell you that you can't call the number anymore.'

'No you didn't. You done told me that on the phone.' She looked keenly at him still. 'This is all to do with the pills you took from my cabinet.'

His eyes seemed to fix on hers then he gazed out to the street where the front door still stood open. He shut the door and took Gigi's arm. At the window he scanned the houses on the other side of the road.

Gigi worked her arm free of his hand. 'What on earth did you want with meds I take for my thyroid?'

'I don't know what you're talking about.'

'Sure you do. You're the only other person that's been in the house.'

He shook his head. 'Look, never mind your meds. That's not why I'm here. I came here to warn you, OK?'

Gigi looked startled. 'Warn me, what do you mean?'

'Not warn you, tell you.' Confusion in his eyes, Earl peered out the window again. 'I'm just saying. I mean, there are people out there who know who you are and . . .' Breaking off, he sat down in a chair as if he was carrying a weight that his legs just would not take. He stared at the coffee table. He stared at the floor. He worked his palms together then curled his hands into fists. 'Gigi,' he said. 'I need you to listen to me. There's a cop in town from out of state. Whatever you do, don't talk to him.'

Gigi watched him drive away and then she went out to her old station wagon. Making a U turn where the road crew was working, she headed across the ward towards the French Quarter. When she got there she turned onto Orleans Street and glimpsed the fine lines of the Cabildo. She drove a couple of blocks before pulling over outside the gates to her nana's house. A little further down the road she could see a black Lincoln parked in a bay with a man in a business suit at the wheel who seemed to be checking his door mirrors. Fitting her key in the lock of the small gate Gigi went into the courtyard. Above her the balcony doors were open and she could see her nana sitting at the table talking to an old man with a shock of silver hair. Nana didn't see her but the expression on her face seemed a little wary. Gigi did not go up; she stepped back out to the street. As she closed the gate she noticed a silver-handled walking cane against the leg of the old man's chair.

*

Nana looked into Tobie's eyes. A pair of china tea cups on the table, she watched him cut a slice of lemon and place it in her cup then take the knife to another. She watched him pour the tea and stir in a spoonful of sugar. 'Like old times, Nana,' he said.

65

'Ain't it just, nothing for twenty years and then you visit with me twice in a couple of days. That's not like you, Rosslyn. In all the years I've been in this city I've never known anyone as calculating as you.' She shook her head. 'You don't do spur-of-the-moment. It's a fact you never did.'

'Maybe I'm getting old,' he said. 'Maybe I'm more spontaneous than I was. They say old habits die hard but that's not how it is with me.'

Nana took a sip of tea.

'How's Gigi?' he said. 'Still singing, is she? Still playing with that band?'

'Yes, she is.' Again Nana looked wary. 'That's twice now you asked about her. Are you going to tell me what it is you want or am I going to have to set here trying to guess?'

'Maybe I don't want anything,' the old man said. 'Perhaps I just like to visit. I always loved this balcony, the view downtown to St Louis. It's special, Nana; and I've not been here in a while. Do you remember the day I came over when all the political shenanigans were going on? The Capitol Building, I mean, that day back in '35?'

Nana looked at him with her face a little pinched. 'Yes,' she said. 'I remember.'

'We had us a wonderful time.'

'Did we? I guess we might've done, but we ain't doing that anymore. I don't care what you said before, this is my place and it has been for a long time.' Getting up from the seat she began to clear the dishes away.

'Don't you want your tea?' Tobie said. 'You always used to like lemon tea.'

She clicked her tongue. 'I'm busy, Rosslyn. I got a life to live

66

and I need you to say what you came to say and then I need you to go.'

'I told you.' His eyes had a glaze to them then. 'I like it here. I'll leave when I'm ready.'

*

Late that afternoon Quarrie took a call from Yvonne at the front desk. Upstairs in his room, he was trying to work out his next move when she told him Lieutenant Colback was on the phone and wanted to see him at his office. Walking out onto Canal Street he spotted the cab parked out front of the American Bank building with the blond guy in the driver's seat.

In silence they drove the length of St Charles to where the Old Post Office dominated Lafayette Square. On the phone Colback had told Quarrie to look out for that building, which was empty and about to be remodelled. Situated at right angles was Old City Hall and the NOPD's organized crime squad occupied the second floor of the building next door.

'Do you want me to wait?' Franklin said as he pulled up outside.

'I'm good.' Quarrie opened the door.

He climbed to the second floor and came out in a spacious lobby with high ceilings that had been partitioned into various cubicles by panels of frosted glass. A young woman in a cotton print dress made copies at a Xerox machine and she directed him along the hall. He could see the lieutenant through the open office door talking to another man wearing a linen suit that looked as if it could do with the touch of a steam iron. Colback motioned for him to close the door and Quarrie considered the second man. He didn't get up and he didn't speak. Colback introduced him as Pershing Gervais, chief investigator with the district attorney's office. Quarrie sat down and hooked an ankle over his knee. 'So what can I do for you?'

Sitting back in his chair Gervais looked him up and down. 'Well, for starters you can stop disturbing the working folks down here.'

Quarrie cocked one eyebrow.

'I had a call from a pharmacist on North Rampart and St Ann. Black guy running a quiet little place for the Negroes, his name is Matthews and he told me you were in his store earlier today not listening to what you were told.'

Quarrie looked briefly at Colback.

'Ring any bells?' Gervais's tone was testy. 'Apparently you went in there demanding to know about one of his patients. You unnerved him, Sergeant, so much so, he gave my office a call.'

'The district attorney,' Quarrie held his eye. 'Why would he do that? If he wanted to make a complaint, why not call the precinct?'

'Because that store used to be part of my beat when I was pounding the bricks and that's why he picked up the phone.'

'Part of your beat, uh?' Quarrie nodded. 'Looked out for it some, I hear you.'

Gervais's expression was suddenly cold. 'Look,' he said. 'You're from Texas. You have no jurisdiction and you're only here at all because the lieutenant said he would vouch for you.' He looked Quarrie hard in the eye. 'We're having a friendly chat right now, but you go around upsetting the natives you'll find yourself back on a plane.'

Eight

At six o'clock Claude Matthews closed the door to his pharmacy. His staff had already gone for the day and he fixed the security gate in place before walking to where he'd parked his car.

Circumnavigating the 700 block he turned back onto North Rampart Street and headed towards the 9th Ward. The radio playing, he was listening to a report from Vietnam where the newscaster seemed to be pointedly avoiding any mention of the day's body count. Switching stations to something a little more light-hearted Matthews drove towards the Main Outfall Canal.

A mile or two further he turned into the driveway of a two-story Creole house on Alabo Street and as he put on the parking brake a blue Malibu pulled up behind. For a moment the pharmacist sat with his hands on the wheel and the engine still running. Then he shut it off. Glancing at the empty windows of his house he got out of the car. Behind him a tall, muscular black man climbed from the passenger seat of the Malibu.

'Mr Matthews,' he said, opening his coat to reveal the grips of a pistol. 'I got someone wants to talk to you so come ahead and get in the car.'

*

Gigi was eating dinner with her nana in the apartment on Orleans Street, smoked brown trout and Cajun salad. They were at the table on the balcony.

'Are you all right, Nana?' Gigi said. 'You seem a little under the weather.'

Briefly Nana looked up at her then concentrated on the fish before taking a sip of wine.

'I'm just fine, Cherie. Tout c'est bon.'

'No it's not.' Laying down her fork Gigi sat back. 'I know when tout c'est bon and when it's not and right now I know it's not. Are you getting sick?'

'No, I'm not getting sick.'

'So what is it then?'

'Nothing, I don't know what you're talking about.'

With another long look at her Gigi went back to her food. 'So who was that this afternoon, that older gentleman with the walking cane?'

Nana looked up sharply.

'He was here when I came by to visit. I opened the gate but you were out here on the balcony so I left you alone. Who was that, Nana? I saw the way you were looking at him. Is it that man bothering you?'

For a moment Nana peered at her then she placed her knife and fork on the plate and pushed it to one side. Working her jaws as if she had something stuck between her teeth, she sipped once more at her wine. 'So you saw the way I looked at him. What is it you think you saw?'

'I don't know exactly, like he'd scared you or something maybe?'

'Scared me?' Nana snorted. 'He didn't scare me. If you saw us why didn't you come up?'

'I know how you are when you got company,' Gigi said. 'You

don't like to be disturbed. Nana, I've seen that man before. He was drunk on champagne at a party on Dauphine Street and he was walking around twirling that snake's head cane.' She seemed to think for a moment then. 'Had to be '63, me and the band were playing Clay Bertrand's carriage house right around Christmas time.'

Nana cleared the dishes away and Gigi followed her through to the kitchen. 'Look,' she said more gently, 'I can see how you are and the only thing that's happened that's any different to usual is that man showing up in his chauffeured car. Who is he? Do you owe him money or something? Is everything OK?'

Laying a hand against her chest the old woman laughed out loud. 'Owe him money, are you kidding me? No, I don't owe him money. I don't owe anybody money.'

Reaching out she gave Gigi a hug. 'I'm fine,' she said. 'Tout c'est bon. Tout c'est bien. It's just a few old memories creeping up that I'd thought I'd forgotten is all.'

*

When Franklin pushed open the door he found Matthews with a blindfold over his eyes and his hands tied to his ankles where he lay on his side on the floor. No windows in the room and no furniture save a single, wooden chair. The pharmacist's glasses lay next to him, one arm bent out of shape and one of the lenses fractured. He half sat up but slumped again and a hint of bloody spittle stained the corner of his mouth. Standing to one side, Franklin let Tobie pass and he sat down in the high-backed chair. Behind him Soulja Blue looked on and Franklin nodded for him to leave them alone.

Matthews tried to sit up a second time but flopped onto his side. Tobie inspected him from the chair. He did not say anything. He just looked at the pharmacist then he gestured to Franklin who gripped Matthews under the arms. Hauling him upright he sat him against the wall. Matthews tried to wipe the spittle from his lip but he couldn't reach because his hands were tied.

'Wipe his mouth,' Tobie said.

'Who are you?' Matthews sounded broken and scared. 'Why have you brought me here?'

'Wipe his mouth,' Tobie repeated and Franklin took a handkerchief from his pocket and mopped the gob of crimson saliva then dropped the handkerchief on the floor.

'Where am I?' Matthews uttered. 'What do you want?'

Tobie eyed him from the chair. 'This morning you had a visitor. I want to know what was said.'

The pharmacist worked his head around the bole of his neck as if he were trying to see. Franklin tightened the blindfold around his eyes.

'The Texas Ranger, what did you tell him?' Tobie sounded irritable. 'Speak, man. I haven't got all night.'

'I didn't tell him anything. He was asking about a patient and I told him I don't talk about patients, I'm not at liberty to say.'

'What else?'

'He had a bottle of pills I'd dispensed and told me they'd been used in a murder.'

'And what did you tell him?'

'Nothing, I told you. I don't talk about patients. I never have and I never will.'

Tobie sat there for a moment longer just watching him. Then he got up and tapped the floor with the tip of his cane.

Outside his chauffeur was waiting and he glanced across the road to where Franklin's taxi was parked. Franklin followed him out and they stood in the darkness then Tobie got in the car. Holding the door open Franklin looked down at him with a puzzled expression. 'What was all that about?' he said.

'I wanted to see him myself.'

'I don't get it. How come we're keeping him here?'

Looking up at him the old man sighed. 'Do I really have to spell it out? His wife will report him missing and in this city "missing" means murdered regardless of whether a body is found. The last person to talk to him was a Texas Ranger claiming to be down here investigating a homicide. That brings in the 3rd Precinct and the fat detective.' He pointed across the Quarter with his cane. 'If Williams was a felon we'll find out his real name.'

'And if he wasn't?' Franklin said.

'What else would he be?' the old man said. 'He knew who ran that office; why else would he make the call?'

*

Quarrie woke to the sound of footfall on metal stairs. Reaching to his boot where it lay on the floor he slid out the snub-nose thirty-eight and they were knocking as he crossed the floor. Opening the door he stared into the unshaven face of an overweight man wearing a baggy-looking suit, his hair slick with a combination of grease and rain water. He was grinding at a plug of chew.

'My name's De La Martin,' he said. 'Homicide, 3rd Precinct.' He pronounced the name "D-La" and considered the gun Quarrie was holding. 'You might want to set that down.'

Quarrie laid the gun on the bureau.

'So you're a Texas Ranger.' De La Martin looked him up and down. 'I've got questions I want to ask you. Best you go put a shirt on.'

An NOPD prowl car was parked outside with two uniforms up front and they drove the short distance to the 3rd Precinct Station House on Chartres Street. A flat-roofed brick building that fronted the narrow road, it was shouldered by similar blocks either side. A pair of arched entrances occupied each end, one with a cut-away curb that looked as if it had been fashioned in the days of the surrey buggy. The other was built around a pair of wooden doors and three windows punctured the wall in between. Parking the cruiser out front the detective made a show of getting Quarrie out then marched him through the arch into the rain-soaked yard.

They took him down a flight of stone stairs that twisted in a narrow spiral. At the bottom was a small landing where two uniforms ushered him past an office with De La Martin's name on the door. Beyond that there was a small squad room and another office where a copier was busy with an incoming teletype. At the far end they came to a room furnished only by a table, chair and a three-sided steel mesh cage. They locked him in the cage and closed the office door, panelled with frosted glass. Quarrie could see shadows passing back and forth and hear the hubbub on the other side. There was nothing to sit on so he squatted cross-legged on the floor.

As soon as the prowl car left the hotel Franklin got out of his cab and locked the door. Waiting for a break in the traffic he crossed to the median with a newspaper folded under his arm. On the other sidewalk he went into the lobby where Yvonne was behind the desk. '3rd Precinct,' Franklin told her. 'I need a key to the Ranger's room.'

Upstairs he unlocked the door and went inside. For a moment he stood in the half-darkness where the drapes were pulled across the window, and studied the unmade bed. His gaze shifted to the chair and bureau beside the door. He took in the confines of the bathroom and nightstand. Then he opened the closet door.

*

Tobie spoke to Dean Andrews on the second-floor landing of the baroque-style office on Baronne. A chubby-looking man in a linen suit, Andrews wore a pair of black-framed Ray-Ban sunglasses as he always did even when he was indoors. He looked a little nervous and considered the older man's snake's head cane.

'Mr Andrews,' Tobie wore an easy smile. 'Rather than us call you for the odd consultancy job now and then, when are you going to take up my offer and join the firm?'

Andrews peered through his sunglasses with lines of perspiration marking his brow.

'Rosslyn F Tobie and Associates,' he said. 'It's a heck of an offer and I'm thinking seriously about it.'

'You're right. It is.' Tobie's smile had faded a little. 'Don't think, Mr Andrews. Make a decision before the offer is off the table once and for all.'

He watched the attorney climb the stairs then went through to his office where two P53 Enfield Muskets were displayed crosswise beneath a painting of Jefferson Davis. Sitting down at his desk he sought through the stack of case files the girl had brought in earlier and then he looked up. Pushing back his chair he crossed to a wall safe behind the door. Working the combination he cast an eye across the bundles of cash and three metal bank boxes, then he reached for a blue paper file. Carrying it back to the desk he sat down once more and considered the name on the front with a thoughtful expression.

*

Sitting on the floor of the metal cage Quarrie went through all that had happened since he got off Mrs Feeley's plane. He thought about Colback and Pershing Gervais. He thought about the pharmacist and a cab driver who'd been there at every turn. He thought about who might've been on the phone to the fat detective who'd shown up at his door.

Half an hour passed and nobody came. An hour went by and he knew they were trying to make him sweat. He was sweating. Despite the fact it was raining out, it did nothing to lessen the weight in the air.

Another hour passed and he spent it sitting on the floor. Then the door opened and the fat man stood there along with a second detective wearing slacks and a short-sleeved shirt. 'How you doing over there?' De La Martin called.

'Oh, it's a regular home from home.'

Head to one side De La Martin worked a palm across the shadow that built on his jaw.

'Texas,' he said. 'We recovered a pair of Ruger Blackhawks from your nightstand drawer.'

'Did you?' Quarrie said. 'That's where I left them, Detective. Fact is I prefer a single action to an automatic and I prefer a pair.'

Two hours later De La Martin was back again with a yellow legal pad and a pen, which he laid on the table as he settled his bulk in the chair. Quarrie got up and pressed a hand to the mesh of the cage. 'Are you kidding, Detective? Locking me up in here?'

'It's where I want you right now. Nothing personal, I don't trust you, Texas. That's all.' De La Martin inspected the nib of his pen. 'So tell me about Matthews,' he said.

Still Quarrie looked at him then he shrugged his shoulders and squatted on his heels once more. 'He's a pharmacist on North Rampart on St Ann.'

A little languorous, the detective worked his molars on the plug of chew. 'You were up there yesterday asking questions only he didn't tell you what you wanted to know. You upset the man, Texas, trying to get him to break a confidence like that. He called the DA's office right after you left. That's how it was, right, you were asking a bunch of questions but he wouldn't tell you what you wanted to know?'

Quarrie did not reply.

'Cat got your tongue there, does it?' De La Martin's gaze was hollow as he peered across the floor.

'Nope, I'm just set here wondering who it was put you up to

this. Pershing Gervais, maybe, over at the DA's office. Was it him that gave you a call?'

The detective laid down his pen. Taking a sodden-looking handkerchief from his pocket he mopped sweat where it scattered his brow. 'Nobody gave me a call,' he stated, 'at least nobody from the DA's office anyhow. Think before you answer my questions, Texas, or we're not going to make any progress at all.'

Once more he picked up the pen. 'So we'll start over, shall we? Where were you at last night?'

'Apart from the hotel, you mean. I had a drink in a bar.'

'Which bar?'

'Cosimo's on Burgundy.'

De La Martin shifted his tobacco from one cheek to the other. 'Cosimo's.' He spoke the name as he wrote it down. 'So you like the Vieux Carré then, do you?'

Quarrie glanced at the confines of the steel mesh cage. 'The old quarter, it started out all right only now I ain't so sure.'

'What time did you show up there?' De La Martin said.

'The bar? I don't know, I guess around eight o'clock.'

'So where were you at before?'

'In my room.'

'Anybody up there with you?'

'Nope.'

'Anybody see you go up?'

'Sure: Yvonne from the hotel desk.'

'What time was that exactly?'

Again Quarrie pressed a hand to the mesh that separated them. 'I'm a cop for Christ's sake. Are you going to let me out of here?'

De La Martin arched a brow. 'All in good time, Texas; I asked you what time you went back to your room.'

'I don't know, four, four thirty, five o'clock maybe, I can't tell you that for sure.'

'So how did you get to Alabo Street? You're not driving. Did you take a cab?'

'I never heard of Alabo Street never mind took a cab.'

The detective sat back in his chair. Working tobacco into his cheek he looked for somewhere to spit. Unable to find any suitable receptacle he leaned to the side and released a mouthful of juice then worked it into the linoleum with his sole. 'Alabo Street is the 9th Ward and Matthews went home last night like he always does right after he closed the store. His car was parked on the driveway when his wife got back with her groceries. When she went in the house there was no sign of her husband at all. You're the last person he spoke to, Texas, and he wouldn't tell you what you wanted to know.'

Quarrie did not say anything.

'All evening Mrs Matthews is waiting but her husband he doesn't come home. She's getting worried now so she gives us a call. We have to hold off for twenty-four hours before someone can be classified as missing though, so there isn't a whole lot we can do. Fact is he never did come home and he ain't ever done that before.' Pushing back his chair De La Martin crossed to the cage. 'So what do you think, uh, you being the last person to see him and all?'

The next time the door opened he saw Lieutenant Colback filling the space. He didn't say anything, he just looked at Quarrie and told De La Martin to unlock the cage.

His car was parked outside and Quarrie got in the passenger

side. Colback didn't start the engine, he just sat behind the wheel and gazed towards the Provincial Hotel.

'So, Lieutenant,' Quarrie looked sideways at him. 'What was all that about?'

'That was New Orleans. It's the way things work down here.'

'You had nothing to do with it then? Not some lesson you thought you'd teach an out of state cop who ruffled your feathers maybe, huh?'

Colback looked round. 'If I wanted to teach you a lesson, believe me, buddy, you'd know.'

'Gervais then I figure.' Quarrie curled his lip. 'So where will I find the sumbitch, uh?'

'You won't.' Colback shook his head. 'Not if you know what's good for you. I just told you, this is New Orleans. Like you said, you're out of state and you're out of your depth as well.'

'When do I get my guns back?' Quarrie said.

'When De La Martin's done with them I suppose. I guess you feel kind of naked without them, don't you? Well, it's like Gervais told you yesterday. You're a civilian here. You only get to carry them because I agreed.'

'So what did you say to him?' Quarrie said.

'De La Martin?' Colback shrugged. 'I told him I'd vouch for you, at least for the time being anyway. I managed to persuade him that you were down here because of a murder in Texas and that you'd cleared it with me. The way things have played out with this pharmacist, I told him it's possible there might be a connection between what you're looking at and his disappearance and that's the only reason he let you go.'

Quarrie stared straight ahead. 'Lieutenant,' he said, 'I pay a visit to the pharmacist and they tell me he calls the DA. The chief investigator hauls me down to your office and the next thing I know that excuse for a cop shows up at my door. I figure somebody's messing with me and that ain't the smartest thing anyone could do.' Taking a package of cigarettes from his shirt pocket he rolled the window down and rested his arm on the sill.

'Listen to me,' Colback said. 'I told you. New Orleans ain't like other cities, it's a cesspool is what it is. Maybe you've got a point and you probably got a beef as well. We need to be clear about something though. Pershing Gervais called *me* yesterday and not the other way round.'

Quarrie did not say anything. He just drew on his cigarette.

'Despite your suspicions it's perfectly feasible that nobody tipped De La Martin off. Matthews went missing and if that happens in this neck of the woods it usually means they've been murdered. When his wife called the department to report it, it's D-Lay she would've talked to.'

'D-Lay,' Quarrie said. 'That what you call him, Lieutenant? Like there's a delay between his mouth maybe when he spits tobacco juice and the workings of a normal brain?' He flicked ash from the tip of his smoke. 'The fact is somebody didn't want me talking to that pharmacist. The question I'm asking is who.'

Nine

When he got back to the hotel Yvonne gave him a disparaging look. Ignoring her he went up to his room and closed the door. Colback was right, he did feel naked without his weapons and it wasn't just the Blackhawks, they had taken the snub-nose as well. Sitting down on the bed he took a moment to think then the phone rang and Yvonne told him he had a call.

It was Van Hanigan in Amarillo and his tone was a little weary. 'So how's it going down there?'

'Captain,' Quarrie said. 'I figure you know how it is already or you wouldn't be giving me a call.' Lighting a cigarette he lay back and propped the heel of one boot against the toe of the other. He told Van Hanigan what had happened and the captain was silent on the end of the phone.

'You're getting some shit back there then?'

'I got the odd phone call to deal with I guess. Someone from the DA's office down there called the Feds on Loyola Avenue and they called the field office here. About an hour ago I had Patterson chirping in my ear.'

'Do you want me out of here?' Quarrie said.

'No, I don't. I want you to find out what's going on. Only do it quickly, will you? I'm too old for the politics now.'

When he hung up Quarrie called the district attorney's office looking for Gervais, but they told him he went out to lunch.

'Yes, mam, I know that,' Quarrie said. 'I'm supposed to be at that lunch but I can't remember what restaurant he said.'

'McAlister's on Canal Street,' she told him. 'You're very late. He's been there quite a while.'

Downstairs, Yvonne told him that the restaurant was just two blocks from the hotel. When he went out he spotted the taxi parked in front of the American Bank building as it always was. Briefly he caught Franklin's eye.

Pushing open the restaurant door he located the DA's chief investigator sitting in a booth with Dean Andrews wearing his black-framed sunglasses despite the low-level lighting inside. 'Mr Gervais,' Quarrie said leaning with his fists on the table. 'I got a question for you. Was it you had me spend all morning locked in a steel mesh cage?'

'Cage?' Andrews looked up. 'Where was that? What sort of cage?'

Quarrie considered him with one cold eye.

'This is Mr Andrews,' Gervais informed him. 'He's a criminal attorney, Quarrie, just so you're aware.'

The man in the sunglasses smiled. 'Aha,' he said. 'The Texas Ranger everyone's talking about. What's this about being locked in a cage?'

'Another time maybe, Counselor.' Quarrie was concentrating on Gervais. 'Detective,' he said, 'I know you don't want me down here. I'm just trying to figure out why. You told me to stop disturbing the working folks, well, let me make a couple of things clear.' He bent a little closer still. 'Kill a man in Texas you have to account for it and messing with me ain't a good idea.'

Outside, he walked back to the hotel. The cab was still parked on the other side of the road and jay-walking between the vehicles he crossed.

'Mr Football Scholarship,' he said as Franklin rolled the window down. 'Whenever I need to go somewhere I look round and there you are.'

'What can I tell you?' Franklin said. 'I'm a cab driver. This is one of my spots.'

Quarrie got in and told him to take him back to North Rampart and St Ann. Franklin drove to the junction and made the U turn. In the mirror he sought Quarrie's eye. 'I heard on the radio just now that the pharmacist where I took you before is missing.' He twisted his mouth at the sides. 'I know what I said yesterday but I can't be driving you around this city if it's going to land me in some kind of jackpot.'

'Relax,' Quarrie said, without looking at him. 'You ain't in a jackpot. You're just along for the ride.'

They pulled up on the 700 block where Quarrie got out and went to the door of the pharmacy. The gate was secured and no lights were on inside. Franklin looked on from where he leaned against the driver's door. 'I guess they're closed on account of how the main man's not there.'

Quarrie glanced towards the river briefly and then along North Rampart Street before turning back to the taxi once more. 'You told me you get around the city. Does the name Matisse mean anything to you?'

Franklin shook his head. 'No, sir,' he said. 'Why?'

Quarrie didn't answer; he just got back in the cab.

Yvonne was in the lobby and the look she had given him earlier became a question about the police being there.

'It's all right,' he told her. 'I'm a cop myself, Yvonne, a Texas Ranger, and that was all just a misunderstanding before.'

Still she looked doubtful. 'Well, I don't like trouble here and if you staying means we got the NOPD hammering on people's doors, I'm going to have to ask you to leave.'

Hat tipped low, Quarrie considered her out of half-closed eyes. 'I can do that,' he said. 'But like I said just now it was a misunderstanding, that's all.'

He started for the courtyard to get some air but paused as something on the table housing the local fliers caught his eye. A handbill half hidden, it was worn at the edges and out of date but the name seemed to climb from the page. 'Gigi Matisse' playing with her blues band at Pat O'Brien's. For a moment he stared then he picked up the flier and took it to the desk. 'This singer,' he said, placing the sheet of paper before Yvonne.

Eyebrows raised, she clicked her tongue. 'That flier shouldn't be there, Sergeant. It's way out of date. She won't be playing there now.'

'I know that, but do you know where else she could be?'

'Gigi Matisse?' Yvonne shook her head. 'No, sir, I can't tell you where she's playing at but she's from the 7th Ward just like me.'

Upstairs Quarrie unlocked the door to his room and stood for a moment before he went in. He was thinking about how that cab driver was parked across the street all the time and he considered the bed and nightstand then turned to the bureau. Tugging out the drawers he went through his clothes then closed the drawers once more. His shoulder holsters were still in the bottom of the closet and he placed them on the bed. On the floor underneath was a folded newspaper and he couldn't recall whether that had been there when he took the room or not. The way the paper was folded looked as if it was meant to cover a hole in the boards but when he checked there was no hole.

Glancing at the front page he saw a piece on the new radio station that HL Hunt had started up in Dallas just a block from KRLD. There was a short column about Muhammad Ali and his stance with the US Army and a major feature on LBJ and his visit to the house on the Pedernales River in Gillespie County where he was born. Other than that it was just stuff about the drought and he placed the paper back where it had been. Behind him the phone rang on the nightstand, Yvonne from the lobby downstairs. 'Look,' she said. 'I'm sorry if I was out of line before, but . . .'

'That's OK, Yvonne: you run a quiet place.'

'Gigi Matisse, y'all were asking about her just now so I called up a girlfriend I know. She told me Gigi lives in an old camel-back house on North Rocheblave if that's any use to you.'

Quarrie had a feeling the taxi would be across the street when he went out and it was. He stood on the sidewalk with his hands stuffed in the pockets of his jacket and regarded Franklin where he sat at the wheel. When the cab made the U turn he told him he wanted to go to North Rocheblave Street.

'Everything all right back there?' Franklin asked as he turned into the traffic. 'You look a little preoccupied tonight.'

'Who're you working for, Mr Football Scholarship? Who's picking up the tab?'

Franklin looked puzzled. 'For the ride? Well, you are. I don't get it, what do you mean?'

'You know exactly what I mean,' Quarrie said. 'You're at the airport to meet me and you've been there every time I come out of the hotel. You run me here, there and everywhere including his office so is it Colback pulling your strings?'

'I never heard of him,' Franklin said.

Quarrie peered out the window. 'What about Pershing Gervais? If it's not that lieutenant then I guess it's him whistling Dixie, huh?'

'Mister,' Franklin said, 'I got no idea what you're talking about. And I told you earlier I'd just as soon not be driving you at all. If you want I'll pull over right here.'

They drove across town with no more words passing between them. As they got to the 7th Ward Franklin glanced in the rear view mirror. 'Did you find that girl you were looking for this afternoon?'

'She's a singer,' Quarrie said catching his eye. 'Plays the blues pretty good, and according to the gal at the hotel she's got a voice like Lizzie Miles.'

Franklin said he didn't know who Lizzie Miles was.

'Nope, I didn't either.'

'You plan on booking her then? Is that what this is about?'

'No, I ain't looking to book her. I got a couple of questions to ask, that's all.'

'So you're a cop then, huh? I kind of figured that.' Franklin lifted a hand from the wheel.

'Sure you did. I'm a Ranger. You know that. Colback told you who I was when he asked you to take me where I wanted to go.'

They continued the rest of the journey in silence and Franklin pulled onto North Rocheblave, a long and narrow road with potholes puncturing the asphalt. Shadows grew up outside the fall of the streetlights and a few blocks further a fire burned in an old oil drum. Quarrie gave him the house number and they pulled up outside a shotgun home with a half-length second floor.

'Camelback,' Franklin indicated. 'That's what they call 'em. Contractor would've built them like that on account of the taxes because the city zoned them same as a regular. I tell you what,' he said, looking over his shoulder. 'The way you've been bitching I ought to take off right now, but this ain't the kind of place to leave a white man afoot, even a Texas Ranger.'

Stepping out of the car Quarrie considered his surroundings. A few blocks further a monolithic elementary school dominated the sidewalk with a payphone out front and a church behind. In the other direction that oil drum burned where a couple of rag pickers squatted on upturned cartons. There was no front yard to the house, just three steps that rose from the sidewalk to a wooden stoop and very little gap either side. Quarrie climbed the steps and knocked. Nobody answered. All was still. Cupping one hand to his eyes he pressed his face to the glass but could make out nothing but shadows inside. Franklin looked on with the window rolled down and his arm on the sill. 'I imagine she's out of town someplace playing with her band.'

Quarrie didn't reply.

'What do you want to do?'

'Where's the nearest bar? If she's a singer she's bound to have played around here. Maybe somebody knows where she's at.'

'It's possible,' Franklin said, 'but I doubt they'll be talking to you.'

They drove past the rag pickers and Franklin made a turn onto another street with fewer houses and a couple of glass-fronted stores. Quarrie could see a wash house and coffee shop, another string of shabby-looking shotgun homes then a run-down bar where juke box music seemed to pulse right onto the street. Franklin pulled up outside and Quarrie regarded the worn-out sign that hung above the door. 'The Feathered Egg,' he muttered. 'You got to be kidding me.'

Franklin looked over his shoulder. 'You sure you want to do this? You're going to be the only white face in there and that might be OK but then again it might not.'

The cab pulled away and Quarrie felt a breath of wind in the air. With another glance at the weathered-looking sign he went in. Dark and gloomy, the lighting cast from naked bulbs hung with colored paper shades that looked like they might be a fire hazard. He could see holes here and there in the shiplap walls and when the wind blew it would break right through. On hot days that might not be a bad thing but when it rained the place would be awash.

The wall opposite the door was devoted to a wooden bar that sported a couple of old-fashioned beer taps fixed into barrels in sawbuck racks. Beyond it the wall panels were fitted with shelves stacked with bottles of liquor. The stools out front had probably been topped with some kind of velour at one time or other but not anymore. A few circular tables scattered the dusty floor and there was a shabby-looking pool table ahead of the corridor that led to the restrooms. Despite all that the place was heaving with people laughing and talking, the hullaballoo only just overshadowed by Etta James's voice pumping from the juke box.

The cab driver was right, Quarrie's was the only white face in there and the moment he was spotted the conversation petered out and the laughter died. Gradually every eye turned his way and he moved to the bar with his hands in his jacket pockets. Nobody spoke. Everybody stared and only Etta James's voice could be heard. Carefully he picked his way through a group of young men wearing jeans and canvas jackets. At the bar he ordered a beer from a big man with a lazy left eye who rolled his good eye across Quarrie's hat.

'Mister,' he said. 'I can get you that beer but you sure this is really the spot?'

Evenly Quarrie looked back.

'Serve the man, Clarence.' A woman's voice, soft and husky, it lifted from further along the counter. She looked around forty and her tightly cut hair was the color of coal.

The bartender poured out a glass of beer from one of the barrels and everyone's attention drifted back to what they had been doing. A skinny-looking man shifted off the barstool next to Quarrie and the woman motioned for him to sit down.

'Well,' she said, 'I reckon whoever you are you're an awful long way from home.'

Taking a seat on the stool Quarrie smiled. 'Can I get you a drink?'

'Sure.' She passed her empty glass to the bartender.

Quarrie broke open a pack of Camels and offered one but the woman shook her head.

'So, you're not from New Orleans,' she said, 'and this ain't any kind of place for tourists. What're you doing back here?'

Quarrie lighted his cigarette. 'I'm looking for Gigi Matisse.'

As he spoke so a couple of people turned their way but still the woman held his eye.

'What do you want with her?'

Quarrie looked keenly at her then. 'Do you know her?'

'Sure I know her. Everybody round here knows Gigi.'

All about them people were talking and the music still played, not Etta James now but the Four Tops. It was getting harder to hear and with that in mind perhaps the woman slipped off the stool and led Quarrie to the far side of the room. They sat down at an empty table and the same group of young men cast inquisitive glances their way.

'So what is it you want with Gigi?' she asked him.

Still Quarrie held her eye. 'What's your name, mam? Who am I talking to?'

'What's your name, cowboy? It's you who's visiting with me.'

'My name's Quarrie,' he said.

'So who are you that you're looking for Gigi?'

'I'm a Texas Ranger.'

The woman sat back in the chair stretching her arms and pointing her fingers. He could smell the perfume she was wearing where it was laced with a hint of sweat.

'So your interest,' she said, 'it isn't personal then, it's professional.'

Quarrie lifted his gaze to hers. 'Have you any idea where she is?'

'With what that girl does for a living she could be just about any place right now.'

Quarrie was peering beyond her to where people were beginning to look their way.

'You still haven't told me why you're looking for her.' The woman gestured. 'Gigi's a friend of mine and you're a cop from out of state. I'm not going to try and figure out where she might be till you tell me what you want with her.'

For a moment Quarrie was still. He looked evenly at her then he reached in his pocket and took out the empty Proloid bottle and placed it on the table between them. 'I want to talk about this,' he said. 'It has her name on it. The contents killed a man and I found it in a hotel room in Texas.'

Ten

A fine rain was falling as Detective De La Martin pulled up outside the Hotel Magnolia. Sitting at the wheel for a moment he loosened the tie at his throat, checked his mirrors then reached for a heavy-duty paper sack where it lay on the passenger seat. Climbing from the car he strode under the arch into the courtyard where lights drifted from the lobby. Yvonne was at the door to the office and her gaze settled on the package he placed on the counter.

'Remember me?' De La Martin said.

Yvonne nodded.

'Is he in?'

'No, sir, I believe he went out.'

De La Martin cocked his head to one side and shifted a plug of tobacco from one side of his mouth to the other. 'You *believe* he went out?'

'He went out,' Yvonne stated definitely. 'He called a taxi to take him back of town.'

'The 7th Ward, what does he want up there?'

Yvonne lifted her shoulders.

'He didn't tell you?'

She shook her head.

Still De La Martin held her eye. 'Do you know why we were here this morning?'

'Yes, sir, I heard on the news how a pharmacist went missing.'

'That's right. Claude Matthews, a gentle soul who never did anybody any harm. On the contrary he did a lot of folks a whole lot of good. Got him a wife at home, kids in college and nobody knows where he's at.' He looked keenly at Yvonne again. 'So do you want to tell me what the Ranger's doing in the 7th Ward?'

'Sir,' she said, 'you know I'm only looking out for the privacy of my guest. Fact is he asked about Gigi Matisse.'

'Who?'

'Gigi Matisse. She's a singer, plays with her band around town. He spotted her name on a flier that was out of date and had me find her address.'

Working slowly at the tobacco De La Martin peered at the photos of jazz musicians hanging on the wall. 'So tell me about him,' he said. 'The Ranger I'm talking about.'

Again Yvonne shrugged her shoulders. 'I don't know what I can say to you. I don't know nothing about him. I guess there's been a couple of phone calls but nothing much apart from that.'

'Has anyone been by since he's been staying here?'

Yvonne shook her head. 'You mean apart from the forensics people and that other officer you-all sent down?'

The detective frowned. 'What other officer?' he said.

'A young man with straw-colored hair, he was in regular clothes like you are and went up to the sergeant's room.'

*

Franklin waited outside the bar until he saw the doors swing open and Quarrie come out. He had his hat pressed to his eyes

93

and his shoulders hunched. Franklin watched him for a couple of moments then flashed his lights.

'Still here then,' Quarrie muttered as he got in the back.

'I told you already, you should be grateful I stuck around.'

When he dropped him at the hotel Quarrie found Yvonne still working the desk. She looked at him a little warily. 'Sergeant, the detective was here just now, the one from this morning. He came by with your guns and said to tell you he was taking them to Lieutenant Colback.'

Quarrie frowned. 'Why would he do that?'

'I can't tell you, sir. But he left me this address.'

When he went back out to Canal Street the taxi was gone. Making his way down to St Charles, he took the trolley car heading for Audubon. He sat with his hat in his lap, thinking about the 7th Ward and the black woman with crew-cut hair. He got off at St Andrew Street and walked with a mist swirling about his legs. Heading towards the river he found the house on Camp Street built in traditional clapboard and set behind a half-height fence made from iron railings that were tipped with fleur de lys. Peering between the cypress trees he saw an Eldorado parked on the gravel driveway. He rang the bell on the small gate and a couple of minutes later it opened automatically and he was greeted at the front door by Colback wearing a pair of chinos and a monogrammed shirt. He showed Quarrie into a spacious, oak-panelled hallway, the stairs overlooked by a series of painted portraits.

'Family, Lieutenant?' Quarrie said.

Colback nodded. 'My wife's folks, no one's related to me.'

On their left was a study where the door stood open to reveal a highly polished desk. Beyond the staircase an archway led to a living room set with leather couches and a brand new color TV.

'Just got her,' Colback told him as they went in. 'Admiral, twenty-three inch and that cabinet you see right there. They were asking five twenty-five but I shook them down to four-fifty including the sales tax.'

He poured a couple of drinks then crossed the hall to his study and came back with the pair of pistols and snub-nosed thirty-eight. Quarrie took a moment to inspect each weapon in turn then slipped the Blackhawks into his shoulder holsters and the snub-nose in his boot. Sitting back, he took in the contours of a room that had an old world, almost historical feel. There was something of the southern gentleman about it he would not have associated with a man like Colback.

'This is a serious place you got going on,' he said. 'I guess you ain't doing badly for a jarhead turned New Orleans cop.'

'The house, you mean? It's been in the family for years.' Colback made an open-handed gesture. 'All these grand-looking homes you see from the street car are still owned by the people that originally built them. None of them ever get sold, just passed to the next generation. Fact is I earn a cop's salary and that caddy outside in the driveway is a present to my wife from her dad.'

He nodded to Quarrie's Blackhawks. 'You know, you're the only cop I ever saw wearing a twin-rig outfit like that.'

'Habit I got into,' Quarrie said. 'The way we work we're on our own most always and sometimes the locations can be pretty remote.' Pausing for a moment he added, 'Still shoot a rifle, do you?'

Colback laughed. 'I can point one I suppose, but shoot, no

sir, at least nothing like I did.' Again he disappeared inside his study and when he came out he was holding a sniper's rifle. 'Souvenir from Korea, though all she does right now is hang on the wall.' He pitched the weapon to Quarrie. 'She's not loaded but I keep her oiled and everything. Smooth as silk. Go ahead and give her a try.'

An M1C similar to the one Quarrie had found in Wiley's bag only this had a four-power scope. The stock was covered with a hand-stitched piece of leather to stop chafing and the barrel tipped with a trumpet-shaped piece of metal designed to hide the muzzle flash.

'Just as she was the last time I used her and that might well've been that hill you were talking about on the phone.' Colback looked on as Quarrie worked the action and inspected the empty chamber. 'Not fired her since and I doubt I could hit a barn door right now even if I was sat on the latch.'

Pressing the stock to his shoulder Quarrie let the hammer down then rested the rifle against the edge of his chair. 'So tell me about the cabbie.'

'What cabbie?'

'The young guy who's been driving me around, told me he was in college.'

Colback looked puzzled.

'Come on, Lieutenant. Level with me. He was at the Lakefront to meet me and he's been outside my hotel every time I came out since.'

'And you think he's something to do with me?' Colback pressed a thumb to his chest.

'You're the only person who knew I was coming. I figure you asked him to keep tabs on me.'

Colback laughed. 'You don't think I got anything better to do?'

'I don't know, Lieutenant. Do you?'

Sitting back in the chair Colback crossed his legs at the knee. He studied Quarrie with his chin high. 'You're unbelievable, you know that? Right now I'm the only friend you got in this city. The pharmacist you hassled is missing. De La Martin was down here just now asking all kinds of questions. On top of that you bust in at McAlister's where the chief investigator with the DA's office is having lunch with one of its more colorful attorneys.'

Quarrie flared his nostrils. 'All right, Lieutenant. I'll level with you then maybe you'll level with me. Those meds I told you about were prescribed for a singer called Gigi Matisse.' He told Colback about the woman he had met just now. 'The way she was looking at me, the expression on her face when I showed her the empty bottle, she ain't who she says she is.'

'You're thinking that was her, huh, only she wasn't about to admit it to you?'

Quarrie nodded.

'And you're wondering how a bottle of meds with her name on it wound up with the guy you shot dead in Texas?'

Again Quarrie nodded.

'Maybe she gave them to him?'

'Yes, sir, it occurred to me.'

'Think you can find her again? Don't go holding your breath.' Colback sat forward in the chair. 'Half the people working the Quarter use an alias. You swing by her house she isn't going to be there.' He gestured with an open palm. 'Listen, what happened in Texas is probably just some lowlife deal gotten out of hand. If it originated in New Orleans and it's organized that's my bag now, not yours. You need to go home, Quarrie. You need to get yourself on a plane. You already shot the guy who killed your man in the hotel room. Go back to Rangering and leave whatever's going on down here to me.' Reaching for his whiskey glass he sipped. 'I'll give you the heads up on anything you need to know but I get the feeling if you stick around much longer thing's are only going to get messy. You want me to level with you I will. You don't know this city like I do and Louisiana is not Texas. We both know the pharmacist is dead and if somebody's giving a dick like De La Martin the workout he'll jump any bone they toss.'

*

Across town on Chartres Street De La Martin peeled his sodden jacket from sweating shoulders and hung it on the back of the chair. With nobody else in the office he went through to the room where they housed the Telecopier and selected a pad of paper from the secretary's desk. He started to pen the message he wanted to send, got half a sentence down before he seemed to change his mind and laid the pen aside. He remained where he was for a moment then walked the hallway and screwed the piece of paper into a ball.

In the corridor he plucked a cone from the water cooler and sought a bottle of Old Crow from a drawer in his desk. Holding the cone against the top he poured and drank as he stared the length of the hall.

*

The Lincoln was parked in the driveway when Franklin drove through the mansion gates. There was no sign of the chauffeur but lights burned in the apartment above the garage. He didn't bother with the front door; he made his way around the back of the house to where Tobie's study doors were open and the fly screen pulled across. He could see the old man in a leather armchair sipping on a glass of malt. Franklin remained in the shadows, his gaze shifting from the chair to a gilt-framed photograph of a young boy on the desk.

'Franklin,' Tobie said. 'I've told you before. To covet a position is not to possess.'

Franklin pushed open the screen door and considered the ceiling fan where it whirled above the old man's head. A little languid in the armchair, Tobie looked up. 'So what've you got to report?'

'We were in the 7th Ward. I just dropped him back at his hotel.' Taking a chair on the other side of the fireplace Franklin cast another glance at the photograph.

'Just nine years old when he died,' Tobie said. 'Rosa was eleven and she managed to avoid the epidemic but not young Ross. Polio initially, when he was in the hospital he contracted meningitis. There wasn't anything the doctors could do.'

'When was that?' Franklin asked.

'1925.' The old man sipped from his glass. 'So what happened in the 7th Ward?'

Franklin told him about the bar and Quarrie's demeanor when he came out. 'I went back after I dropped him off. She was in there all right and she talked to him but I don't think she told him who she was. He wasn't fooled though, I could see that. First thing tomorrow he's going to be back at the house.'

Tobie sat in silence, the glass in his hand and his hand on the arm of the chair. Franklin looked at him then he looked at the walking cane and finally the photo of the boy once more. 'You should let me kill him,' he said. 'I've been driving him around and he's not as tough as you think.'

'That's your considered opinion, is it?' Tobie sipped his whisky. 'It's not about that, I told you. It's about covering all the bases and not creating any more problems than we've already got. We don't kill him; we work him, at least for the time being anyhow.'

'So what's the plan?'

'The plan is to keep doing what you're doing.'

'He suspects me.' Franklin gestured. 'He thinks Colback had me show up at the airport so he could keep an eye on him.'

Tobie looked beyond him then. 'I can see how he'd come to that conclusion. He's not stupid. Let him think what he wants.'

'What about the pharmacist? He's still alive. Shall I tell Soulja Blue to get rid of him?'

'No,' Tobie said. 'Hold off on that for now. I have a use for his body. When the time comes it needs to be fresh.'

Franklin nodded. 'So you've got a plan to deal with Quarrie. Are you going to tell me what it is?'

'Not right now. I'll tell you when you need to know.'

'What about Texas, Wichita Falls? We still don't know who Williams really was or what other information he might've had.'

'I've been thinking about that and it was probably only the photograph,' Tobie said. 'Don't worry; we're not taking any chances. So long as Quarrie doesn't know anything we don't, then we're up with the play.'

'I don't understand why we don't just ask the supplier.'

Tobie's expression darkened. 'I told you. I don't want to do that. Our relationship with him is not only delicate, it's specific. Without him no case is closed and a closed case is how we built our reputation.'

Getting up from the chair Franklin poured himself a drink. 'So what about Gigi?' he said.

Tobie pursed his lips. 'What can she tell him exactly?'

Franklin shrugged. 'That her meds were stolen. Apart from that I don't know. I don't know for sure what she's been told. Moore said it was only his Christian name.'

'Perhaps she'll heed the warning.'

'She's already spoken to him once.'

Finishing his whisky Tobie handed him the empty glass.

'You've been visiting with her nana,' Franklin said. 'That address on Orleans Street.'

'How do you know about her?'

Franklin snorted. 'How do you think I know? You had me take you there after the fundraiser so I looked up the address.' He poured another whisky and Tobie sat with the glass clutched to his chest.

'So what do you want me to do about Gigi?'

'Kill her,' the old man said.

Eleven

Gigi left the bar an hour after Quarrie and walked to her beaten-looking sky-blue Nomad. Behind the wheel she caught a glimpse of her face in the mirror and her eyes looked a little haunted. Parked cars lined both sides of the road and she studied them carefully before starting the engine.

She drove home keeping to the speed limit and making sure she didn't run any stop signs. There were no prowl cars around though, and she pulled up outside her camelback house and stared at the darkened windows. Almost as if she didn't want to venture inside, she remained where she was for a minute before finally opening the door. Locking the car she paused on the sidewalk gazing along the road to where wood burned in the oil barrel and the rag pickers hunched by the flames.

Inside the house she pulled the living room drapes then took a bottle from the cupboard in the kitchen and pressed crushed ice into a glass. Lacing it with a sprig of mint she poured a measure of bourbon and was about to screw the cap back on the bottle when she poured a little more. Opening her purse she found cigarettes and a book of matches. On a whim she picked up the phone and dialled Earl's number but all she got was the tone.

*

When Franklin left the mansion he topped up the cab with gas. Half an hour later he turned onto North Rocheblave Street for the second time that evening and as he approached the camelback house, he could see the oil barrel still burning. He watched as the flames seemed to leap from the darkness then drove past Gigi's house where her station wagon was parked with one wheel up on the curb. No lights showed upstairs or down. He pulled into a space and considered the school and the church and that burning oil barrel.

*

Gigi lay in bed with her eyes wide open. She was staring at the ceiling where patterns of light broke up the shadows that grew up from the corners of the room. She heard a car make the turn outside and trundle the length of the road. She heard it slow when it came to her house. She sat straight, back stiff, then she got out of bed and crossed to the window. She saw the car drive past and pull over a little way down the street. Craning her neck she thought she could make out the unlit sign of a cab. She could hear the engine ticking over and then it was switched off. No door opened. Nobody got in or out. For a moment longer she stood where she was then she reached for her dress.

*

As he climbed from the cab Franklin stuffed the Beretta into the waistband of his pants. He felt inside his jacket, brought out a switchblade and flipped it open. Carefully he worked the blade against his palm, closed it and flipped it a second time.

He stared at the house, his gaze shifting to the proximity of its neighbors, then he walked to the steps. He stood there taking in the confines of the glass-panelled front door before climbing to the stoop. From the pocket of his jacket he took a pencil light and panned it over the lock.

*

Gigi saw him get out. She saw him approach her steps and stuffed her feet into the mules she'd been wearing when she went out. Grabbing her purse she rushed to the window at the back and lifted the sash. She heard footfall on the sidewalk, the creak of wood as he came up the steps. She was trembling. She bit her lip as she reached for the rope ties that held the fire-escape ladder in place.

*

Franklin had the flashlight between his teeth as he worked the knife against the door where the edge met the jamb. It was old and warped and he fed the blade a little way into the gap. Taking care to make sure it did not snap he slid the blade down to where the tumbler secured the lock. Slowly he worked it up and down and at the same time he twisted the handle. Nothing gave, but he kept working the handle and pried the blade in behind the lock.

*

Gigi had the ladder unfurled and it tumbled all the way to the ground. She could hear scraping sounds coming from downstairs and poked one leg out the window and tried to swivel around. Her dress caught on the sill and she couldn't get it clear then a piece of material tore off. Now she pivoted so her back was to the world outside and her hands on the window frame. Her other leg clear, she lost her shoe and it fell to the yard. Quickly she climbed down the ladder and dropped to the ground. She bent for the fallen shoe, her weight resting on the heel of the other; she could feel it sinking into the grass. As she stood up again she peered through the kitchen window. The doors in line, she could see all the way to the front of the house where the door was wide open.

*

Franklin stood very still. Ears pricked, lips parted, he sought any movement from the shadows within. His gaze seemed to fix on the open doorway that led to the kitchen. No sound. No movement back there. To his left were the stairs. A shotgun home, there was no hallway and he started climbing the wooden steps. When he got to the landing he stopped. The bathroom was on his right and a short expanse of walkway led to a window that overlooked the street. The rest of the upstairs was a single bedroom. The boards groaned a little as he moved his feet. One hand on the wall he paused for a second to listen then opened the bedroom door.

The breeze hit him. The window at the back wide open, the bedroom was empty though the bed had clearly been slept in. He stood there with his features taut and his eyes blank. He closed the blade and slipped the knife in his pocket. Then he crossed to the window and looked out over a tiny yard. He could see a half-height chain link fence that led to another

105

yard and another after that. Still he stared then his attention switched to the window ledge and the rope ladder.

*

Quarrie woke early and went outside to find the taxi parked as it always was on the other side of Canal Street. Franklin was in the driver's seat with his eyes closed and his head against the window. He jerked upright as Quarrie opened the passenger door.

'Mr Football Scholarship,' Quarrie said. 'It's time you and me had a talk.'

Franklin swivelled round in the seat with his back to the window as Quarrie got in. He had his jacket open and the heels of his pistols visible. 'I'm not exactly known for my patience,' he said, 'so you might want to keep that in mind.'

'Look, Mister, I'm just a cab driver. I ...'

'No you're not. You told me you were in college on a football scholarship. Which college? What faculty? Where's the campus?'

Franklin lifted his palms. 'All right, all right, I'm at LSU. But you're right; the lieutenant did ask me to keep an eye on you.'

'Colback?' Quarrie said.

Franklin nodded.

'I talked to him last night and he reckoned he had better things to do than pay you to be watching me.'

'Of course he did. He's not going to admit it. But the fact is he lives on Camp Street and he tossed a few bucks my way. Do you want me to drive you over there so we can ask him?'

Quarrie held his gaze. 'What did he want you to do?'

'Nothing really: he just needed to know where you were going and who you were talking to.'

They drove back to the 7th Ward with Quarrie still in the passenger seat. Lifting a hand from the wheel Franklin gestured. 'What can I tell you? I'm sorry.'

Quarrie just looked at him.

'So we're going back to this woman's house again. What did she do exactly?'

'Keep your mouth shut and drive the taxi.'

As they turned onto North Rocheblave Quarrie spotted Detective De La Martin by the open trunk of his Ford. Franklin pulled up behind and Quarrie got out. De La Martin closed the trunk and came around with his jacket undone and perspiration coating the front of his shirt. 'Texas,' he said. 'I didn't expect you back so soon, not after you were here last night.'

Quarrie looked at him then back to where Franklin was sitting in the cab. De La Martin followed his gaze and took in the boyish features and yellow hair.

'How did you know I was here before?'

'Well, first off the desk clerk at your hotel told me how she gave you this address and second . . .' De La Martin pointed to the open front door.

Quarrie had his hands in his jacket pockets. 'Somebody broke in here and you figure that was me?'

'You were looking for her. I was in The Feathered Egg last night and according to some folks I spoke to, you were sitting down with her, only she didn't tell you who she was.'

Quarrie nodded. 'That's right,' he said. 'But she knew that bottle when I showed it to her. I figure she gave those meds to the man I shot dead in Texas.' He stepped past the detective, went up to the door and could see where the lock had been pried open. He looked more closely still and took in how the door itself was warped a little where it met the jamb at the tumbler. 'This ain't me, Detective.' He jerked a thumb over his shoulder. 'Mr Football Scholarship back there will tell you he took me to that bar and then my hotel on Canal Street. After that I was at Colback's house picking up my weapons. It's a fact he's been paying that asshole to keep an eye on me.'

Again De La Martin squinted at the man behind the wheel of the Impala. 'Well, he ain't doing a very good job.'

Quarrie followed him into the house and up the stairs. In the bedroom the detective pointed out the open window and rope ladder where it hung to the ground. He indicated a tiny piece of black material that had caught on a splinter of wood. 'See that?' he said. 'If it wasn't you in here last night, who-all it was, looks like they left in a bit of a hurry.'

Quarrie took a good look at the sliver of material. 'Detective,' he said, 'that's the color of the dress she was wearing last night so I figure this has to be Gigi.' Gaze taut, he scanned the rest of the room and saw that the bed sheets were ruffled and the drapes drawn all the way across the front window. 'If she's climbing out the back then she's running from whoever it was busted in here, and maybe that was a home invasion and maybe it wasn't.'

'What do you mean?' De La Martin looked quizzical.

'I mean maybe it wasn't just a house breaker. Maybe she knew who-all it was or at least what it was they wanted.'

On the dressing table was a photo of the woman he had spoken to in the bar last night. She was with a much older woman whose hair was cut just as short only it was the color of snow. Back at the window he dropped to his haunches and studied the lip of the window, the wall underneath and the wooden floorboards directly in front. 'There's nothing here,' he said, 'no flakes of wood on the sill save the one where the material is caught. There are no marks in the wall paint and no scuffing up of the floor.' He shook his head. 'There was no struggle here, Detective. I figure she heard whoever it was and lit out.'

He led the way downstairs to the kitchen with De La Martin following behind. The back door locked, Quarrie took a kerchief from his pocket and wrapped it around the key. Outside he stood on the wooden step and studied the grass. There was not much to see but he moved to where the rope ladder trailed its final rung then bent to squat on his heels. He looked very carefully now, a hint of something where the grass was broken, an indentation in the dirt. 'She climbed down all right,' he said. 'That mark was made by the heel of a woman's shoe.'

'What mark?' De La Martin looked where he did. 'I can't see anything.'

'Sure you can if you look.' Again Quarrie pointed out the split blade of grass and the hole in the dirt. 'The heel of her shoe, Detective, she was standing right here.'

'Well, she's still missing,' De La Martin stated, 'her and the pharmacist both.' He stepped up close and looked Quarrie in the eye. 'I'm a homicide detective and you're a suspect. Don't leave town, OK?'

Out front Quarrie walked back to the taxi and bent to the window. 'We're done,' he said to Franklin. 'You can tell Colback I don't need babysitting.'

Franklin opened his mouth to say something but then he

caught the look in Quarrie's eye. Quarrie watched as the cab drove away and turned back to where De La Martin was sitting in his Ford.

'So Colback had that guy keep an eye on you, that's what you're saying?'

Quarrie nodded. 'I guess he figures if he's vouching for me he wants to know what I'm doing.'

'Him and me both, Texas. I don't want you poking around up here so why don't I give you a ride?'

'Thanks, I'll make my own way.'

He walked beyond the church to a Minit-market that had a dining room in the back. Taking a seat he laid his hat on the table and took out cigarettes. A waitress came over and poured coffee. Quarrie smoked a cigarette, thinking about De La Martin breathing down his neck and the fact that Colback was keeping tabs on him. He thought about Gigi Matisse and the bottle of prescription medication and the hunch he had that it wasn't her who'd given it to Wiley.

The waitress topped up his coffee and asked him if he wanted anything to eat. He shook his head, thinking about that sliver of material on the window ledge and the photograph of the older woman on the dressing table. On the wall outside the mensroom he found a payphone together with the phone book hanging on a length of wire. He had a last name and that woman looked like she might be a relative so he flicked through the pages till he found an address. Lifting the receiver he dialled. It took a couple of rings then a woman's voice sounded.

'Mrs Matisse?' Quarrie said.

'Ms,' the woman told him. 'Who is this?'

'Mam, I'm sorry to bother you. I was looking for Gigi.'

'I haven't seen her.'

'You don't know where she might be? I'm looking to book the band, but I can't seem to get a-hold of her.'

'I haven't seen her,' the woman repeated. 'Not for a couple of days now.'

Quarrie thanked her and hung up. Back at his table he asked the waitress if she could call him a cab.

*

When Gigi fled her bedroom she climbed the fence and hid in the neighbor's yard remaining absolutely still as a shadow appeared at the window. From there she had made her way to the church and spent the night in an alcove beyond the pulpit where she could see anyone who came in the front door.

Now she stood on the corner and stared at an NOPD prowl car parked outside her house. There was nobody at the wheel but she could see that the place had been taped off. She watched for a while then walked to the phone booth outside the church. Pretending to make a call, she stayed there until she saw two uniformed cops come out of her front door and a couple of minutes later the prowl car took off. Purse hanging over her shoulder she walked back towards the house looking as far up the street as she could and back the way she had come. She did not go in. She got in her car and drove off.

*

Quarrie was on the phone to Colback in his hotel room. 'Lieutenant,' he said. 'If you want someone keeping tabs on me I get that, but why lie about it? What's the big deal?'

He heard Colback let go a breath. 'You know what?' he said. 'For a while now I've been humoring you but you're beginning to piss me off. I told you how it was last night. If I wanted to keep an eye on you I wouldn't use a cab driver, I'd use another cop. Get that through your skull, why don't you?' The phone went dead and Quarrie put the receiver down. He sat there for a moment shaking his head then someone knocked on the door. Still he sat there and whoever it was knocked again more urgently and he got to his feet.

'Yeah?' he called. 'Who is it?'

A woman's voice answered. 'Gigi Matisse. Sergeant, I need to talk to you.'

Twelve

When he opened the door he found her on the walkway in the torn black dress. Her eyes were hunted, she was shaking slightly and he ushered her into the room. He checked the courtyard below then closed the door and locked it. Gigi perched on the bed. She took a package of cigarettes from her purse and shook one out but her hand was shaking so badly she couldn't strike the match. Quarrie took the cigarette from her and lighted it himself.

'I'm sorry.' Gigi sounded a little breathless. 'I didn't know what else to do. I think someone is trying to kill me. Last night they broke in my house.'

Quarrie looked at her with his head to one side. 'I was there just now,' he said. 'You should've told me who you were when we spoke last night.'

She sucked on the cigarette. She shook her head. 'I couldn't. I'm taking a chance as it is.'

'I figured you had to know what went down in Texas,' Quarrie said. 'Did you?'

'No, I didn't. That was the first I'd heard of it.'

'So you didn't give anyone that bottle of meds?'

'No, I didn't.'

'You sure? You lied to me once already. Why should I believe you now?'

'I didn't lie. You asked me if I knew who Gigi was and I told you everybody did.'

Quarrie sat down on the chair by the door. 'So if you didn't give up the meds, how'd they end up in Texas?'

Gigi didn't answer. She drew on the cigarette. She worked her free hand up and down her thigh.

'Last night,' Quarrie said. 'Tell me what happened.'

'I was asleep in bed when someone tried to get in.'

'Did you see them?'

'Only a shadow on the street and then afterwards at my window, I never saw a face. I didn't have time to do anything except grab my purse and climb down the fire escape.' She looked fearfully at him. 'I didn't know what to do. I was so scared all I could think about was hiding so I went to the church. There's nothing to steal so it's never locked.'

'All right,' Quarrie said. 'If you didn't know about Texas and you didn't give anyone those pills, what happened? Did somebody warn you off?'

Eyes bright now, she nodded.

'Who?'

'Earl,' she said. 'It was Earl that told me. When I called him on the phone he said it was being disconnected then he showed up at my house. He was so pale I asked him what was wrong and he told me to stay away from anybody asking questions.'

'Who is he?' Quarrie asked.

'I guess he's sort of been my boyfriend.' She made a face. 'But he's white and I'm black so it wasn't like we were a couple or anything. I can't tell you his last name. I never asked and he never told me.' She took a moment to think. 'I met him in the Quarter one night back at the end of January and I've been seeing him on and off I guess ever since.'

She started to cry, covering her face with her hands where she sat on the bed. Quarrie stood at the door and gave her a moment. 'It's all right,' he said gently. 'You're safe here. No one can get you. You set tight for a minute or two. If you want to use the bathroom to get cleaned up then go ahead. I'm going to rustle up a pot of coffee.'

*

Franklin was in the phone booth at the A&G Diner a couple of blocks further up Canal Street. A film of sweat on his brow, he scraped his fingernails over his palm. 'I told you she wasn't there. She must've known someone was coming. She was gone when I got in the house.'

'Find her,' Tobie stated. 'Don't let me down, Franklin. Not a second time. I'm warning you.'

Franklin leaned a shoulder against the glass wall of the booth and stared across Canal Street. He was about to say something else when a vehicle caught his eye. A weary-looking Chevrolet Nomad with sky-blue paint, it was parked on a meter directly across.

'Rosslyn,' he said, 'I've got to go now. I'll check with you later. OK?'

*

Quarrie went out to the sidewalk and peered across four lanes of traffic. He couldn't see the taxi parked anywhere so he went back to the lobby where Yvonne had made a pot of coffee. She placed it on a tray together with a couple of cups and he carried it upstairs. Gigi opened the door when he knocked and he locked it again and unhooked his shoulder holsters. Gigi glanced at the guns as he laid them on the bureau and she seemed a little calmer.

'Thank you,' she said, 'for letting me in here, for listening to me and not sending me away. Maybe I should've talked to you last night but after what Earl told me I needed time to think. I needed to figure things out.' Pausing for a moment she sighed. 'Right now they got my house taped off. I don't think I can go back there anyway, and I don't want to talk to the cops. I could go stay with my nana for a couple of days but I don't want to worry her and I don't know if I'd be safe.'

'Is that the lady in the photograph,' Quarrie asked, 'the one on your dressing table?'

Gigi nodded.

'I talked to her on the phone.'

'You did?'

'I was looking for you but she said you'd not been over in a couple of days.' Eyes half-closed he squinted. 'The meds, Gigi: the Proloid. *Did* you give them to someone or did somebody take them from you?'

Gigi's hand was shaking again as she took a sip of coffee. 'I don't know for sure,' she said, 'they just went missing.'

'Missing? What does that mean exactly? Did you lose them or did somebody take them?'

'It means I had them in my bathroom cabinet but when I needed them they weren't there.' She plucked another cigarette from the pack and lighted it. 'I think it was Earl who took them, though when I asked him he denied it. But then he would of course.' She shook her head. 'I didn't know that second bottle was gone till I woke up the other day with my muscles in spasm.'

'Second bottle,' Quarrie said. 'You telling me this happened before?'

'Yes, it did. Last time I thought I'd lost them on account of how they'd been in my purse and I had to go back to the pharmacist.'

'When was this?'

'February, I think it was; a couple of months back at least.'

Quarrie watched as she crossed to the window and peered out over the courtyard.

'Gigi,' he said. 'Tell me about Earl.'

Hunching her shoulders she turned to face him again. 'I hadn't seen him for a week or so then I try to call and he's all irritable and nervous on the phone. He tells me the line's being disconnected. After that he shows up at my place and tells me things had changed and I can't call him anymore. I could see he was frightened and I'd never seen him like that before.' Flicking ash she puffed at the cigarette. 'Those meds were dispensed by Mr Matthews and I heard on the radio how he never showed up at home. What happened to him?' she said. 'Where is he?'

'I don't know,' Quarrie told her. 'But I talked to him and I talked to you. Now he's gone and someone came after you. Last night, tell me what happened again, every detail, Gigi; don't leave anything out.'

Gigi repeated the events of the night and when she was finished Quarrie looked sharply at her. 'You think it might've been a cab?' he said. 'You didn't say that just now. What kind of car was it, Ford, Chevy? Did you see?'

She shook her head.

'And you couldn't pick out the driver?'

'I told you, all I saw was his shadow. The car was too far away and by the time he was at the front door I was hauling ass out the back.'

Still Quarrie stared at the floor. 'So tell me more about Earl,' he said. 'Who is he? What does he do for a living?'

'I can't tell you what he does. He never told me that, and like I said, I never knew his last name.'

Quarrie squinted at her.

'That's not unusual, not in this part of town; people use different names all the time. He told me if I asked no questions he'd tell no lies and that was just fine with me.' She gestured. 'He bought me jewelry and stuff from Royal Street, things I could sell if I had to.' She looked at the floor. 'He's married of course; I ain't so dumb as I don't know that. But life ain't easy for a black woman down here and the fact of it is there ain't much money to be made with the band so you just have to take what you can get.' She looked back at Quarrie then. 'Earl never told me what he did for a living and I never asked. But the way he carries himself I figure he might be a cop. I know cops, been hassled by them all my life. Earl's got a cop's eyes and a cop's bearing. I've lived here long enough to know.'

Thirteen

Franklin crossed the busy road and walked around the station wagon. The doors were locked and the trunk secure, but he could see a roll of Life Savers on the dashboard together with a tube of lipstick and a package of tissues. Hands on his hips he stared as far as the sign for the Magnolia where it jutted ahead of the Savings & Loan. Making his way back across the street once more he went into the diner and picked up the phone. 'Do me a favor,' he said when the call was answered. 'Call the club on Bourbon and Governor Nicholls. Tell Soulja Blue he's not done yet. I want his ass down here on Canal Street.'

*

De La Martin turned at the railroad station and headed towards the river. As he drove he worked a palm through his hair and spotted the taxi parked in a bay. Glancing in the mirror he switched lanes and pulled his Ford in behind. No sign of the blond-haired driver, he got out of his car and walked around the cab considering the sign on the roof and the meter, the shortwave radio fixed to the dash. He looked at the hood and the trunk and took a note of the license number. Then he got back in his Ford. The radio crackled and a voice came over the receiver. 'Are you out there, Detective, pick up?'

De La Martin unhooked the transmitter from its housing.

'Copy that,' he said. 'What's up?'

'Marjorie reckons a teletype was sent last night and there's no entry in her log. She's asking if it was you and why you didn't fill out the papers.'

*

Ten minutes after Franklin put down the phone the Malibu SS pulled up to the curb outside the Hotel Magnolia. In the passenger seat Soulja Blue glanced at his driver. He told him to park a little way down the street and wait. Then he got out of the car. Shaven head and yellow whites to his eyes, he straightened the flaps of his Nehru jacket.

*

Quarrie picked up the phone and asked Yvonne for an outside line. Dialling the organized crime squad he waited to be connected. Finally Colback spoke in his ear.

'You got some nerve calling me again.'

Quarrie glanced briefly at Gigi. 'Lieutenant, quit jawing and listen for a minute, will you?'

*

Soulja Blue strode into the hotel courtyard and glanced at the metalled walkway before stepping into the lobby.

'Can I help you, sir?' Yvonne spoke up from the desk.

'I need a room for the night.'

'We can do that I think, yes, we can.' She indicated for him to sign the register and he considered the list of names.

'How about 33?' he said. 'Always been my lucky number.'

'Yes, sir, 33 is fine. That'll be sixteen-fifty including the sales tax.'

The room was two doors further along from Quarrie's and Soulja glanced at the window as he passed. Inside, he left the door on the latch, took an automatic from his pocket and slipped out the magazine. Popping out the topmost round with his thumb he pressed it back and slipped the magazine home once more. Then he laid the gun on the nightstand and picked up the phone.

*

When Quarrie finished talking to Colback he peeled a cigarette from his pack and tapped the inscribed end against the base of his thumb. 'All right,' he said, turning to Gigi. 'Lieutenant Colback's coming down in a piece and he wants to talk to you. When you're done either you can go with him to some kind of safe house or I can take you to your nana's apartment.'

Gigi frowned. 'I don't trust the NOPD.'

'I don't suppose you do. But I figure you can trust Colback; someone's playing him for a joker right now same as they're playing me.'

Letting her take a moment to think he opened the closet and picked up the folded newspaper.

'What is that?' Gigi asked.

'It's a copy of *The Dallas Times Herald* and I ain't sure if it was here when I took this room or not.' He folded the paper away. 'Anyway, you can't go home so unless you got anyone else, it's your nana's place or whatever Colback suggests.' He glanced over his shoulder. 'Is there anywhere else you can stay?'

Gigi shook her head. 'There's the band I guess, but I don't want to do that. There used to be a cousin lived back my way but he left town a couple of years ago. Took him a loan out with Soulja Blue and couldn't pay the vig. Soulja don't take kindly to folks not paying what they owe so he took up a ball peen hammer. My cousin left out after that, I mean just as soon as he got done with Charity Hospital. Soulja never did get his money back, though he did try to lay that debt on me.'

'Who's Soulja Blue?'

Gigi looked grim. 'He's a black man I've known since I was a kid. Got him a club on Bourbon and Governor Nicholls where white boys get to take it to women like me. I'm talking about the same way their great-grandpappies used to back in the day. From outside it's a regular drugstore, but there's a club in back and a show every night like a Catholic Mass only with colored girls getting naked and rooms for anything those white boys want to do after.' Her eyes were heated then. 'Soulja don't care what happens just so long as the mess is cleaned up. If a girl's been beat so bad nobody wants her anymore they have to pay what it costs to get him another.'

She drank the rest of her coffee. 'I think I will call Nana. I ain't up for the NOPD.'

'All right,' Quarrie said. 'Do that and when the lieutenant gets here we'll take you over to her place.'

'You don't need to do that,' she said. 'I got my old Chevy parked up the street.'

'We'll follow you then,' Quarrie said. 'Make sure you get there safe. She looks like you, your nana, same hairstyle. How old is she?'

'She's eighty. But she's not actually my grandma, she's my aunt.

Nana's her Christian name and I guess she raised me pretty much on account of how my momma died when she was having me.'

Peering beyond him then she started talking as if the shock of having her life threatened had hit home suddenly and all she could do was focus on things that were familiar and close. 'I don't mean by herself,' she said. 'Two old mammies from the 7th had me come live with them and I guess that was on account of Nana was a woman on her own and she lived a particular kind of life. That life didn't fit with children so they took care of me but Nana paid for everything and I visited with her all the time. I remember being at her place on the weekend when Lizzie Miles would come around and maybe it was on account of Lizzie that I got into singing. She and Nana used to go at it from time to time; you know, butt heads and all because of the way Nana lived and Lizzie being a Christian girl. I'll be all right with Nana. She keeps a piece in the house and she'd shoot anyone who tried to get in. Haitian, old-time Creole, she speaks French a lot of the time and when she gets mad she falls into the patois and there ain't no following her then.' Breaking off she smiled. 'She's done pretty well for a woman on her own. That place where she lives at on Orleans Street, one of her lovers bought it back in the day.'

'One of her lovers?' Quarrie arched a quizzical brow.

Again she smiled and got up off the bed. 'Don't worry; it sounds a whole lot worse than it is. It's what I said before about women like us and the way things have to be. Nana had a few lovers in her time and when she was done with them she made sure she was a little further on than where she'd been. This guy was around for a while I guess, old white family from way back when. Plenty of money and younger than her. Course he had him a wife at home but don't they always,' she said.

Fourteen

Half an hour later Yvonne called up to tell Quarrie that Colback had arrived. Leaving Gigi to phone her nana he went downstairs and found the lieutenant sitting at one of the tables in the courtyard with a cup of coffee. 'So do we understand each other finally?' Colback's tone was edged with a hint of sarcasm.

'We better,' Quarrie said.

'I guess she's upstairs then. Is she all right?'

Quarrie sat down. 'She's doing OK. She was a little shaky when she knocked on the door.'

'So what about this cab driver?'

'Last time I saw him was on North Rocheblave Street.' Quarrie took the business card from his wallet and a slip of paper fell out. The note he had found on Wiley after he shot him, one word scribbled – *Jacinto*.

'What is that?' Colback said.

'It's the name of a street in Dallas.'

'So what's the significance?'

'I don't know. I found it in the pocket of the feller I shot back in Texas.' Stuffing the note away again he placed the business card on the table.

'This all you got?' Colback inspected the card where only the company name and phone number were printed. 'The cabbie never told you his name?'

'No, he didn't. But he shouldn't be hard to track down, the number's right there on the card and that cab is a '65 four-door Impala.'

'Have you called this number?' Colback said.

'Not since talking to you.'

'But he told you it was me paying him to keep an eye on you?'

'Yes, he did.'

'So who's he working for then?'

'Beats me, Lieutenant. Pershing Gervais maybe; the kid told me how he's the quarterback in college and it might be he's making the passes but there's someone else in charge of the play.' Taking off his hat he placed it crown up on the table. 'That other thing I told you about. You got any ideas about this feller Earl?'

'A cop she was talking about.' Colback pushed out his lips. 'I made some calls but don't go hanging your hat. If he's in the job we don't know if it's the city or the sheriff's department, which means we could be talking Jefferson Parish or Bernard, Plaquemines and St Tammany probably as well. Earl isn't exactly an uncommon name in these parts, is it?'

Quarrie looked the length of the courtyard to the traffic out on Canal Street. 'Gigi told me he was the one who warned her to stay away from me. Said how he came around her house in the 7th Ward so jumpy he could barely get the words out.'

Colback was quiet for a moment, sipping from his coffee. 'When we talked on the phone you told me you thought it was a photograph in that hotel room back in Texas. The guy you shot, what was his name again?'

'Wiley.'

'Wiley, right: so did he burn everything? There wasn't anything in those ashes you found that might give us some kind of clue?'

'Nope, all that was left was mush.'

'What about the kid you said he had with him?'

'Henderson?' Quarrie made a face. 'He swears he never saw the photo, and with what-all he's staring down the barrel of right now he'd be running his mouth if he did.'

Colback peered beyond him. 'So they burn a photograph and tip a bunch of pills down some poor bastard's throat. What do you know about him?'

'Nothing,' Quarrie said. 'Right now we're waiting on the NCIC.'

*

From the crack in his door Soulja Blue saw Quarrie walk the gantry and make his way down the steps. He saw him heading for the back of the courtyard where he disappeared from view. Then he opened the door and strode along the short landing with the automatic held at his side. When he got to Quarrie's room he knocked.

*

Downstairs Colback glanced at his watch. 'I got a meeting to go to,' he said. 'Let me have a word with this gal real quick, see if she's got the sense to let me take her somewhere we can protect her.'

Quarrie led the way upstairs to his room. There was no

answer when he knocked and no sound from inside. The door wasn't locked and, with a glance at Colback, he went in. The room was empty, no sign of Gigi: the door to the bathroom stood open but there was nobody there.

'So where is she?' Colback said.

Quarrie didn't answer; his gaze settled on a scrap of paper on the nightstand beside the bed. He picked it up and studied three words scribbled in an unsteady hand. 'She's gone to her nana's house,' he said.

Colback pumped the air from his cheeks. 'Did she tell you she was going to do that?'

Quarrie was still studying the note. 'She said she had a vehicle parked up the street but I told her we'd cover her till she got there.'

'Do you have an address?'

Quarrie gave him the address for Orleans Street he had found in the phone book.

'Soon as I'm done with my meeting I'll give her a call,' Colback said. 'If you talk to her in the meantime, tell her I'll have a prowl car make regular sweeps.' He turned for the door. 'And by the way, if you get hold of that cab driver – make sure you let me know.'

*

In the room two doors down Gigi lay on her side, her mouth stuffed with toilet paper and her hands tied at the base of her spine. Her eyes were wide as she stared at Soulja where he sat on the chair with his forearms resting on his thighs. He was staring at her and his gaze had dulled till there was no expression at all.

He was listening to the two men talking on the walkway out-side. Gigi started to murmur and he lifted a finger to his lips. She was silent again, and he picked up the sound of footsteps receding and the door to Quarrie's room as it was shut. Still he sat there and then he got up and came over to the bed. Sitting down beside Gigi his free hand fell to her hair. Fingers stiff he worked them against her scalp and she shut her eyes, drew her legs up tight and tried not to wet herself.

*

Franklin's cab was parked outside Stein's Clothing a little fur-ther along Canal Street from the hotel. He had the collar of his jacket turned up and the radio playing Marvin Gaye. He sat up a little straighter as Lieutenant Colback came out from un-der the hotel arch and walked half a block before he got in his unmarked car. A minute or so after that Quarrie appeared and Franklin watched as he made his way to the corner.

Fifteen

There was no one in the lobby when Soulja Blue came down the steps with his jacket slung over his arm to hide the automatic. He had Gigi's hand hooked through the crook of his other arm and together they walked out onto Canal Street. Glancing towards the trolley car tracks, Soulja signalled to his driver and seconds later the blue Malibu was hugging the curb. Forcing Gigi into the back, he climbed in beside her and the driver pulled out into the traffic. Soulja sat with his arm around Gigi's shoulders.

'They say what goes around comes around, don't they?' he muttered. 'The hippies, I mean, in their communes and whatnot. I think they might have a point. I mean, your cousin lit out owing Soulja money and here I am getting paid.'

Gigi was shaking. She could not speak. She could smell leather and the scent of cologne. They drove across the Quarter to Bourbon Street and down to the junction with Governor Nicholls. The car pulled up and the driver got out, a more slightly built man wearing a dark suit and white shirt. He bound Gigi's eyes with a strip of cloth then Soulja pushed her out of the car and she was on the sidewalk breathing in the stench of the river. She felt the driver grab her again and she was bundled through a door and across a floor to where she felt strands of metal brush her face. Another door was opened and she could hear the sound of church music echoing from somewhere behind.

Manhandled along a narrow corridor she came to a flight of stairs. She felt a hand at her back and was forced up those stairs and along a landing where the blindfold slipped. The driver reached to tie it again but not before Gigi glimpsed a corridor with doors leading off and one of the doors was cracked. Beyond it she caught sight of a middle-aged black man slumped on the floor with his hands tied and blood staining the front of his shirt. Then she was past and the driver shoved her up another flight of stairs and along another corridor. He opened a door and she was forced inside and across the floor to a rancid-smelling bed. Thrown onto her back she felt drops of water spilling from some leaking pipe above as the driver secured her hands and feet. His breath all over her face, she twisted her head away. She heard the sound of the door opening and closing and all that was left were the strains of that organ drifting from two floors below.

She did not know how long she lay like that, it could have been minutes, it could've been hours, but then she heard the door open and twisted her head to the side. Whoever was there did not speak, but she could hear the music from downstairs and it was louder and laced with intermittent voices. 'Who's there?' she cried. 'Who are you? What do you want?'

Silence, nothing, there was no sound in the room, even the dripping had stopped.

'Who are you?' she cried again. 'What do you want with me? Why did you bring me here?'

'Gigi Matisse from the 7th Ward who won't do what she's told.' A man's voice so close to her ear she physically jumped.

'Who are you?' she said. 'What do you want?'

'I thought Earl made it perfectly clear. He warned you what would happen. All actions have consequences, Gigi. There's no such thing as an action that does not have a reaction. Talking to strangers, sleeping with white men; not doing what you're told.'

Gigi opened her mouth to say something but could not find any words. She felt a hand on her shin and a shudder worked through her as that hand climbed to her knee. 'On top of everything else there's the money now as well. Your cousin, we settled his debt with Soulja Blue so now it's us you owe. We know you can't pay in cash but it's not cash we want, it's you.' He was silent for a moment then he said, 'You're going to die here. You need to know that. You're never going to see your nana again or any of your friends, none of the boys in your band. You'll live only as long as it takes to pay off what we gave Soulja Blue.' She felt him get up off the bed and pad across the floor. Then she heard the sound of the door being opened and closed.

'Hear that?' he said. 'That's a sound you'll be begging me to silence. Open and closed. Open and closed. Before we're done you'll scream for me to slam it once and for all.'

*

Quarrie bought a pack of Camel regulars from the kiosk outside the Shell Oil building. Standing on the corner he peered towards the river as he tore the cellophane away.

Back in his room he sat on the bed and considered the slip of paper Gigi had left on the nightstand. He phoned the number he had called earlier that morning and the same woman answered as before.

'Ms Matisse,' he said. 'My name's Quarrie. I called you this morning.'

'Yes,' she said. 'What can I do for you?'

'Is Gigi there?'

'No, she's not.'

'But you talked to her on the phone? I mean since I last spoke to you.'

'Yes, I did, a little while ago. She told me she was on her way.'

'But she's not there yet?'

'I'm expecting her sometime soon.'

'All right, mam. Thank you. Do you think you could do me a favor? When Gigi gets there would you ask her to call me at the Hotel Magnolia?'

He waited twenty minutes but there was no call. Picking up the phone he dialled the number again but this time there was no reply. Replacing the receiver he worked fingers through the stalks of his hair. He was aware of a yawning sensation in his gut and that could've been trepidation but it could've been the fact he hadn't had anything to eat and it was well past noon.

He walked up Canal Street towards the A&G looking for a gap in the traffic. Up ahead he could see an NOPD cruiser double parked and a cop in uniform writing a ticket for a car that had overstayed the meter. As he passed Quarrie noticed the car was a battered-looking '55 Chevy Nomad painted a pale kind of blue. There was something familiar about it and he paused for a moment on the sidewalk.

'This outfit yours?' Spotting his interest, the cop called across the roof.

'No, sir.' Quarrie pointed to the A&G. 'I'm headed for the

diner yonder and I'm wondering how you're going to be if I skip the light and cross right here.'

'Why don't you try me and see?'

Touching a finger to the brim of his hat Quarrie walked on towards the pedestrian light. He didn't get that far, however; the car was bugging him and he stepped into the doorway of Zales Jewelers. He waited until the cop was done with the ticket and had climbed back into his cruiser. Then he started down the sidewalk again, his gaze all over that vehicle as he came up on the passenger door. A roll of Life Savers on the dashboard, a stick of lip gloss; bending closer he cupped his hand to the glass. He could see nothing inside that identified the owner though, and headed back to the hotel.

'Yvonne,' he said when he walked into the lobby, 'did anybody check in here this morning?'

She nodded. 'Just the one man, I think. Why?'

'What man? What did he look like?'

'He was colored, pretty well built I guess. Nice clothes. He had no hair, that's right, his head was shaved.'

'Did he have any luggage with him?'

'Excuse me?'

'Did he have any luggage with him?'

'Actually, now that you mention it, I don't think he did.'

'What room did you give him?'

'33,' she said. 'He told me that was his lucky number.'

Quarrie stood with a palm pressed to the counter studying the illegible squiggle in the register. 'Is he up there now?'

'I don't know, sir. I can't tell you.'

He looked squarely at her then. 'You ain't going to like this,' he said. 'But I need you to give me your pass key.'

Climbing the stairs he drew a Blackhawk from his shoulder holster and made his way along the walkway past his room. No sound from inside 33, lightly he knocked and nobody spoke so he knocked a little louder. 'Room service,' he called. 'I got the coffee you ordered.'

Still there was no answer so he fit the key in the lock and tried to turn it but the door was already open.

The room was empty; no sign of it ever having been occupied save the way the bedclothes were ruffled slightly. He checked the bathroom but it hadn't been used. As he turned he glanced at the bed once more and the nightstand where a pad of paper sat alongside a ballpoint pen. There was nothing written on the pad, but when he looked more closely he picked up the slightest of indentations.

Returning to his room he sat on the chair by the door and stared at the floor. That was Gigi's Nomad with a ticket on the windshield, he was sure. Picking up the phone he dialled the number for Orleans Street but again there was no reply. He hung up and thought about calling Colback's office but it occurred to him that no sooner had the lieutenant shown up than Gigi had disappeared.

He was trying to work out where they could have taken her. Then he remembered something she had said and tried to get his head around what that would mean. Opening the door he stepped out onto the landing then changed his mind and went back into the room. Sitting down on the bed he reached for the phone. Yvonne gave him a line and he dialled the ranch back in Texas and it was James who answered the phone.

'Hey, bud,' Quarrie said, 'what're you doing?'

'Not much. It's too hot to be outside right now. Mama Sox

made lemonade and Miss Eunice put a pitcher in the ice box here at home.'

'Well, save a drop for me, uh, don't be drinking it all.'

'Where are you?' James said. 'When're you coming back?'

'I'm still in New Orleans right now, but I'll be home pretty soon. Listen, can you go get Pious for me, ask him to come to the phone?'

'He's right here,' James said, 'him and Miss Eunice both. We've been doing some of those word games I told you about.'

'Anagrams, what you said you were doing in school?'

'That's right. Dad, I'm better than Pious and I'm only ten years old.'

Quarrie laughed. 'Don't let him hear you say that. Can you put him on the phone?'

He waited a moment then Pious spoke in his ear. 'What's up, John Q? What's going on?'

'Bud, I'm still in New Orleans. Does Mrs Feeley have any plans for the plane?'

'Right now, you mean? Not that's she's told me. Why, what's on your mind?'

'I need you to fly down here. There ain't a cop in town I can trust. I got something I have to do and I'm going to need someone in back of me.'

'All right, I'll gas her up and be at the Lakefront soon as I can.'

'Pious?' Quarrie said.

'What?'

'Before you leave out, fetch the twelve-gauge pump from my room.'

*

Rosslyn Tobie walked the path in his garden with one hand behind his back and in the other the cane. Like a reluctant dog Franklin followed a few paces behind. At the summerhouse Tobie considered where Spanish moss clung to the branches of live oaks despite the weight of the breeze. 'So she's at the club on Bourbon and Governor Nicholls?'

Franklin nodded. 'I spotted her car when I was talking to you and figured out where she was.'

'And that was the Ranger's room, which means she spoke to him and that wasn't what we agreed.' The old man shaded his eyes. 'I told you to deal with her properly.'

'I know you did and I tried.'

'Like you tried in Texas with Wiley?' With a shake of his head Tobie walked more purposefully towards the house. 'Why isn't she dead? Why is she with Soulja Blue? Why, when I order you to do something, do you only half do it? You elicit no confidence at all.'

A little crimson at the jowls, Franklin came alongside. 'You told me to pay Soulja Blue what her cousin owed.' He flapped a hand. 'I figured she could cover that debt before she dies. It'll make me feel better about parting with the dough.'

Tobie stepped through the French windows into his study and laid down the walking cane. 'Just get rid of her,' he said. 'I don't care about the money. I don't want anything else going wrong. Just kill her as I told you to.'

'All right,' Franklin said. 'If that's what you want. I'll do it tonight, take her over to Algiers and dump her somewhere downriver.'

'Make sure you do.' Crossing to his desk Tobie picked up his diary. 'Where are we with the 28th? What's happening? Is everything in place?'

'Everything bar Wiley,' Franklin said. 'You still haven't told me what we're doing about him.'

Tobie looked beyond him. 'What exactly did that bitch tell the Ranger? Does he know about Moore?'

'He knows he exists, that's all. I told you, all she knows is his first name. She doesn't know where he lives or who he works for.' Franklin looked at him then with his head to one side. 'Despite the way you've treated me I'm not as incompetent as you seem to believe.'

'You don't think so?' Tobie scoffed. 'You're forgetting the railroad, the box car, the dead man in Wichita Falls.'

Sixteen

Quarrie phoned the tower at the Lakefront Airport and they gave him Pious's ETA. It was getting dark outside now and he needed a vehicle. Selecting a wire coat hanger from the closet he untwisted the hook and worked the metal until it was straight. Then he fashioned a smaller hook in the end and slipped the hanger inside his jacket.

Keeping one eye out for prowl cars he walked back to Gigi's Chevy. He stood on the sidewalk at the passenger door, making sure he was unobserved then slid the coat hanger between the door frame and the window so he could lift the lock. With the door open he dropped behind the wheel and felt under the dashboard for the wiring loom. He sought the two power wires that linked to the battery and separated them. Ignoring the electric shock the wires gave off he twisted the strands of copper together, then unhooked the back of the ignition barrel. Working the starter wire loose he had to clear away some of the plastic coating with his pocket knife, then he touched the starter to the battery wires and the engine fired into life.

Shifting gear he pulled out into traffic and followed the signs for the lake. Halfway there he turned into an Enco station, bought a street map and located the Lakefront Airport. He was watching his mirrors for any sign of a tail, but as far as he could tell nobody was back there and he got to the airport just as Pious walked out of the freight entrance. He wore jeans and a Carhartt and carried a long flat, canvas hold-all. Quarrie flashed his headlights.

'Good to see you, bud,' he said as Pious got in. 'No issues with Mrs Feeley and the plane?'

Pious made a face. 'Actually she made a point of telling me that the plane ain't mine and it ain't the property of the Rangers either, said for me to remind you.'

Quarrie reached to the dashboard and unfolded the street map. With his index finger he traced a route from the Lakefront to Bourbon and Governor Nicholls.

'Where'd you get this outfit?' Pious said, glancing at the interior of the car.

'It belongs to a gal called Gigi who's in a spot of trouble right now.'

*

Franklin called the club from his apartment on Washington Avenue. 'Soulja,' he said. 'Gigi Matisse, you got her till midnight only. After that I'm going to need you to load her up and bring her out to the Point.'

'I thought we were working her,' Soulja's voice came back at him. 'I thought she was here to stay.'

'Well, she's not. She's done down there. I'll be waiting for you at the warehouse, no later than twelve, OK?'

*

At eleven o'clock Quarrie parked the station wagon on the corner of Bourbon Street and Governor Nicholls. Switching off the engine he stared through the windshield towards the entrance of what looked like a regular drugstore. Pious shifted the weight of the shotgun where it lay across his thighs. 'That's the spot, huh?' he said. 'So, how do you want to play it?'

For a moment Quarrie was still. 'Gigi told me the club's for white men only so I'll go in while you wait with the car. If I'm not out in fifteen minutes I want you to storm the place like you're raiding foxholes back in Korea.' Unzipping his jacket he worked it over his shoulders and unbuckled the holsters. 'You better take these,' he said, passing Pious the Blackhawks. 'They're bound to frisk me but I got a snub-nose in my boot and you'll know if they find it, I promise you.' He got out of the car and tossed his hat onto the back seat. Then he crossed the road to the drugstore and paused for a moment in the glow of the streetlamps. The building was pretty ropey compared to some in the block, the wooden shutters at the upstairs windows chafed and weather-beaten and a number of shingles on the roof were missing.

Inside, a young woman wearing a little too much make-up was sitting behind the counter reading a paperback novel. Ahead of her was the cash register and a rack of candy bars, a cooler full of Dr Pepper. A selection of paperback novels, the kind of pulp she was reading, was stacked in another rack that swivelled on a spindle. Beyond that was yet another rack holding cheap sunglasses and greeting cards. It looked like a regular store but considering how the block extended it was a whole lot smaller than it should be.

Conscious of the way the girl was looking him up and down Quarrie took in one door at the far end of the room and another to the side that was covered by a metal fly curtain.

'Can I help you, sir?' the girl said.

Quarrie was studying the fly curtain. 'I thought maybe you could but I guess I must be mistaken.'

The girl was on her feet. 'What were you looking for? A little something extra, was it?' She passed a hand under the counter and he heard a buzzer sound through the wall.

A couple of minutes later the curtain peeled back as the door beyond it opened and a slim, black man appeared. He wore a dark colored suit over a roll-neck sweater and for a long moment he looked at Quarrie. Beyond the door was a short corridor that came out in a small lobby. The black man led the way and Quarrie could hear what he thought was organ music and he had not heard it before the door opened. The man indicated for him to spread his arms out wide and Quarrie did that, determined to bring his knee up hard if those hands delved too close to his boots.

'It's fifty dollars for the show,' the man said. 'Anything you want after that is extra, but it's fifty bucks for the show.'

Quarrie did not have fifty dollars. Taking his money clip from his pocket he fingered a ten-dollar bill.

The black man twisted his lip. 'A ten spot,' he said. 'Are you kidding me?'

'Take it easy, brother. Town like this, I keep my stash where no one can pick my pocket.' Putting the clip away Quarrie bent to his boots.

The man glanced towards the corridor and when he looked back Quarrie had the snub-nose under his chin. 'You got a new girl they just brought in. You're going to take me to her and you're going to do it nice and easy.'

He walked the man ahead of him and as they passed the room where the music was playing, he glimpsed a gaggle of white men sitting in what looked like church pews while a string of naked black girls knelt at a mock altar before them. At the foot of the stairs the black man hesitated and Quarrie prodded him with the pistol. They climbed two sets of stairs and the man led him to a threadbare room with broken boards on the floor and a metal framed bed where Gigi was stretched with her feet secured at one end and her hands tied above her head at the other. She was bruised around the face, one eyelid all puffed up, her lip bloodied and broken. Naked save a soiled white sheet, her eyes were closed but Quarrie could see she was conscious and she was trembling.

'Gigi,' he whispered softly.

She opened her eyes, but her pupils were vague and glassy.

Savagely Quarrie brought the heel of the gun down on the black man's head. He let out a moan, buckled at the knees and started to topple over. Grabbing him around the chest Quarrie lowered him to the floor as soundlessly as he could. Quickly he worked at Gigi's fastenings. She started to speak. She started to weep, spittle breaking from her lips; she closed her eyes very tightly. Stripping away the bonds that held her ankles Quarrie lifted her with the sheet still wrapped and carried her to the window.

'Can you walk?' he said. 'Gigi, we have to get out of here and I need you to walk. Can you do that for me?'

'I can walk.' She was sobbing; half-stifling the sound with a hand to her mouth she tried to speak again but he hushed her.

'It's all right,' he whispered. 'It's OK. My buddy's outside with your Chevy.'

At the window he lowered her down so her feet were on the floor but still he supported her weight. Wrapping the sheet more tightly about her he stripped off his jacket and threw it around her shoulders. Hauling on the sash he pushed at the shutters till they flapped open. Pious was across the road standing by the driver's door of the station wagon. Making a whirling motion with his hand Quarrie signalled for him to bring it over.

'All right.' He turned back to Gigi. 'Now we go down. If I tell you to run you run and you don't look back. That guy outside's called Pious. If anything happens to me just do whatever he tells you.'

She was clinging to him, almost sobbing again as they went down the narrow stairway. He could hear other women in other rooms and by the sound of things in the chapel the mass had taken a new turn. Gigi was barefoot and stumbling. He guided her beyond the chapel door and then they were in the lobby. A shout went up and, as he kicked open the door to the drugstore, Quarrie saw a huge man with a shaven head appear behind them.

Outside, the station wagon was bumped up to the curb with the driver's door wide and the engine running. Pious was on the sidewalk with the shotgun in his hands and Quarrie was half-walking, half-running, trying to shield Gigi.

'Get down, John Q,' Pious yelled at him.

Quarrie shoved Gigi to the floor. He was on top of her, trying to spin around while Pious levelled the shotgun. Before he could get a shot off the door beyond the curtain was slammed. On hands and knees Gigi was scrabbling, Quarrie was scrabbling; together they made it to the door and tumbled onto the sidewalk.

In the driver's seat Quarrie stamped on the gas, the back end fishtailing as they careered the length of the block. He hauled hard on the wheel to stop it crashing into a lamp post and the car rocked with a sawing motion. They drove Governor Nicholls towards the river with Quarrie watching in the mirror for headlights. Making the turn he cut deeper into the Quarter and a few minutes later they pulled up outside the Orleans Street apartment. Pious got out of the car and pressed the bell on the wall and then they were inside the narrow driveway with the steel gates closed behind them. A door on their right was already open and beyond it they came to a courtyard dressed with palmetto and baby oak trees. Italian tiles on the floor, it was lit by carriage lamps with stairs climbing in a spiral to the gallery above where the old woman from the photograph was waiting. 'Cherie,' she called, 'qu'est ce qu'il se passe ici?'

'Rien, Nana, everything's fine.' Gigi was stumbling for the stairs and Pious caught her before she fell then carried her up with Quarrie keeping one eye on the street behind them.

'Ms Matisse,' he said to the elderly woman, 'I talked to you on the phone. I'm a Texas Ranger, mam. Gigi's hurt and needs a place to hole up in.'

The apartment was spacious and cool with tall ceilings and full height, rectangular windows. The furniture was so delicate and individual it looked as if it had been there since the days of the Spanish. Under Nana's direction Pious carried Gigi through to a room where a bed was made up, a sphere in each corner of the iron bedstead embossed with a coiled serpent. Gently Pious laid Gigi down and she looked past him to where Quarrie stood in the doorway.

'Mr Matthews,' she sobbed. 'The pharmacist, I saw him back there, they had him tied up in a room and there was blood on his shirt, his glasses were smashed. He . . .'

'All right,' Quarrie said. 'It's all right now. Take it easy.'

Nana followed them in from the hall and Quarrie could see she was trembling. 'What happened?' She looked at Quarrie. 'What went on here? What happened to my baby?'

Taking off his hat Quarrie held it at his side. For a second or two he regarded Gigi's battered features then he glanced through the open door beyond the hall, to where Pious was watching the street from the balcony.

'What happened to her?' Nana repeated.

'I don't know exactly, some men took her to a club on Governor Nicholls.'

'Soulja Bleu.' The old woman's eyes were wide and he saw the way a shiver worked her shoulders. Lifting a hand to her breast she blessed herself then kissed the tips of her fingers.

'We got her out of there pretty quick,' Quarrie said, 'but I can't tell you what happened because she hasn't had time to tell us.' He glanced once more across the hallway. 'She can't stay here for long because sooner or later they're going to find this apartment. When she's rested I'm going to have Pious fly her back to the ranch where we live at in Texas.'

He and Pious remained in the living room while the old woman filled a basin with warm water and took a bag of cotton balls to the bedroom so she could bathe Gigi's cuts and bruises. Pious sat in a high-backed chair with his fingers entwined across the flat of his stomach. 'What do you reckon they done to her?'

Quarrie didn't answer. He picked up the phone, dialled 911 and asked for the 3rd Precinct. When dispatch put him through, he told them to get hold of De La Martin and let him know where the pharmacist was. Hanging up once more, he dialled again and asked the operator to connect him to the

Department of Public Safety in Amarillo. 'This is Sergeant Quarrie,' he said when the call was answered.

'John Q,' the dispatcher came back. 'Where are you?'

'I'm out of state right now. Are there any messages for me?'

'Yes, sir, Captain Van Hanigan wants you to call him.'

Nana came out of the bedroom and quietly closed the door. She looked puffy about the eyes but she seemed composed enough as Quarrie and Pious got up from their seats in the living room.

'I imagine you boys could do with a drink,' she said, waving them down. 'I know I sure could.' Her voice was a little shaky. 'I keep julep mixed if y'all want one.' She went to fetch the drinks and Quarrie called his captain at home. 'It's Quarrie,' he said when Van Hanigan answered. 'I just talked to Amarillo and they said you wanted to speak to me.'

'That's right, I did. I thought you'd want to know that we had those fingerprints confirmed by the NCIC.'

Quarrie sat more upright. 'Got us a match then, do we?'

'Yes, we do, but it didn't come from the felon register. Strangest thing,' Van Hanigan said. 'The NCIC told me that right after your request went in they had something from the coroner's office down there in New Orleans. It was very specific, wanting them to check police records rather than the felon register. I asked them who it was sent the request but they couldn't give me a name. Said it was just a scrawl on the paperwork. Anyway, it turns out the dead guy's real name was Trace Anderson and I can't tell you why he checked into The Roosevelt under an alias, but I can tell you he used to be a cop. NOPD, John Q. I made a call and they told me he quit about six months back. There's an address on Esplanade Avenue.'

Seventeen

Earl kept one eye on the windows of his office from the diner on Tulane Avenue. He had a cup of coffee before him and his hand shook every time he took a sip. He saw the lights go out and not long after that a car came up the ramp from the underground parking garage. A few minutes later he pried a dollar from his clip, placed it on the table and left. Outside on the sidewalk he stood bathed in neon that echoed from the signs of competing bail bond companies.

On the other side of the road he made his way down the ramp to the parking garage and entered the coroner's office through the same door he had before. Walking quickly he took the stairs to the back corridor and glass panelled office where the Telecopier was still plugged into the outlet. A role of flimsy-looking paper seemed to peel from the drum. As he tore it off a hint of perspiration moved on his brow.

In the parking garage he got behind the wheel of his car and unrolled the sheet of paper. He read it through then read it again and then he started the engine. Reversing out of the space he swung up the ramp before the gates were closed for the night. The heel of a palm on the wheel he drove across town, keeping his eyes on his mirrors. When he got to North Rampart Street he drove downtown as far as Esplanade Avenue then turned for the river and made his way to where the railroad tracks hit the wharf. With the window rolled down and the smell of diesel in the air, he spun all the way around and faced the way he had come. He passed the apartment complex on his right and turned at the next corner then drove another half a block before he stopped. For a few moments he sat at the wheel with his hands in his lap staring at his reflection in the rear view mirror.

When he got out of the car the rain was coming down and he grabbed his trilby from the passenger seat. He looked up and down the block then across the road to where the various houses and apartments seemed to radiate with light. Fixing the hat he buttoned his coat to the rain then walked as far as the corner. There he stopped and cast a glance towards North Rampart then again in the direction of the river. With no one around, he plucked a two-piece set of lock picks from his coat pocket and studied them in the fall of the streetlight.

*

When Quarrie opened the bedroom door Gigi was lying in the half-light that broke through the window. He sat on the edge of the bed and took her hand and she gripped his fingers tightly.

'How're you doing?' he asked her.

'He was there as soon as you left.' Gigi's eyes were alive with fear. 'Soulja Blue. How did he know where I was?'

'I don't know yet, Gigi. I aim to find out.'

She closed her eyes then broke down crying and it was a couple of minutes before she was able to compose herself. Quarrie was holding her hand as Nana appeared from the hall-way. Gigi looked up at her then back at Quarrie and her voice was shaking. 'A man came to the room where you found me. I

148

never saw his face, I just heard his voice. They blindfolded me when they took me into the club. That man said I didn't listen. He said I'd been told to stay away from you but I went ahead and talked to you anyway. He told me that behavior like that had consequences. He said my cousin's debt had been paid. The money he owed, they had the note and I had to pay but . . .' She broke down again as the sobbing swept her.

Quarrie left Nana to comfort her and went back to the living room where Pious was keeping vigil at the window.

'Anything going on out there?' Quarrie said.

'No, sir, all's quiet.'

Quarrie picked up his shoulder holsters from the arm of a chair. 'I'm going to take the car and check that address Van Hanigan gave me. If anybody shows up while I'm gone, make sure they know you got a shotgun.'

He drove the short distance up to North Rampart Street then swung north once more, watching for anybody watching him. At Esplanade he made a right and headed for the river and Decatur Street, which ran parallel with the railroad. A mist seeped from the Mississippi to shroud the rain-washed asphalt and he slowed as the glare from his headlights reflected against the windshield. Hardly tickling the gas, he passed Bourbon Street and Royal, after that Chartres Street where they had held him at the 3rd Precinct Station House. Pulling into a bay just ahead of the Decatur Street junction he switched off the engine and gazed towards the brick-built apartment complex on the other side of the road. Locking the car door he checked for signs of surveillance then crossed the road and vaulted the gate. Now he stood looking up at the metal gantry where flickering gas lamps cast shadows at each apartment.

Earl saw the car pull up and Quarrie get out and square his hat. He saw him cross the road, hop the gate and walk the court-yard to the gantry steps. Easing an automatic from inside his jacket he held a paper file in his other hand and stepped around the end of the block. There was no way out back there, it was just an alcove where the garbage cans were stacked. With Quarrie on the steps already he had no choice but to crouch in the shadows.

The apartment was the last in line, and, as Quarrie approached, he could see a handful of letters lying in front of the door. He stopped, stood still for a moment then took another couple of paces and saw that the door was ajar. Easing back a fraction he pressed his body in close to the brickwork and peered beyond the pool of light that bled from the gas lamps.

Just yards away, Earl crouched with perspiration rolling down his cheeks. His palm was damp where he gripped the auto-matic. He did not move. He did not breathe. He just rocked on his haunches hidden by the shadows thrown out from the trash cans.

Keeping his back to the wall still Quarrie eased up to the door. The front window was on the other side and no light drifted from inside. He could feel the breath in his throat and a pulse at the skin of his temple. He scoured the darkness, listening intently, but there was no sound save a horn carrying from a boat somewhere on the river far off. He studied the door where it was cut from wooden panels and sectioned by foot-square panes of glass. Reaching out with his left hand he pushed at a square and the door swung in.

*

Earl listened with the automatic cocked. His gaze seemed to stretch as the door opened with the hint of a creak and then there was silence. Nothing, no movement, then he heard the scrape of a boot on the gantry.

*

Quarrie stepped into the apartment with his pistol levelled at the shadows. He swung left and right but there was no one there. Standing on unopened mail he took in a kitchen and living room, a TV set against the wall. At the back was a desk and chair and metal steps that climbed to a mezzanine upper floor.

*

Outside, Earl rose to his full height and stuffed the automatic into his pocket. Quietly he took off his shoes. He could hear movement from inside the apartment, the sound of footfall on metal stairs. Pinning the file under his arm he picked up his shoes and drew the gun from his pocket.

*

On the balls of his feet Quarrie climbed to an open-plan bedroom at the top of the stairs. Halfway up he stopped, conscious of what looked like the crack of a bathroom door. No light, just a duller shade to the darkness; he stood in the middle of the staircase for a second or so then started up again. He was almost at the top when the slightest of noises made him pause. He looked down to where the shaft of light fell from the lamp outside and he thought he saw a shadow that hadn't been there before. For a long moment he concentrated on that patch of darkness but nothing stirred.

*

Earl could see him through the open door and as soon as Quarrie got to the bedroom he emerged from the shadows and made his way along the gantry in his socks. Making no sound he got to the stairs and paused to look back, but there was no sign of pursuit and he padded all the way down. At ground level he stepped under the gantry where he could not be seen and slipped his shoes back on. Listening for any sound from above he crept to the outer wall.

*

There was nobody upstairs. Quarrie checked the bedroom and bathroom but there was nobody there and he made his way back down. At the door he gazed the length of the gantry then walked around the corner but all he could see were garbage cans. As he turned again he glimpsed a man in a coat and hat making his way up Esplanade. He stood there watching till the figure was swallowed by mist then turned back to the apartment once more.

Holstering his gun he studied the desk at the back of the room where he could pick out the silhouette of an anglepoise lamp. He switched it on and took in the parameters of the room. A studio really, it was compact but modern with tiled floors and copies of Warhol paintings hanging from naked brick walls. Picking up the fallen mail Quarrie found mostly bills, the gas company, power company; there was a phone bill but nothing hand-written at all. He closed the door and carried the pile of mail over to the desk.

The living area was made up of a couch and La-Z-Boy armchair. A TV set occupied one corner together with a record player with a seven-inch copy of 'Eleanor Rigby' on the turntable. With half a smile, Quarrie recalled being asked to shadow The Beatles for a night last year when they stayed at The Cabana in Dallas.

Sitting down at the desk he could see that the top drawer had been forced. Searching through it he found nothing save a pad of yellow legal paper, an expensive-looking fountain pen and a box of business cards detailing Trace Anderson as a freelance feature writer. He considered what Van Hanigan had said about the coroner's office and figured that whoever had been down here was the person who sent the teletype. Given the way the door was open it had probably been earlier that evening. That meant anything that could've told him what was going on would almost certainly have been taken. Even so he checked the rest of the drawers and found a diary where April 28 was underscored heavily in red. That was just a few days from now and he stared at the empty page. Nothing written down, no hint as to why it had been marked. He laid the diary aside.

Rummaging further he located an empty 8 × 10 inch envelope addressed to Anderson with the postage mark stamped in Dallas. The envelope had been sliced at the top and something was scribbled on the back. Holding it up to the light he read the words *Adapt or Die* and remembered the screwed up sheet of hotel notepaper he had found in the trash at The Roosevelt. *Liberty*, one word printed there and three more on the back of an envelope that had been mailed in Dallas. He thought about the slip of paper he had taken from Wiley's wallet and how San Jacinto was a street in Old East Dallas. Returning his attention to the drawers once more he found another pad of paper and placed it with the first one. Buried right at the back was another of Anderson's business cards, only this had a New Orleans phone number hand-written on the flip-side.

Quarrie stared at the number then he laid the card on the desk and crossed to the kitchen. He went through every cupboard and every drawer but found only cutlery and crockery so he turned to the shelves and coffee table. Finding nothing there, he went back to the desk. He tore open the phone bill and ran his eye down the list of numbers. One stuck out, the area code was Dallas but he didn't recognize the number. Folding the page he slipped it into his pocket then picked up one of the pads of paper. Like a flip book he worked his thumb over the heel of the pages but found nothing. Taking the other one he got right to the back before he stopped. The final page was fractionally thicker than the others and pressed between it and the cardboard backing was a black and white photograph.

He bent the stem of the lamp a little further over so he could study the image properly. A couple of uniformed police officers, they were escorting two civilians past a set of steel mesh gates as a third civilian approached from the other direction. The second cop was a good distance behind the second civilian and both he and the cop out front carried shotguns they were holding easy. Quarrie frowned. From a law enforcement point of view the picture didn't add up. If those two uniforms were escorting the other two men then why were the weapons easy? Why was a third man passing the other two heading the opposite way? That would never happen, not if those men were under guard, anyone trying to pass would be directed well away. Something was wrong here but he couldn't figure out what it was. Holding the picture up to the light he stared at the second civilian. A young man wearing a pea coat and sunglasses, he had his head tilted so his gaze was fixed on the floor. There was something familiar about him. Quarrie knew he had seen him before. He looked again and as he did he felt the hairs stand up on his forearms.

Eighteen

In the back seat of the Lincoln Tobie stared through the glass divider that kept their conversation from the ears of the chauffeur. 'So what you're telling me,' he said, 'he got her out of there before you went back?'

Franklin nodded.

'I told you not to fail me.'

'And I told you to let me deal with him. But you wouldn't let me do that and you won't tell me why. It doesn't make any sense.'

'That doesn't alter the fact that twice now you've let that woman slip through your fingers. I told you what he was capable of. What happened in that club was proof if you think we needed any.'

They were quiet for a moment then Franklin turned to him. 'To hell with this, Rosslyn, I can take him out. I've done it before.'

'No you haven't. Not like this, not somebody like him. He gunned Wiley down without batting an eye. But that's not the point. I've told you how we're going to play it and nothing has changed. I already know who's going to kill him but that's only going to happen when I can ensure no comeback from the Rangers.'

'And how're you going to do that exactly? You tell me you have a plan for him and a plan for Matthews, but Matthews is still alive.'

'You can kill him now, but do not dispose of the body.'

'Jesus Christ. Will you tell me what's going on?'

Tobie smiled, only there was no laughter in his eyes. 'The endgame,' he said. 'That's what's going on. Where I deal with the mistakes you made and ensure the 28th is delivered exactly as we said it would be.'

'So you're not going to postpone then even though we've got this going on?'

'I told you, we don't postpone. We never have.'

'So how're we going to play it? Wiley's dead and it's too late to do anything about that.'

'Only if you believe it is.' Tobie looked sideways at him then. 'Improvise, Franklin. We adapt. We overcome like we've always done.'

'But you said it yourself our whole reputation has been built on a closed case.'

'And so it has.'

'So what about now? How can we go ahead?'

'I told you to leave that to me. The rest of it, the room, the money order, is everything in place?'

*

As dawn broke Quarrie was on Chartres Street outside the 3rd Precinct Station House watching De La Martin as he parked his Ford. The detective's suit looked bagged and sweaty, his necktie not fastened at the collar. He locked the driver's door and spat tobacco juice in the gutter.

'Did you get my message?' Quarrie said.

'It's early, Texas, I've not yet had my coffee.'

Quarrie followed him into the relative cool of the building and down the narrow flight of stairs to where De La Martin's office was crammed with desk and chair and a sorry-looking air conditioner. With a glance at Quarrie he stripped off his jacket, eased the weight of his suspenders up over his shoulders and considered the pile of papers gathered on his desk.

'Did you find him?' Quarrie said. 'Claude Matthews, he was in that club. I called last night to tell you.'

They were interrupted by a knock on the open door and a young woman came in with a mug of coffee which she placed carefully amid the paperwork on De La Martin's desk.

The detective fastened the mug with a paw. 'What with everything you got going on right now, I'm surprised to see you back on Chartres Street.'

'What do you mean?' Quarrie said.

'I mean Matthews and Gigi Matisse.'

'I just told you where Matthews was.'

'And the club singer?'

'She's safe.'

'Is she? I've only got your word for that and it's only your word to Colback that she was ever in your hotel room in the first place.'

'Are you kidding me, Detective? You still think I broke into her house? Right now she's at her nana's apartment on Orleans Street. Go talk to her if you want but you're wasting time here. Matthews was in that club and . . .'

'If he was, we both know he won't be now.' De La Martin sat back. 'When I got your message I sent a prowl car down right away but all they found was a drugstore in total darkness.'

'It ain't a drugstore, it's a whorehouse.'

'I know what-all it is, but that doesn't change the fact nobody was home and if he was there he isn't going to be anymore.'

Quarrie was halfway down the corridor when De La Martin called him back. 'Before you go,' he said. 'What do you know about that blond-haired guy who's been driving you around in the cab?'

Quarrie turned to him with one hand in a jacket pocket. 'Why're you asking?'

The detective still held his mug of coffee. 'I'm just curious. Who is he? What's his name?'

'I don't know his name. He told me he was working for Lieutenant Colback. I told you that already.'

'And is he?'

'Not according to Colback.'

'That what he said?'

'That's what he said. He also told me that if someone's giving you a workout you'll jump any bone they toss.'

Back at Nana's apartment Quarrie showed the photograph to Pious. 'The second civilian,' he said. 'That's the guy who's been driving me around in a taxi.'

Pious looked at the picture more closely, taking in the blond hair and leather pea coat.

'So where was this taken?'

'I don't know, but I think it came out of this envelope.' Quarrie showed him where it was postmarked Dallas.

Gigi was in the bedroom and he knocked on the door. She looked better than she had last night and Nana had tended to her cuts and bruises.

'How you doing?' Quarrie said.

159

'I'm all right, I guess.'

He showed her the photograph and asked if that was the man in the cab. For a long time Gigi studied the picture then she twisted her lips. 'It could be,' she said. 'I told you, all I saw was a shadow.'

Leaving her alone again Quarrie went through to the bathroom and splashed cold water over his face.

When he came out Nana and Pious were in the living room with the balcony doors open, though the air was sticky and humid. With the scent of salt in the air, Quarrie figured a storm was on its way. 'Nana,' he said, 'is it all right if I use the telephone?'

'Sure.'

Lifting the receiver he dialled the number on the business card the cab driver had given him and a woman answered. 'I need a ride,' Quarrie told her.

'Sorry, sir, but we're not running the service today.'

'You're not, huh?'

'No, I'm afraid the cab's in the shop for a tune up.'

'All right,' he said. 'Do me a favor and have Mr Football Scholarship call John Q at the Hotel Magnolia.'

'Mr Football Scholarship?' she said.

'That's right. The driver, he's been running me all over town since I got here, but he never did tell me what his name was.'

'All right, I'll pass the message on.'

'So what is his name?'

'I'll pass the message on, sir.'

'Where am I talking to you by the way? I got your business card right here, but there's no address.'

'We're out of town, sir. Thank you for calling. Have a nice day.'

*

When she put down the phone the young woman got up from behind her semi-circular desk. Nodding to Dean Andrews as he came down the main stairs, she pushed open the glass doors to the Tobie Foundation and walked the corridor to the old man's office. He was behind his desk with a paper file lying open before him.

'What is it, Joanna?' he said.

'The Ranger just called asking for a taxi.'

'And what did you tell him?'

'That we're not running the service today.'

'Does Franklin know?'

'Not yet, you told me to make sure I told you if he called before I spoke to anybody else.'

Closing the file Tobie clasped his hands together. 'Thank you, Joanna,' he said.

*

'Nobody home then, huh?' Pious commented as Quarrie hung up and Gigi came through from the bedroom.

Quarrie got to his feet. 'Gigi,' he said, 'I had to tell Detective De La Martin where you were and I don't trust him. I don't trust Colback. I don't trust any of them and I figure nowhere's safe for you in New Orleans.'

Gigi looked fearful again.

161

'I think you ought to get out of town and the best way to do that is to fly back to Texas with Pious.'

Gigi looked at him and then at Pious. She looked doubtfully at Nana. 'I hear you,' she said. 'But I've a mind to stick around. They broke in my house and they took me to . . .' The words tailed away and she turned again to Nana. 'I don't think I should run away.'

'I don't think you should either. Your cousin done that and we never did see him again.' The elderly woman's gaze seemed a little distant. 'Nobody likes running but, whether we like it or not, it's a fact that there are some fights we just can't win.' She crossed the room to a Queen Anne cabinet, opened the drawer and took out a thirty-eight like the one Quarrie carried in his boot. 'There ain't much I haven't seen in this city and it's a fact anybody getting into this apartment without I allowed it isn't getting out again. But John Q is right, nowhere's safe anymore and if you stay here I'd worry for you and you'd worry for me. You need to get quit of this place, Cherie. I want you to do as he says and go to Texas with Pious.'

*

North of the lake Earl told his wife he had some work to do and closed his study door. Sitting down at his desk he unlocked the top drawer, took out the file he had found in Anderson's apartment and flicked through the pages. The trace of a smile on his face, he sat back in the chair and lifted one foot to rest against the lip of the desk. Again he regarded the file then he closed it and entwined his fingers at the back of his head.

Out in the hall he picked up the phone and his wife called to him from the kitchen door.

'Do you want some coffee, hon?'

Earl put down the phone and went through to the kitchen where he slipped his arm around her waist. He kissed her full on the lips and she looked up in surprise.

'Do you know how long it's been since you did something spontaneous like that?'

'Too long,' Earl told her. 'And I'm sorry about that. I've let things slip but it'll be different from now on. That pressure I told you I was under, all that stuff with work, I think I'm done with it finally.' Back in the hallway he picked up the phone. 'This is Earl,' he said. 'Let me speak to Pershing Gervais.'

Nineteen

Gigi had no clothes to take to Texas so she and Pious went back to her house. Quarrie stayed behind with Nana just in case anybody showed up at the apartment. He had his pistols but Pious had the twelve-gauge shotgun and Quarrie figured two black people in the car would be less conspicuous in the 7th Ward than if one of them was white.

Watching Nana move about the apartment he thought she seemed a little pensive. But then she was bound to be, a woman her age, and he tried to take her mind off it.

'Mam,' he said stepping out to the balcony. 'This is a real sweet spot you got here, the apartment and all, the views down to the cathedral.'

Nana came out and stood next to him. 'I knew how it was going to be the moment I set eyes on it. When I'm gone everything goes to Gigi. She's all I got in the world and nobody works harder than that girl. I've been listening to the music coming out of Motor City right now and she's as good as any of it, I swear.' She looked askance at Quarrie then. 'Do you have family back in Texas?'

Quarrie stared the length of the street. 'I got a ten-year-old son,' he said. 'His momma passed on a year after he was born.'

'Oh, I'm sorry.'

'That's OK; it was a long time ago.'

'So you bring him up on your own?'

'Technically I suppose I do, but there're plenty of folks around when I'm working and I seem to be working a lot. James is pretty much used to it now and he's in school of course. I talk to him all the time.' He smiled then fondly. 'Just yesterday he got done telling me how he'd been learning what an anagram was.'

'Anagram, huh.' Nana smiled. 'Making words out of other words, I remember doing that myself.'

The phone rang in the living room and she went to answer it. Quarrie remained at the balcony doors as an NOPD cruiser made its way up the street. He watched it slow down as it came to the apartment then the driver eased on up to the junction.

'John Q,' Nana spoke from behind him. 'It's Lieutenant Colback. He wants to talk to you.' Quarrie took the phone from her and sat down in a chair. 'Lieutenant,' he said. 'What's up?'

'That's the question I was going to ask you. I had De La Martin on the phone just now telling me how you'd been taking the law into your own hands.'

'If you mean what happened on Bourbon and Governor Nicholls, there was no time to call you up.'

'Really.' Colback sounded unconvinced.

'It doesn't matter, Lieutenant. Nobody got shot and I got her out. That place needs raiding by the way, but the fat detective seems reluctant to do it.'

'So is Gigi there? I want to talk to her.'

Quarrie thought about that. 'She ain't here right now but she'll be back.'

'So who's looking out for her?'

'A buddy of mine. She ain't coming to you, Lieutenant. If you want to talk to her, you're going to have to come to us.'

He hung up the phone and considered Nana where she

leaned in the doorway with her arms folded. 'Is that all right with you, mam? Better he talks to her here where I can look out for her.'

'You don't trust him?' Nana said.

Taking his smokes from his pocket he shook one out. 'No, I don't. First of all I had that cab driver tell me it was Colback paying his wages and then he shows up at the hotel. Soon as he does Gigi is missing, and I ain't much of a one for coincidence.'

'So what's going on here?' she said. 'What's all this about?'

Quarrie worked the air from his cheeks. 'Mam, if I knew I'd tell you. I swear.'

He slid the photograph from the envelope once more and considered the set of steel mesh gates, trying to work out where the picture had been taken. He studied the blond-haired man and knew he was not mistaken. He studied the cop out front trying to figure some kind of collar insignia. He couldn't make it out and Nana didn't have a magnifying glass so he laid the photo aside and sought the business card he'd found in Anderson's drawer as well as the phone bill with the Dallas number. Picking up the phone again he dialled that number first and a woman answered. '*Fort Worth Star*, can I help you?'

'The newspaper?' Quarrie sat forward where he perched on the chair.

'That's right, sir, how may I direct your call?'

'It doesn't matter. Thank you, mam, you already answered my question.' Hanging up he thought for a moment then picked up the phone once more and called the number on the back of the business card.

'District Attorney's office,' a man's voice this time. 'Investigation, this is Earl.'

Quarrie felt the muscles tighten where he gripped the receiver.

'Earl Moore speaking,' the man repeated.

'Sorry, sir, I got the wrong number.' Quarrie put down the receiver aware of sweat on his palm that seemed to bead from the Bakelite.

He heard a vehicle out on the street and stepped onto the balcony. It was the station wagon and he called out to tell Nana that Gigi was back then went down to open the gates. When the car was inside he locked the gates once more.

'Gigi,' he said, as she climbed from the driver's seat, 'I just spoke to someone at the DA's office called Earl Moore.'

For a moment she stared.

'We don't know it's your guy but I found the number on a business card at that address on Esplanade Avenue.' As he was speaking they heard another car pull up outside the gates. Gesturing for Pious to get Gigi upstairs Quarrie drew a pistol and was at the small gate as the bell rang.

'That you, Lieutenant?' he called.

'It's me,' Colback replied.

Slipping the gun back into its holster Quarrie opened the gate.

He led the way upstairs to the living room where Gigi was sitting on the couch. Her nana was in her bedroom and didn't come out. Pious was on the balcony with the shotgun in his hands and Colback arched one eyebrow. 'Looks like a regular Alamo you got going on here, doesn't it?'

'Pious,' Quarrie said. 'Do you remember this guy, hill 500 back in Korea, that feller in the trees with the long barrel?'

'They flew a sniper in.' Pious was still looking at Colback.

'That was you?'

'It might've been.' Colback looked him up and down then turned his attention to Gigi. He took in the cut on her lip and the bruising. He tried to smile. 'I'm sorry about what happened to you. Are you all right now, feeling any better?'

Gigi looked up at him but did not return the smile.

'Do you want to write up a statement or anything like that, make an official complaint?'

'Why would I do that?' she said. 'I don't see the point.'

Colback looked at her in surprise. 'You were abducted, beaten . . .' He glanced back at Quarrie. 'I just swung by that address on Bourbon and Governor Nicholls and it's all locked up right now, but . . .'

'You won't find him,' Gigi stated. 'It don't matter whether I make a complaint or not, it's Soulja Blue we're talking about.'

'I can put him away,' Colback told her.

'I doubt it, Lieutenant. You see, for a black boy out of the 7th Ward he's sure got a lot of white friends.' She looked up at him again. 'The way he runs that club and all, you know what I'm talking about.'

'So what am I doing here?' Colback asked.

'I don't know, Lieutenant. You're the one wanted to come.'

Colback told her to call if she changed her mind then he walked the hall to the door with a shake of his head.

Quarrie followed him out. 'I talked to De La Martin,' he said.

'Yeah, he said as much on the phone.'

'I told him what you told me, Lieutenant, and he seemed pretty tickled by that.'

Colback held his eye.

'Do me a favor. Tell him you've seen Gigi for yourself now so he can strike me off his list.'

'I guess I can do that.' Colback started down the stairs. 'You got a problem with trust, do you know that? I keep telling you. Despite what you think, I'm not the enemy here. I'm the only one batting for your team.'

*

When he was gone Quarrie checked the time on the hall clock. Conscious of the phone call he'd made before Gigi got back, he glanced at Pious where he came in from the balcony. 'I'll drive you out to the Lakefront,' he said. 'What time are you fixing to leave?'

'Just as soon as I talk to Mama and let her know we're coming.'

'John Q,' Gigi interrupted them. 'What about the DA's office? You told me you spoke to Earl.' She lifted the phone from its cradle. 'There's one way to find out if it was him or not. Let me give him a call.'

Taking the receiver from her Quarrie put it down. 'Not from here,' he said. 'If anybody's checking the only connection they've got to this line right now is a man's voice and a wrong number. Where's the nearest payphone?'

They walked to the corner and made the call and it was her boyfriend all right. He seemed surprised to hear from her but Gigi told him she'd run into someone downtown who said he worked for the district attorney. She told him she wanted to see him as soon as possible and he suggested they meet in Lafayette Square. She hung up the phone and walked back to the apartment with Quarrie watching the sky as the wind picked up and the first drops of rain began to fall.

*

When Earl put down the phone he sat for a moment with his hands in his lap and his brow cut in narrow lines. Glancing up he saw Gervais in the corridor talking to one of the ADAs. Gervais caught his eye and Moore looked back. Then he got up and walked the corridor to the coffee room. He stood with his back to the worktop and stared at the linoleum floor. He poured a cup of coffee, took one sip then put it down and went out to the landing where he looked down on the melee of newsmen that filled the foyer below. Taking the stairs he pushed his way through the gathering and walked a block in his shirt sleeves to a payphone on the corner. A breeze in the air, he glanced at the sky where it was rippled with bruise-colored cloud.

'This is Earl,' he said, when he was put through. 'Gigi Matisse just called. I don't know how she knew where to get hold of me but you told me to let you know if she called.'

'What did she want?' the voice said.

'To see me of course, what else would she want?' Earl looked up and down the street. 'I told her I'd meet her.'

'Where?'

'Lafayette Square at noon.' Again he glanced at the sky. 'Though with the way the weather's looking right now that might not be such a good idea. You need to know something,' he stated, his tone a little more confident. 'This is the last piece of business I do for you. I'll find out what she wants and report back. After that it's over. You told me I needed to consider the nature of our relationship. Well, I've done that. Right now there's nothing you can do to me that I can't bring back to you. You got that? I'll talk to her and I'll tell you what she said. After that we're through.'

*

On the far side of Tulane Avenue Franklin sat in his cab outside a bail bond company. He watched Earl in the phone booth getting animated, saw him hang up and then gaze the length of the road. He looked on as he walked back to his office past the crowd of reporters camped on the courthouse steps. Picking up the radio he pressed the transmit button. 'I've got Earl Moore in a phone booth. If it's us he's talking to I want to know what was said.' Clipping the handset back on its housing he sat watching till the investigator disappeared inside the building. A couple of minutes later the radio crackled and the woman's voice lifted from the speaker. 'Are you out there, Franklin? Pick up.'

'Gotcha,' he said, lifting the transmitter.

'That was him all right. There's a meeting set for Lafayette Square.'

*

As they went down to the station wagon Quarrie handed Pious the envelope containing the photograph he had taken from Anderson's apartment. 'I want you to hang onto this for me, bud,' he said. 'Take good care of it, will you?'

'Sure,' Pious said with a grin. 'I'll put it under my pillow.'

171

Quarrie drove them out to the Lakefront with Gigi sitting next to him and Pious in the back with the shotgun. When he pulled up outside the freight entrance Quarrie got out and walked them to the plane. Pious helped Gigi into the co-pilot's seat then handed Quarrie the gun.

'So what're you going to do?' he said.

'When I'm done with Earl I'm going to hunt down that blond-haired cab driver.'

The storm broke as Quarrie drove back to the city. By the time he hit Canal Street the rain was coming down in stair rods; with the wind gusting off the river it swamped the windshield to the point where the wipers could barely cope. The dashboard clock read ten minutes to twelve already and the meeting was set for noon. He drove along St Charles with not much traffic on the road and hardly anyone braving the sidewalk. As he got to the square he drove past Colback's office and looked up to see the lieutenant in the second-floor window talking to his secretary. Concentrating on the road again, he made the turn in front of the Old Post Office.

*

Franklin saw the pale blue station wagon as he opened the trunk of his cab. Parked on the corner of Girod Street, he spotted Quarrie behind the wheel but Quarrie did not see him. Franklin retrieved a flat, aluminum case from the trunk and walked to the fire escape. Flight after flight he climbed until he came to a broken window and used the edge of the case to punch out the remaining shards.

He made his way through the empty corridors and every step

he took seemed to echo off naked walls. He walked to the stairs and climbed to the next floor and the floor after that. He kept climbing until only the stairs to the roof remained. At the top he paused with the door to the rooftop open and placed his case on the concrete floor. Popping the catches he rocked back on his heels and hummed to himself as he began to assemble the sections of rifle from compartments of closed cell foam.

*

At street level the rain beat against the roof of the car. Quarrie drove the length of the post office and pulled up at the stop sign. The road clear, he made another left and was on the far side of the square from Colback's office. He drove that street then turned right and parked the car. Then he killed the engine, checked the pistols under his jacket and reached for his hat where it lay on the seat.

*

His rifle ready, Franklin checked the scope then made a couple of tiny adjustments with a screwdriver before closing the case and leaning it against the wall. Still humming he pushed open the door to the rooftop and walked out into the rain. At the parapet wall he gazed across the haze of gray where the storm clouds wrapped the tops of the taller buildings. For a moment he stared, then his gaze fixed on the park below where the grass was bisected by concrete footways that broke from the cover of trees. Settling the weapon he put his eye to the scope to test the distance then he adjusted the sights once more.

Quarrie strode into the tree-lined square. Hands in his pockets he walked with the brim of his hat pulled low. He kept walking until he came to the middle and stopped where the paths converged. Briefly he looked back the way he had come but there was nobody there. He glanced to his left, taking in the trees, then he gazed towards Old City Hall. A movement to his right caught his eye and he picked out a young man in a tan-colored raincoat and short-brimmed hat standing thirty yards away. He was looking at his watch. He was looking over his shoulder. He was looking up and down the square.

*

Franklin had Quarrie in his rifle sights all the way from the station wagon to the footway, only losing him for a second in the trees. He picked him up again as he walked the path to the middle of the square.

*

Earl faced the Old Post Office Building and Quarrie looked him up and down. The investigator considered him for a moment then his gaze shifted to the path behind.

'She's not coming,' Quarrie told him. 'I'm a Texas Ranger, but I figure you know that already. You need to talk to me, Earl. You need to tell me who it was had you tell Gigi to avoid me. You need to tell me why you stole a bottle of meds and gave them to that blond-haired guy.'

High above them Franklin had Quarrie in the crosshairs and his breathing was shallow in his chest. He kept his eye to the scope then eased his head back a fraction and worked the muscles in his neck. He sighted again and there was no waver from the barrel at all. Exhaling very softly, finger to the trigger, he squeezed.

Twenty

Pious got the plane airborne and they flew low into the west under a mass of puce-colored cloud. In the co-pilot's seat Gigi had a set of headphones over her ears and a smile on her face as she watched him handle the instruments.

'Pick Feeley paid for me to get the hours in,' Pious explained through the phones. 'He's the feller used to own the ranch where we're going only he passed away a couple of years ago. When I got out of Leavenworth John Q got me a job and my momma and sister had already come out from where we used to live at in Georgia. I kept all the vehicles running and I guess the old man was impressed enough with the work that when the notion of a plane come around, he figured someone better learn how to fly.'

'He didn't want to do it himself?' Gigi said.

'No, mam, I guess he figured he was too old by then and Mrs Feeley wouldn't have allowed it besides.' Lifting a palm he smiled. 'Anyways, that's how I got my license and one of these days I'll quit the ranch and start flying freight or something on my own.'

Gigi was gazing out of the window at the ground below. 'You know,' she said, 'this is the first time I've ever been in an airplane.'

'Ain't so many folks like us ever gets the chance.'

'No kidding.'

'The only way to travel,' Pious said. 'Just a few years back it'd take thirty hours on the railroad from Dallas to Chicago. Now, if you leave by ten you're there by noon on a plane.'

Gigi looked a little troubled. 'Pious,' she said, 'just now you said how you'd gotten out of Leavenworth. Are you talking about the federal pen?'

Pious nodded. 'Back in '51 me and John Q served in Korea. I was accused of being a coward after I brought what was left of my platoon down off a hill. We were under so much fire it was suicide to stay there, but nobody wanted to hear that so I was court-martialled for disobeying an order. They'd have shot me if John Q hadn't written President Truman. The letter appeared in *The New York Times*, a bunch of lawyers got involved and in the end I only did a five-spot.' He looked a little bitter then. 'That's still five years of my life they took away and there ain't no getting them back.'

*

De La Martin was sitting behind his desk reading a report and listening to the rain on his office window when one of his colleagues came through with a teletype.

'This just came in from the NCIC,' he said and placed the sheet of copier paper before him. The detective studied the page for a few moments then got up and lifted his jacket from the back of his chair. Folding the paper he tucked it into a pocket and made his way out onto Chartres Street where he splashed through the puddles to his Ford.

*

The rain hit the north shore ten minutes after it swept New Orleans. The wind lashing the chalet-style roof of Moore's house, his wife was sitting at the kitchen table with the phone to her ear as she arranged a flat-pack box with an assortment of candy.

'Yes, he seems a little different now,' she said. 'Just this morning he was talking about the pressure he's been under at work and that's what was keeping him in the city.' She listened for a moment then she said, 'No, it was nothing like that. I admit I did begin to wonder, but it's the pressure of work as well as those night classes he's been taking since last fall.' As she spoke she placed a bar of Turkish Taffy in the box then arranged two bags of Boston Baked Beans. 'No,' she said. 'I'm fine, really. Like I said, I was worried for a while but he was lovely to me this morning. He sort of swept me up in his arms and he hasn't done that in months.' Again she paused. 'Come over? No, I can't right now. I'm putting together a candy box for Simon's birthday.'

After she hung up she added more candy to the box till it bulged like a store display. The phone rang again and she lifted the receiver. 'Hello?' she said. 'This is Jean Moore.'

'Mrs Moore, I'm glad I caught you, just a quick call from your husband's office. He's had to go out of town for a few days, Baton Rouge and then Shreveport. It's a case he's working and he asked me to call and tell you if he doesn't phone tonight you're not to worry.'

Mrs Moore sat up a little straighter. 'I had no idea a trip was coming up. He didn't say anything to me.'

'That's because he didn't know. It just came up this morning and the DA wanted Earl on it. He didn't have time to call before he left, so I said I'd let you know. When he checks in with the office I'll tell him we spoke.' The phone clicked to the dialling tone and Mrs Moore let the receiver hang in her palm for a moment before returning her attention to the box of candy.

*

The rain fell, the wind howled across the park and Quarrie saw Earl's legs buckle. His hat came off and his coat flapped open to reveal a holstered automatic. He was on his side in the soaking grass with one arm thrown out, the fingers stretching briefly before he was still.

*

There was barely any sound from the silenced barrel and hardly any kick. For a moment Franklin kept his eye to the sights then lowered the rifle and stepped away from the parapet. Bending to retrieve the spilled cartridge case he slipped it into his pocket and walked back to the stairwell door. Inside he took a cloth from the gun case to wipe away the water then he disassembled the weapon and packed each component away.

When he was finished he retraced his steps through the building until he came to the window that overlooked the fire escape. There he paused and took a look at the watch on his wrist before crouching with his back to the wall. Outside the rain still fell and all he could hear was the rattle against metal rungs. After a while he got to his feet and peered outside, but instead of climbing onto the fire escape, he went back to the stairs. He took them all the way to the ground floor and the rear of the building where he passed through the old restaurant kitchens and pushed open the fire exit doors.

*

On the ground Quarrie took cover. Ducking into the shelter of some trees he looked up at the Old Post Office before scanning the alley that ran alongside. Pistol drawn, he sprinted across the road and cut down the alley towards Girod Street. To his left was a fire escape where metal steps climbed the wall in a zig-zag with balconies fixed in between. He started up the steps, the soles of his boots slipping on iron that was polished with so much rain. Passing a broken window he kept on climbing till he made it to the top of the building and could see how the roof was shaped in sections like a series of staggered steps.

The Old Post Office was not square or oblong even, it formed a sort of C shape and he moved from the top of the fire escape to the parapet that overlooked the square. From there he could see the middle of the roof and the left-hand tower. Nobody was down there and he could see no way to get down unless he jumped and that was two full floors. Visibility was poor with so much rain. The world was gray and the city grayer still. He looked back to the street and glimpsed a panel truck making its way down St Charles in the direction of the French Quarter. Turning to the park once more he sought Earl's body but it was nowhere to be seen. The patch of grass between the trees was bare and for a long moment he just stared. It didn't make any sense. And then it did. That truck just now. A couple of men with hessian sacks: as soon as he left they were there.

Twenty-one

Mama Sox and Eunice were up on the dust-blown plateau to greet the plane. Banking sharply Pious made a pass above the ranch buildings before setting the Piper down. Gigi climbed from the cockpit and Eunice slipped an arm through hers as if she was an old girlfriend that she hadn't seen in a while. Together they walked down to the house. James was home from school and he came out of Quarrie's cottage and Pious introduced him to Gigi. They all went into the Noons' house where Mama Sox had lemonade on ice. She poured a glass for each of them and fetched a plate of chocolate brownies. After that she left them to it while she crossed to the bunkhouse to start preparing supper for the ranch hands. Eunice showed Gigi to her bedroom, making sure she knew that she wasn't putting anybody out because whenever John Q was away Eunice slept over at his house.

Left alone, Gigi sat down at the dressing table. A little tremor in her shoulders she studied her face as tears slipped onto her cheeks. For a while she cried with no sound then she lay down on Eunice's bed, drawing her knees to her chest and hugging them until she was coupled in the fetal position.

That's where she was when Pious knocked on the door a little while later to tell her she was welcome to take a shower if she wanted. He saw the way she was curled on her side with tears spilling soundlessly and for a moment he just stood there.

She didn't send him away. She looked up and there was fear in her face and panic in her eyes and quietly Pious sat down. 'Is there anything I can do?' he said. 'Anything I can get you?'

Gigi tried to wipe the tears away. 'Just hold me, Pious. Just hold me.'

*

Quarrie got back in the car with his breath steaming like a newborn calf. He didn't start the engine; he just sat there staring at a windshield opaque with running water. Cracking the window a fraction, he tried to get his head around what had just happened. Earl shot dead when the shooter could've taken him. Why didn't they do that? Why not just take him out and be done with it? What was it the investigator could've told him that they could not allow him to know? In his mind's eye he could see Wiley on that dirt road with a shotgun wedged to his hip and an M1C in the duffel. He could see Scott Henderson across the table in the interview room swearing before God that he didn't know any more than he'd already said. He thought about that and he thought about the photograph he had found and the date Anderson had underscored in red.

When he got back to the hotel he changed his clothes and took the rain-soaked bundle down to Yvonne and asked her to have them laundered. Heading back to the car he drove to Orleans Street where he spotted a black Lincoln Continental parked half a block from Nana's apartment. A man in a business suit was at the wheel with his gaze alternating between the street ahead and the mirror on his door. Quarrie eased the station wagon up to the sidewalk and glanced at the apartment where the balcony windows were secured against the rain.

Inside the courtyard, he could hear voices from above and spotted Nana on the landing with her hand gripped by an elegantly dressed older man with a mane of silver hair. Keeping out of sight, Quarrie could not make out his features but he did catch the wary expression in Nana's eyes. He stepped behind palmetto trees as the old man came down the steps carrying a silver-handled walking cane. The old man did not see him as he crossed the courtyard to the small gate and stepped out into the street. Quarrie heard an engine fire followed by a high-pitched whine as the Lincoln reversed. After that there was only the rain.

He climbed the steps to the apartment aware of the look still in Nana's eye. 'Who was that guy?' he said.

'Oh, nobody you'd know. Just someone I haven't seen much of in a while.' Leading the way inside she closed and double-locked the door. 'Well,' she said. 'When Gigi calls she's going to want to know what happened.'

Quarrie let go a breath. 'Earl was murdered. Somebody shot him before he could talk to me.' Moving into the living room he checked the street. 'If Gigi calls ahead of time it's up to you if you want to tell her. I'm going to phone the ranch tonight so I'll be talking to her then.'

The old woman did not reply.

'Nana,' he said. 'The way this is playing out right now I don't think me being around you is any safer than when she was here. I want you to call me if you're worried about anything, but I'm going to try and stay out of your hair.'

'I understand,' she said. 'Don't worry about me. I can take care of myself. I'll be fine.'

He headed for the door then turned. 'There's something I wanted to ask you. That club on Bourbon and Governor Nicholls, did Gigi tell you what happened?'

*

When he left the apartment Tobie instructed his chauffeur to drive across town to the office on Baronne. The concierge was there to open the door and Tobie made his way inside. He stepped into the elevator and climbed to the second floor where the receptionist looked up from behind her desk. Tobie walked the hall to his office and found Franklin at the window with his back to him and his hands in the pockets of his gabardine jacket.

'I suppose you know what you're doing,' Franklin said. 'Taking Moore out instead of Quarrie, it goes against every instinct I know.'

With barely a glance at him Tobie took off his coat and hung it on the back of the chair.

'Soulja wants to know what to do with the pharmacist's body.'

'Tell him to ice it for now. I'll let him know when we're ready.'

Franklin considered the old man's desk, the pair of muskets and the painting of Jefferson Davis. 'All this history,' he said. 'Such a sense of heritage, how is it you only ever gave me your middle name?'

Briefly Tobie looked up.

'It doesn't even mean anything.' Franklin threw out a palm. 'It's just an initial. The F doesn't actually stand for anything. So where did *Franklin* come from?'

'You want to talk about that now?' Tobie said. 'Our lands in Kentucky: one of my grandfather's bucks.'

'You named me after a slave?'

'It doesn't matter what your name is or where it comes from. Full blood or not you'll get what's coming just as long as you step up.' The old man could see the lump in Franklin's throat. 'You need to show me a capability that so far is conspicuous by its absence. Don't make the mistake of thinking you're the only half-breed I have running around. It's a fact you're merely the eldest.'

Franklin turned to the window with his shoulders hunched. 'My mother told me how this would be. She warned me to stay away from you because I'd never be accepted. She told me if *she* wanted to see you she had to wait till you called.' His voice was low in his chest. 'She said she wasn't allowed to contact you. She was forbidden from phoning the house.'

'Of course she was,' Tobie said. 'I'm an attorney, a business-man with a wife. She doesn't need other women calling our home.'

Franklin turned to face him again. 'She always wondered what would happen if she stepped out of line and broke the rules.'

For a moment the old man stared. 'You can tell her from me – if she wants to find out all she has to do is pick up the phone.'

For a couple of moments neither of them spoke. Then Franklin flared his nostrils. 'So now Earl's dead, what're you going to say to the clients?'

Tobie shrugged. 'I'll remind them the service we've delivered has been far in excess of anything they actually paid for.'

'And they'll accept that?'

'They have no choice. They know our obligation is over. We fulfilled our mission three years ago and did them a favor back in February. Everything since then has been a bonus.'

'We still don't know about Williams,' Franklin stated.

'We will.'

'So you'll talk to the supplier?'

Tobie clicked his tongue. 'Franklin, you need to understand that every facet of any organization has its specific function. If boundaries are crossed they become blurred and a boundary that's blurred is no longer a boundary at all. To make the kind of request you're suggesting might seem a small thing to you, but in reality it's anything but. Change the game halfway through and people start to believe they're more important than they actually are. They begin to take liberties.' Breaking off for a second he stared. 'That's when things can get messy.'

There was a knock on the door and the girl from reception came in with a tray of coffee. When she was gone Tobie turned to Franklin again. 'I've been running this operation since I was younger than you are now and I've never let any difficulty get the better of me. Every step has to be taken at exactly the right moment. To incept a plan is one thing, to stick to it and not deviate, quite another.' He nodded to the walking cane. 'The baton passed to me when my father died and since then we've neither postponed nor cancelled an engagement. That's because I understand what it is that we really do here. I understand what the people we work for believe in. This isn't just a business. It's a way of life that echoes the history, the very fabric of this country.'

'That's one opinion,' Franklin stated.

186

Tobie's gaze seemed to sharpen a little. 'You don't share the sentiment then?'

'I didn't say that.' Franklin gestured. 'But when all's said and done it is a business. Business is about risk and reward and as far as this situation is concerned the risk seems greater than the reward.'

'Managing the risk is part and parcel of the process,' Tobie reminded him. 'Earl's behavior was unfortunate and it's the same with Gigi.' He made a dismissive gesture with the flat of his hand. 'It no longer matters because he's dead and she will be.'

He poured coffee into his cup and put the pot down without pouring one for Franklin.

'Speaking of Earl's behavior, there's something else we need to consider.' He peered at the younger man then. 'On the phone he told us that the meeting in Lafayette Square was the last piece of business he'd do. I'm told he was confident, arrogant, sure enough of himself to sound threatening.' Lifting the cup to his lips he took a sip of coffee. 'He's never been that way before so something changed and I want to know what that was.'

*

When he left Nana's apartment Quarrie drove back to North Rampart Street then took the one way system to Bourbon. Making a left he crawled to the junction with Governor Nicholls and found the drugstore locked and bolted. He drove on towards Esplanade Avenue but slowed again when he spotted a panel truck parked up ahead. It could've been the one he'd seen from the roof of the Old Post Office Building, but he wasn't sure. Parking the station wagon he paced all the way around the truck then peered through the driver's window. The seats were littered with Styrofoam coffee cups and sandwich wrappers. A copy of an old newspaper lay on the floor and the ashtray was full of butts. There was no window into the back, however, and none in the side panels or rear doors either.

He drove back to the hotel and phoned the DA's office on Tulane Avenue. A receptionist answered and he was about to ask for the district attorney, but changed his mind and asked for Moore instead.

'He's not here, I'm afraid,' the woman told him. 'He went home at lunchtime after catching a chill in all this rain. I'm not sure when he'll be back. What's it regarding, sir? If it's in connection with an ongoing case I can put you through to the chief investigator?'

Quarrie thought about that for a moment. 'Sure,' he said. 'That would be useful, thank you.'

A minute later Pershing Gervais came on the line.

'This is Ranger Sergeant Quarrie,' Quarrie told him. 'You remember me from Colback's office?'

'I remember you from McAlister's. What do you want?'

'I want to talk to Garrison.'

'The DA, he's not in right now. What do you want with him?'

'I need to tell him about Earl Moore.'

'What about him?' Gervais said.

'He was murdered in Lafayette Square.'

Gervais told him to come into the office but he couldn't come armed. Unstrapping his shoulder holsters Quarrie considered leaving the guns in his room, but instead he carried them downstairs and asked Yvonne if there was somewhere she could lock them away. She looked a little doubtful but he held her eye and she told him he could use the safe.

*

Franklin left Tobie in the office and went down to his taxi. He sat for a moment drumming fingers on the steering wheel then drove as far as the drugstore two blocks down the street. Inside there was an old-fashioned phone booth and he closed the doors. He sat down on the stool and dialled the number. He waited and no one picked up so he hung up and redialled. Again he waited and it took a little while but finally the phone was answered.

'About time,' he said. 'I started thinking I had the wrong number.'

'What do you want?'

'Wichita Falls: we weren't able to secure either his real name or an address. I want you to get that for me and call me on the warehouse phone.'

*

Quarrie stowed the snub-nose in his boot then drove to Tulane Avenue and the criminal court building that housed the district attorney's office. Parking in a side street he left his hat on the seat and cigarettes on the dash then walked back to Tulane where he spotted the mass of photographers gathered outside the main entrance. Adjacent to the court building was

189

the coroner's office. As he went in he was thinking about the teletype the NCIC had received and the fact that Moore had worked just across the hall. He stood in the foyer for a second or two then spotted a sign for the stairs that led to the underground parking garage.

It was dark down there with the bays poorly lit and not much light drifting from the ramp that led to the street. A number of cars were parked and he could see the unmarked door Gervais had told him about. Behind it was an elevator that ascended directly to the district attorney's private bathroom. Crossing the concrete floor he paused at the door and looked for the button to call. Lights flared from a car parked over by the ramp. Lifting a hand to his eyes he tried to see who it was but the lights were blinding. When he turned again he stared into the barrel of a pistol.

Twenty-two

A black man with a shaven head. Quarrie picked out the pigment of steroids in his lifeless eyes. It had to be Soulja Blue and he wasn't alone; another man emerged from the shadows, the one from the club with a band aid covering the cut on his head. He held a Colt forty-five in his hand and he stared at Quarrie. Passing the weapon to Soulja Blue, he searched him and found the snub-nose in his boot. Pocketing that, he marched him across the parking lot to where the cab was parked at the heel of the ramp. Behind the wheel Franklin stared. The man with the band aid opened the door and Soulja nudged Quarrie in the back. As he bent to get in Band Aid hit him with the grips of his pistol.

He woke to a pain in his head that was more like a noise. He could taste blood in his mouth and felt bilious. He had no idea where he was but intermittent shafts of light seemed to break up the wall across from where he lay. He was on his side. He could not move. At first he thought his feet were bound but they weren't and neither were his hands. Blinking slowly he could see shadows crossing and re-crossing those strips of light, he could hear machinery and voices. Something was moving beneath him. Gaps in the floor, whatever it was down there, it was shifting back and forth and it took a moment before he got his head around how that could be. Water; he was lying on a floor made from old wooden planks and that was the river he could see.

He could smell something, a kind of metallic tang in the nostrils; it took a moment before he worked out it was tomatoes. Pressing a hand underneath his stomach he maneuvered himself up and sat with his back to the wall. He tried to figure this out: the river beneath, and those strips of light were gaps in walls made from vertical wooden planks. A storeroom of sorts; on his left was a metal door and another made of wood. He could hear voices again and picked out shadows of workmen criss-crossing the warehouse floor.

He tried to get to his feet. It was awkward, he was unstable and swayed with one hand out to the wall. Gradually he felt a little strength return to his limbs and stood tall. His mind was mud; the parking garage, Tulane Avenue, he'd been on his way to meet Gervais. Stumbling a little he put one eye to a gap in the wall and saw a pair of forklift trucks transporting pallets of tomatoes beyond an up and over door and depositing them on the wharf.

He must've passed out again because when he opened his eyes he was sitting on the floor with his back to the wall and all the machinery had been shut off. Forcing himself to his feet he could see that the door to the wharf was still open but there was no sign of the longshoremen now. Moments later a car pulled into the warehouse and stopped outside the storeroom door. A shiny blue Malibu SS, he could see it through the gaps in the wall.

*

In an office at the far end of the warehouse Franklin put down the phone and sat with his hands clasped together on the desk.

Getting up he opened the venetian blinds and saw Soulja Blue get out of the car. He watched as his driver unlocked the door to the storeroom and dragged Quarrie out. They marched him across the floor to the office. Franklin did not say anything. He stood behind the desk while the man with the band aid made Quarrie sit on a high-backed chair.

'Mr Football Scholarship.' Quarrie held Franklin's eye. 'I guess it wasn't Colback paying you after all.'

*

Tobie ate an early dinner with his wife. Halfway through the entree his butler appeared and hovered a little uncertainly at the dining room door.

'What is it, Benson?' Tobie said.

'There's a telephone call for you, sir?'

'I'm eating dinner. You can see that, man. Can't it wait?'

'Yes, sir, I know, sir, and I already told them. But they were insistent. They said it was very important and you would want to take the call.'

*

Franklin perched on the edge of the desk, Quarrie in the chair with his hands hanging down by his sides. Soulja Blue stood in the corner and Band Aid had his gun just inches from Quarrie's eye.

Quarrie stared into Franklin's face. 'I fly into town and you're there. I visit Matthews and he disappears. I talk to Gigi and you go after her then you shoot Moore when you could've shot me.

So tell me about Wiley. What was the deal with that M1C?'

'What did you find in Anderson's apartment?' Franklin said.

'So you know about him then, huh. Was it De La Martin that filled you in?'

'What did you find?'

'You mean apart from a photo? When was that taken? Where was it taken, uh?'

'I know about the photograph,' Franklin stated. 'You need to tell me what else you found.'

'Who was the other guy in that picture with you?'

'I asked what else you found.'

'That photo got a man killed. A bottle of drugs ground into powder to make it look natural. What was all that about?'

'So you didn't find anything else. There wasn't anything, was there?' A smile on his face, Franklin got up from the desk.

'There was a date.' Quarrie looked keenly at him then. 'April 28, that's just a few days from now.'

Franklin stopped. He seemed unsure of himself for a second then he glanced at Soulja where he stood with his arms across his chest. 'Lock him up again,' he told him. 'I want the two of you back here as soon as you're done so we can take him out to the bayou.' He turned to Quarrie again. 'You have no idea how long I've been waiting to kill you.'

'Good luck with that,' Quarrie said.

*

He sat on the storeroom floor peering through the slatted boards as river water washed around the pilings. As soon as they had locked him up again Soulja Blue and the other man had taken off. Franklin had stayed in the office for a while but he had gone as well now leaving Quarrie alone. In the bands of light that pierced the walls he considered how those boards were old and warped. He could see they were held together by rusty-looking flat-head screws and he was thinking that if he could pry a couple out he might be able to create a gap large enough to drop through. But he had nothing to work with save his fingernails, and he hadn't given much thought to the reality of being in the Mississippi River with the kind of currents that carried down here.

As he hunched forward on his heels he felt the edge of his belt buckle chafe his belly. A western design, the buckle bore the longhorn emblem favored by the Rangers, rectangular and flat-fronted; the edge might just be narrow enough. Stripping the belt from the loops in his pants he took the buckle in both hands then tried the edge in the groove of the screw.

With a little maneuvering he managed to get some purchase and began to work the buckle back and forth. It was slow going, laborious; the buckle kept slipping but he carried on, not knowing how much time he had before either Franklin or those other two came back. Finally he got the first screw taken care of and was into the second then the third. Four screws clear, he could raise one piece of planking but he needed the width of two. He worked on but the buckle started slipping again and the light was fading now. Every so often he thought he heard the throb of an engine on the road outside but nobody came. He worked harder, applying all the pressure he could muster on the head of each screw; he was into the second length of board as the darkness became complete. Sweat on his brow, the flimsy weight of his shirt sticking to him, he was almost done when he finally did hear the throaty tones of a muscle car. Moments later the Malibu pulled into the warehouse again and the engine was shut off. Weapons drawn, the two men from the club came striding across the floor.

Quarrie tried to pry that second plank free but it stuck as if he had missed a screw. Peering into the darkness he could see there were no more screws. He had got them all but the wood was so old and expanded with water it had sealed. He stamped on it. Again and again he stamped and from the warehouse he heard a shout. One last time he brought down his boot heel and finally the board sprang loose.

They were at the door as he plummeted into chill, gray water that washed him against the wooden pilings. The wind knocked out of him, he hung there directly beneath the storeroom floor. A stripe of bubbles lit up the darkness as someone fired a shot and he grabbed the piling. The current pried him free and he floundered again for a moment as bullet after bullet came down. Somehow he got hold of the pole once more and used his feet to get himself all the way around. Now he was away from the gap in the boards with the piling between him and the hole in the floor. He surfaced and sucked a breath with the water slapping his face and the lights of the city jagged and broken up in a haze. It was all he could do to stop the current dragging him out from under the wharf. He could feel it tugging at his body with freezing fingers where the tide had swept up from the gulf. Clogged with salt and sand, he was conscious of drags and eddies, whirlpools that would suck him down.

The shooting had stopped but he could hear the sound of voices and he had to move. With open water not being an option, he bobbed from piling to piling gradually working his way downstream. He could hear nothing from above anymore and could see very little below. He was going with the current heading away from the warehouse towards Algiers Point. At the fifth piling he saw a series of plywood boards fixed between it and the next with one board on top of the other reaching up like a laddered wall. The topmost lip of the topmost board was only a few feet below the underside of the wharf and there was a gap in the boardwalk itself that looked large enough to climb through. But he was still too close to the warehouse and dare not risk it now. He had to keep moving. They would be looking for him. There was no way they would take a chance on his drowning; they'd want to make sure.

He drifted on aware that his boots had filled with water but he could not kick them off. He was trying to stay in the weaker current close to the shore and use the pilings as buffers to keep him under the wharf. If he ended up slipping clear they would either spot and shoot him or he would be swept mid-river and drown.

They launched a boat. Just a few minutes later he heard the whine of an outboard and someone was shining a light. He swam with that light seeking him out and tried to figure how far he was from the point. He was thinking about the Canal Street Ferry. If he could get out of this river without being seen, he might get to the point and cross. But he was not out of the river. Right now there was no chance of getting out because he could see that skiff and it was hunting him down.

It came in close and he dipped below the surface to avoid the light. Arms wrapped around the piling again, he fought to keep from bobbing up like a cork. He could see the light from under the water bright even there in the murk. It seemed to remain for an age as the boat made a circle and came around once more. He thought his lungs would burst or he would open his mouth, take in water and drown. But the light faded finally and he let go his hold, broke the surface and breathed.

The light was fifteen yards away and he watched it recede as the boat headed towards the point. They were in front of him now so he turned back the way he had come and swam for all he was worth. Hand over hand against the current, he made it to one set of pilings and held on while he caught his breath then kicked for the next. All the time he was moving the boat was going the other way and he had to get out of the river before they returned.

At last he was back at those vertical boards and reached for the lowest point where he could grab on. The current swept him hard up against it then tried to pluck him free but he managed to retain the hold. He tried to climb but it was much more difficult than he'd thought. The boards were slick with river water and diesel and there was not much space for his fingers to grip in between. Twice he tried and twice he slipped but the third time he managed to cling on long enough to haul himself up at least a little way. Then he lost his grip and slipped again. Treading water for a moment he gripped with one hand then reached for the next hold. Hand over hand, he used his knees to work his way up the slats until he was perched on the topmost board in a squat.

Pushing up with the flat of his hands for balance he was right underneath the wharf now and crouched like a sitting duck. But they didn't see him. They came back in their skiff and shone their light over the surface of the water but he was no longer in the water and the darkness was absolute. They passed on by and he waited till the sound of the motor began to die away before he reached for the gap. Moments later he had his elbows on the wharf and swung himself up. He sat there for a few seconds breathing heavily with his feet still dangling through the gap then he pulled off his boots and emptied the water out. Gazing back across the river he saw the skiff turn to make another sweep. He lay flat on the boardwalk as it came in so close he could hear voices and pick out Soulja Blue where he sat in the prow.

When they were gone he put his boots back on and made his way to the warehouse keeping to the shadows. There was no sign of anyone around and he jogged the access road until he came out on River Street. From there with his clothes sticking to him it was street lamp to street lamp all the way to the ferry at Algiers Point.

Twenty-three

Detective De La Martin climbed from his vehicle and stepped between a pair of prowl cars parked outside the apartment complex on Esplanade. Lights burned in the windows of various condos as uniformed officers from the 3rd Precinct took statements from the residents.

A siren sounded as the detective walked across the courtyard to where another couple of officers were standing underneath the gantry sheltering from the rain. When they spotted him they stepped aside and De La Martin's attention was fixed on the shadows beyond. 'Somebody got a flashlight?' he said.

One of the officers unhooked a heavy-duty battery cell from his belt and handed it to him. Upending it over his shoulder De La Martin cast the beam across the alcove where the garbage cans were housed.

The body was slumped in the corner with the head at an awkward angle and one arm buckled underneath. The dead man's eyes were closed. He still wore his tortoiseshell glasses, though one of the lenses was smashed. Casting his gaze over the bruised and bloody torso De La Martin spat a stream of tobacco juice on the ground. He handed the flashlight back to the uniformed cop then climbed the gantry steps. With a glance across the courtyard he made his way to Anderson's apartment at the end of the block. There he paused for a moment before he opened the door and went in.

When Franklin got back to the warehouse he could see the door to the storeroom was open. Standing in the doorway he spotted the hole in the floor. He heard the whine of an outboard motor and walked out onto the wharf. He stood watching the lights from the skiff as Soulja made his sweep. He stared across the water to the city beyond and then back again to the boat. Soulja was in the prow with a flashlight and he must've picked out the shadow on the wharf because he sent the beam his way. Franklin did not move. The boat came in close and the revs died away. No sound but the slap of river water. Soulja looked up at Franklin and the blond-haired man looked back.

*

The ferry docked at the Canal Street steps and Quarrie got off. He was about to head for his hotel room but then another thought occurred to him and he set off along the boardwalk instead. He followed the railroad tracks as a switcher came rattling past pulling a dozen empty freight cars. Gauging the speed Quarrie figured it was moving slowly enough that he could grab a rail and hang on.

Jumping off just before they made the siding at Governor Nicholls, he walked towards Decatur Street and when he got to Esplanade Avenue he stopped. He could hear the sound of a siren howling and spotted two NOPD prowl cars parked at the entrance to Anderson's apartment complex. Another cruiser pulled up and two cops in uniform got out. Still he could hear the siren and he watched as a coroner's ambulance came down the road and made a U turn before it pulled up. Keeping to the shadows he looked on as the back doors were opened and the crew hauled a gurney out. A mass of people seemed to spill from the other apartments and were ushered back by uniformed cops. Moving closer now Quarrie could see lights on in Anderson's apartment and he picked out a couple more uniforms up there as well as the detective from Chartres Street. He was about to make his way over to the steps when it occurred to him that Mr Football Scholarship probably believed he was dead right now and he might want to keep it that way.

Remaining in the shadows for a while longer he watched as the two men from the ambulance came back with their gurney loaded and ushered it through the gates. As they did so an arm worked loose from the blanket and dangled briefly before they tucked it away.

When he got back to the hotel Quarrie found Yvonne still working the desk. 'The clothes I gave you before,' he said. 'Have they been laundered yet?'

Half an hour later he was back at Gigi's station wagon with his guns strapped on, taking in the confines of the criminal court building where the district attorney's office occupied the second floor. Leaving the car he peered across the road to the plethora of bail bond companies that gave the area a seedy feel. He spotted a 'Grayling Security' panel truck parked in the side street where a single wooden door was set in the office wall. On a fire escape abutting the building across, he crouched on his haunches to wait.

*

Franklin followed him from the hotel. Parking a good way down the street from the coroner's office he waited a couple of minutes before getting out of his cab. Opening the trunk he stared at the rifle case then reached for his leather pea coat. He transferred the Beretta from his waistband to the hip pocket, closed the trunk and walked up the street. When he got to the corner he stopped. The wind had picked up and it ruffled his close-cut hair. Nothing but shadows; he could see the security truck, but nothing more.

Back in the cab he drove to Baronne. Lights burned in the foyer but there was no concierge. He didn't stop; he drove to his apartment and parked. Upstairs he unlocked his door and tossed his keys on the drinks bureau. Reaching for the light he paused. A shadow in the corner where it should not be, someone was sitting on the Toledo chair.

*

Quarrie heard the side door in the coroner's building open, followed by the echo of footsteps on the gravel road. He could see an elderly-looking security guard walking towards the truck with the door to the office ajar. Moving out from where he was hidden by the fire escape he was across the road and inside the building heading for the stairs he had taken before.

In the gloom of the parking garage he stood for a moment letting his eyes grow accustomed and picked out the base of the ramp where the main gate was secured. No cars down there now, he remained at the foot of the stairs to make sure he was alone before crossing to the unmarked door in the wall. Thinking back to earlier he tried to recall what Gervais had told him, but there seemed no obvious way to call. There was no button in the fascia that he could see. There wasn't much light to work with either and he had to feel his way, running fingers up and down the outer pillars, but he located nothing there. He searched again and again before finally he felt a button as part of the concrete wall. He pressed it and nothing happened at first then he heard a hiss and clunking sound as the elevator began to make its way down. Opening the doors he eased aside a set of concertinaed gates and two minutes later he was facing another set of gates and a door. The district attorney's private bathroom; despite everything he'd been through he was able to manage a smile. This was as novel a way of gaining entry to any public building as he'd ever come across before.

The DA's office was capacious and panelled in wood. Bookshelves lined the walls where legal tomes bound in leather were stacked all but ceiling to floor. The door to the corridor was locked and there was no sign of any key. Quarrie studied the mahogany desk where it dominated the middle of the room. Set right in the center it seemed a little incongruous but then he remembered reading somewhere that District Attorney Garrison was convinced the entire office was bugged.

Easing back the chair he dropped to one knee and inspected the drawers where only the top one was locked. It was an old desk and he could see a tiny gap between the edge of the drawer itself and the underside of the top. Looking closer he picked out the flat black bar where it was secured.

He went through the other drawers but they contained nothing of interest save a couple of unused diaries and some of Garrison's business cards. Flicking through the diaries Quarrie thought about how the 28th was only three days from now.

Placing the diaries back in the drawer he noticed a box of paper clips. Selecting a couple he stretched them out then wove the two lengths together so he had a single pin that was double the thickness it had been before. He placed that on the desk before taking another two clips from the box and repeated the process, only this time he fashioned a hook. For the next few minutes he worked at the tumbler with the pair of picks. Finally it dropped and he was able to slide the drawer open and wipe sweat where it gathered on his brow.

The drawer contained four separate piles of paper files each secured twice over with a series of elastic bands. Sitting down in the DA's chair Quarrie took a long hard look at them, and when he was satisfied he could replicate exactly how they were bound, he stripped the bands away. He went through the files very carefully, Pershing Gervais on his mind and what had happened to Moore. There was nothing in the first few files but then he saw the name 'Bertrand' printed next to a photograph of a gray-haired man with dark circles dragging the flesh beneath his eyes. Alongside the name was a question mark and next to that someone had written *Clay Shaw*.

Elbows on the desk, he read the file and pored over that photograph once more. He was thinking about the reasons Gervais had given him for using the back door, the fact that half the world's media had been camped out front ever since DA Garrison rejected the findings of the Warren Commission and accused Shaw of being involved in a conspiracy to kill President Kennedy three and a half years before.

Looking further down the page Quarrie came across the name *Dean Andrews* scribbled with a note alongside. The attorney he'd met in the restaurant eating lunch with Pershing

Gervais; he studied that note with a frown. Then he laid the file to one side and opened another but didn't find anything there. He went through the next and the next after that and laid those two aside. Opening the last one he discovered another photograph clipped to the cover inside. A weird-looking guy, he was clearly bald and sporting an impoverished orange wig. His face appeared to be coated with some kind of greasepaint and fake brows had been applied above his eyes. On the opposing page was a dead person's report from the New Orleans Police Department stating that his body had been found in his apartment eight weeks before. There was a note suggesting he'd been in fear for his life, but it wasn't that which caught Quarrie's eye.

Twenty-four

Franklin switched on the light and saw Tobie sitting on the Toledo chair. 'Rosslyn,' he said. 'I almost shot you. What're you doing here?'

Tobie did not say anything. He held the cane across his knees and there was a briefcase next to him on the floor. Franklin took a pace towards him and the old man levelled his gaze.

'What's happened?' Franklin said. 'How did you get in here? What's going on?'

The old man indicated the cane. 'You covet this. You always have. Forged in Ohio in 1865. Three nines fine, it's the purest silver money can buy.'

'I know what it is and I know when it was made.' Franklin's gaze had a bite to it now. 'The transparency of lineage: something that's denied me. Of course I want it, it's mine.' Quiet for a moment, he said, 'What're you doing here, old man? What's all this about?'

Tobie got up off the chair. Holding the cane by the handle he flipped it so he gripped the shaft. 'I'm not so old that I cannot cut you down.' Moving closer he stared. 'You took unilateral action. You deviated from the plan.'

'I made a decision,' Franklin said.

'Like the one you made in Texas, you mean? We've had this conversation before.'

Placing his gun on the bureau Franklin eyed him and the old man echoed his gaze.

'So where is he?' Tobie said. 'What happened? Is he dead?'

Franklin didn't answer. He reached for a glass.

'Is the Ranger dead?' Tobie said.

Franklin stood with his back to him and his shoulders hunched. 'It's me in the photo, my neck on the block . . .'

'I asked you if he was dead.'

Franklin shook his head. 'No, he's not dead. He's still alive. I used Soulja and one of his goons. They blew it. He got away.'

In silence the old man stared.

'I sent them to search Anderson's apartment. I had to be sure. *We* had to be sure. We had to know if there was anything else.'

The old man stepped away from the chair. His back to Franklin briefly, he held the cane at his side.

'I know what you said,' Franklin went on, 'but I couldn't wait for that fat detective to get his answer. Quarrie already knew.'

'So you talked to the supplier after all.' The old man looked back at him again.

Franklin nodded. 'He made a call then phoned me back.'

'How much did it cost?'

'Enough, but it was worth it. They didn't find anything and a copy of the photo was all Quarrie had.'

'But you didn't kill him. He got away?'

'I told those fools to wait. I told them I wanted to kill him myself. But he got out of the storeroom into the river.' He nodded. 'Yes, he got away.'

'Where is he now?'

'The last time I saw him he was heading for the coroner's office. He knows about the 28th.'

Tobie sat down on the chair.

'He doesn't know what's planned. But he's not stupid. Wiley had an M1C.'

Tobie was silent for a moment then he looked up. 'So he was at the coroner's office, which means he knows about the elevator, the parking garage?'

'It's the entrance Gervais told him to use.'

'Then right about now he'll be snooping round Garrison's office. You say you used Soulja Blue?'

'Him and his driver, we grabbed Quarrie in the parking garage and took him to Algiers. That's where they fucked up. They're dead men walking. They just don't know it yet.'

'Oh, I think they probably do.' Tobie seemed to consider the painting hanging on the wall. 'Franklin,' he said, 'despite appearances to the contrary your decision might not be as costly as it would appear. Not only will those two niggers know they're on borrowed time, so will he.'

'Quarrie you talking about? I don't follow. What do you mean?'

Tobie turned to face him once more. 'There's something you don't know. After you talked to the supplier he called me at home. It wasn't only Quarrie and De La Martin who were in touch with the NCIC. They received another teletype from the coroner's office the day after Anderson was killed.'

Franklin furrowed his brow.

'Earl,' Tobie stated. 'It had to be. It's why he was so bullish on the phone.' He paused for a moment then. 'He'd been in that apartment before Quarrie ever got there. He must've found Anderson's paperwork, what he was working on, what he planned to expose.'

Franklin looked a little pale.

'It doesn't matter,' the old man said. 'If he found something, Quarrie hasn't seen it and that keeps us ahead of the play.'

'Rosslyn,' Franklin was shaking his head. 'We have to forget about the 28th. We have to deal with this properly. We have no choice but to postpone.'

Reaching for his briefcase the old man took out a paper file. 'I told you we don't do that. There's no need. We're going to kill two birds with one stone.'

*

Quarrie stared at the ceiling of his room. He'd driven back to his hotel with all he discovered in the DA's office rattling around in his head. He didn't remember sleeping, but it was light out in the courtyard and he was still in his clothes.

'Nana,' he said when the old woman answered the phone. 'It's John Q. Did you speak to Gigi at all?'

'Yes, I did. I told her about Earl.'

'How'd she take it?'

'As well as can be expected, I suppose.' She was quiet for a moment then she said, 'Have you heard the news?'

'What news?'

'They found that pharmacist, at least his body anyhow. It was all over the radio just now and it's in the newspaper. Have you seen the *Picayune*?'

'No, I haven't,' Quarrie said. 'Look, I wanted to ask you something, that older guy you were talking to yesterday. Who is he? What's his name?'

For a moment Nana did not reply. He heard her draw a

breath and sigh. 'That was Rosslyn Tobie,' she said, 'Rosslyn F to be precise. He's a lawyer and businessman. I hadn't seen him in a whole bunch of years then about a week ago he showed up out of the blue.'

'Why would he do that?' Quarrie said.

'I don't know. There's no accounting for what he does. He's a big noise in this city, got him a law firm and he's the chairman of some charity too. There was a fundraiser just the other day and they were all there, the great and the good.'

'What kind of charity?' Quarrie said.

'It's called the Tobie Foundation. I don't know much about it really. When he used to talk to me it wasn't about that, it was business and politics mostly. I'm talking the southern kind. Sometimes I hear him on the radio now and then plugging what he's doing with various projects for unfortunates and whatnot. The office is on Baronne.' She sounded unimpressed. 'He can talk all he wants, but I've lived in this city almost seventy years and never saw any lives he changed.'

She was quiet for a moment then. 'John Q,' she said, 'I understand this city. I know the kind of people we got down here and I know what they can do. If I were you I'd leave this be now and go on home.'

'I can't do that, Nana,' Quarrie said.

'Yes you can and you should.' He could hear a change in the timbre of her voice. 'Looks to me like you're messing with the kind of folks nobody messes with, you understand what I mean? What they're saying in the paper, the way they're saying it, somebody lit a fire under you and they're pouring on gasoline.'

Hanging up the phone Quarrie went down to the lobby and

found a copy of *The Times Picayune*. Leaning on the desk he read the headline where they were calling him a 'loose cannon' then cast his eye over the rest of the page. The reporter seemed to know everything that had happened from the Chartres Street escapade with De La Martin to how he was supposed to have threatened Pershing Gervais. There were comments from a couple of patrons at the bar in the 7th Ward and another about how he had caused a disturbance on Bourbon and Governor Nicholls. His visit to the pharmacy was noted and that he was the last person to see Claude Matthews alive. There was a quote from De La Martin about the body being found on Esplanade Avenue and how he was close to making an arrest.

When he got back to his room he called Amarillo and spoke to Van Hanigan. 'Captain,' he said, 'I need you to do something for me.'

'What's up, John Q? What's going on down there? I've still got Patterson rattling my cage.'

'Clay Shaw,' Quarrie said, 'the businessman the DA just indicted. I need information: who he is, who he hangs out with; that kind of thing.'

'Clay Shaw?' Van Hanigan said. 'Why? What the heck's going on?'

'I ain't sure yet.' Quarrie worked a pistol from its holster and studied it. 'I'll let you know just as soon as I do.'

Twenty-five

Colback was on the phone when he walked the corridor past the Xerox machine. The lieutenant looked up as he closed the door then told whoever he was talking to that he'd call them back. For a moment he didn't say anything, he just sat back in his chair.

'Well,' he muttered finally. 'I heard you were meeting with the district attorney, how'd that work out for you then?'

Quarrie stared across the desk.

'Pershing Gervais gave me a call. Said you'd phoned him with some mad-fool story about one of their investigators, but when he tells you to come to the office you don't show.'

'I did show,' Quarrie said. 'I went down to the parking garage just like that sumbitch said. Only it wasn't him waiting for me, it was the cab driver I thought was working for you.'

'So you don't think that anymore?'

'It wasn't just him,' Quarrie went on, 'had him two colored guys along from that club. One of them whacked me over the head and when I wake up I'm in some warehouse on Algiers Point.'

Colback studied him across the desk. 'You're telling me Pershing Gervais set that up? So why would he do that? And why call me?'

'I don't know, Lieutenant, but he was the only one who knew I was going to be in that parking garage.'

Quarrie squatted on the chair across the desk. 'Earl Moore,' he said, 'the cop I told you about, the one who stole Gigi's meds.' He pointed out the window. 'He arranges to meet Gigi in the park but when I show up instead of her somebody shoots him dead.'

Colback stared at him then. 'Who shot him?' he said.

'I don't know but they were pretty good with the long barrel, that's all I can say.'

Colback's gaze was chill. 'Are you trying to suggest it was me?'

Quarrie shook his head. 'I saw you in your window. It's why I'm set here now.'

Still the lieutenant stared. 'Quarrie, I don't know what's wrong with you but I'm tired of you yanking my chain. Pershing Gervais might be an asshole but he didn't have you picked up. For your information Earl Moore is home in bed with the flu. His wife called in and said how he'd caught a chill.' Picking up his briefcase he stood up. 'I don't have time to talk to you right now. I got a meeting to go to with the Feds.' He looked closely at Quarrie then. 'I just had the ASAC on the phone about the article they wrote in the newspaper. He wants to know why I told De La Martin I'd vouch for you. Normally I'd tell him to go fuck himself, but with the headlines you've been making he's got a point there, wouldn't you say?'

He was gone and Quarrie sat staring at the bay windows for a couple of moments then got up from the chair. Outside he gazed beyond the benches across Lafayette Square. The sun was so fierce where it reflected off the concrete he tugged at the brim of his hat. No wind and a stifling heat to the day, it was as if there had been no storm at all. He thought about what

Colback had said just now and the comment he'd made about Earl. He thought about Gervais. He thought about Mr Football Scholarship and those two hoodlums from yesterday.

The same overly made-up girl was working the counter in the drugstore when he went in. He had his badge on his chest and the twelve-gauge pump in his hand. He pointed to the metal fly curtain off to the side. 'That door over there, whatever you do to get them to open it I want you to do it now.'

The girl's face was the color of chalk. Quarrie heard the buzzer sound and a couple of moments later a metallic click as the door opened and the man with the band aid came out.

Shotgun against the base of his spine, Quarrie marched him across the road to the car. He had him drive while he sat in the back. Heading north from the Quarter they drove beyond mid-city making for the fairgrounds and Quarrie spotted a sign for Holt Cemetery. 'The graveyard yonder,' he said.

The black man parked the car and they passed through a set of rusting iron gates that echoed the ragged-looking fence. The cemetery was shabby and unkempt. Graves had been dug in the traditional fashion rather than as tombs above ground like they were closer to the river. Overhead the sun was still a molten ball but clouds were building again in the south. Headstones gathered at the base of an old oak tree, haphazard and coated in moss and lichen; most seemed to tilt at awkward angles where the soil had shifted beneath.

A sour expression on his face, the black man sat on a stone that was so sunk into the ground only about six inches showed.

'You're a dead man,' Quarrie said. 'You know that, don't you, whether it's them or me.'

The man just stared.

'The moment you don't find me in the river you're history. So is Soulja Blue.'

He didn't say anything; he just peered beyond Quarrie with a hunted look in his eyes.

'Been on your mind some, you been thinking about that blond-haired guy. You figure there's no point running because there's nowhere to run to, leastways nowhere far enough away.'

Still the black man stared.

'What's your name?'

Mouth hooked into a grimace, he looked at the ground.

'I asked your name.'

'Fuck you,' the black man said.

Quarrie cracked him across the face with the barrel of the shotgun. Blood spurted; he fell off the stone and rolled on his side. Using the toe of his boot Quarrie rolled him onto his back then pressed a heel into his sternum till he gasped. 'Mister, I asked your name.'

'Vernon.' He had blood pulsing from his nose. 'My name's Vernon, all right.'

'You're bleeding, Vernon. Go ahead and wipe your face.'

Vernon got to his feet and Quarrie told him to sit back down on the stone. Perching again he wiped the blood from his nose on his sleeve.

Quarrie looked doubtfully at him then. 'If you really don't believe you're dead already I'm pretty sure your boss does. So where's he at?'

Vernon shook his head.

'Soulja Blue,' Quarrie said. 'The man with the shaved head who figured out a way to give those good old southern boys exactly what their granddaddies got. A black man who lets white

216

folks beat up on his own people. Gigi told me how he don't care what happens so long as it's covered with green.' He curled his lip. 'She told me she knew him when he was just a bitty kid living across the street. So what happened to him, Vernon, how'd he turn out like he did?'

Vernon looked coldly at him then. 'I don't know,' he said. 'Just got to figure the meaner side of folks I guess.'

'So what about you?'

'What's it matter to you?'

Quarrie laughed. 'It don't,' he said. 'I couldn't give a shit about you or your boss, but right now whether you know it or not I'm your best chance of seeing out the day.' He indicated the badge on his chest. 'This is all that stands between you and one of those graves right there so best you be talking to me.'

In silence Vernon stared.

'They'll kill you,' Quarrie said. 'You know it and I know it and so does Soulja Blue. It's only a matter of when and where and if they make it quick or slow.' He peered closely at him now. 'Yesterday you let me escape and I showed up at the drugstore just now. How long do you figure it'll be before word gets back to that blond-haired guy?'

Still Vernon stared.

'What do you call him by the way?'

'I don't call him anything,' Vernon said.

'But you do know who he is.'

He shook his head.

'Sure you do. You work for him. You must know who he is.'

'I don't work for him. I work for Soulja Blue.' More blood dribbled from Vernon's nose and he wiped it on his sleeve.

'Who is he? Where will I find him?' Quarrie said.

'He drives a taxi. That's all I know.'

Quarrie thought for a moment then he said, 'Yesterday, after we had that little get-together in the office, you locked me up and then took off. Where'd you go, Vernon? What did you do?'

'We didn't go anywhere,' Vernon said.

Quarrie moved a little closer to him then. 'Buddy, I nearly drowned in that river and I figure that was down to you. I told you, you're dead already. You don't speak up, I'll kill you right here, right now.'

'I ain't talking,' Vernon said. 'Do what you got to do.'

Quarrie let go a sigh. 'All right then, we're done. You want to be an asshole I got no time for that. Kneel down with your back to me.'

Eyes wide Vernon looked up.

'I said, on your knees with your back to me.' He levelled the shotgun at his head.

'All right, all right.' Vernon held up his hands. 'I'll talk to you; tell you what you want to know.'

Putting up the gun Quarrie stepped back under the tree. Head to one side he looked beyond Vernon for a moment where he perched on the stone. 'So where was it?' he asked him again. 'When you left out of that warehouse where'd you go?'

'Back to the club.' Vernon gestured. 'That's where Matthews was at, the pharmacist, we had to dump his body and it was in a freezer back at the club.'

'You took him from his house on Alabo Street?'

Vernon nodded. 'I was driving; it was me and Soulja Blue.'

'Who killed him?'

He did not reply.

'Who killed him, Vernon? I ain't going to ask you again.'

'It wasn't us,' Vernon said. 'It was that blond-haired guy.'

Quarrie looked evenly at him then. 'He was there when you brought Gigi in. That was you and your boss at my hotel. He was there, wasn't he, the blond-haired guy? What did he do to her, did you see?'

'I don't know. I wasn't there.'

'I need a name, Vernon: what's his name?'

'I can't give you a name. I don't know his name. He just drives that cab. I don't know who he is.'

'What about your boss? What about Soulja Blue?'

'I don't know, man. I can't tell you. You'd have to ask him.'

'The body,' Quarrie gestured with his gun, 'why Esplanade Avenue, why that apartment block?'

'I don't know.' Vernon lifted his shoulders. 'I didn't get told.'

'It was just the two of you, though?'

Vernon nodded. 'After we locked you up he told us to get over there and dump the body. He said how he wanted us in that apartment looking for papers or photographs, any kind of writing or notes.'

'What sort of notes?' Quarrie said.

Vernon shrugged.

'What about phone numbers maybe or dates?'

'He never said nothing about no phone numbers, but he did tell us to look out for dates.'

Quarrie peered at him now. 'What dates, Vernon? What did he say?'

'He mentioned April 28.'

'Why? What's happening then?'

Vernon shook his head. 'I don't know. I ain't dumb enough to ask and he sure as hell ain't going to say.'

Quarrie didn't ask any more questions, he just leaned against the tree. Taking off his hat he worked a hand through the sweat in his hair. 'All right,' he said. 'We're done here. You're still alive and if you want to keep it that way you'll get a-hold of Soulja Blue.' Putting his hat back on he rested the barrel of the shotgun against his shoulder. 'Tell him I'll be at my hotel. After what he did to Gigi I ought to drag his ass from here to Texas so he better come talk to me.'

Twenty-six

He did not receive a call, though he waited the rest of the day. As darkness fell he left the hotel and drove the short distance to the 3rd Precinct Station House. Directly across the road was a seafood place and he had a hunch De La Martin wasn't married therefore dinner would either be bar food somewhere or To-Go. Inside he found him sitting at the end of the counter hunched over a bowl of dirty rice and red beans with a pile of steaming crawdads on a sheet of newspaper. He had a shot of bourbon and a half-glass of beer back of that, but his focus was the food.

Quarrie sent a beer down the bar and briefly De La Martin glanced his way. A minute later Quarrie was on the stool alongside him resting an elbow next to empty shells.

'You got some nerve walking in here, Texas.'

'You think so?' Quarrie said. 'After what I read in the paper this morning I wanted to talk to you.'

The big man concentrated on his food.

'I told you the pharmacist was in that club and you didn't want to break down the door. Next thing I know you're up on the balcony and his body's on a gurney from the coroner's crew.'

Pushing away the empty bowl De La Martin wiped his fingers on a napkin and screwed it into a ball. He drank the beer Quarrie had bought him then nodded to the bartender once more.

'Did somebody give you a call?' Quarrie asked him. 'Or was it you picking up the phone?'

De La Martin spoke without looking at him. 'You don't listen, do you, Texas? Wasn't it just the other day I told you to think before you opened your mouth?'

'So you're not working for whoever's behind this? I'm talking about that blond-haired guy.'

De La Martin snorted. 'You know, for someone that just about everybody in this city wants to bust right now, you surely like to run that lip.'

'Esplanade Avenue after hours, that ain't your style, Detective, so what were you doing up there?'

De La Martin adjusted his weight where he seemed to strain the legs of the stool. 'What do you know about that apartment? It's a fact we found a bunch of different fingerprints. Am I'm going to find some of them are yours?'

Quarrie did not reply.

The detective pumped the air from his cheeks. 'Jesus, the mess only gets messier, doesn't it? So never mind me then. What were *you* doing up there?'

'Anderson,' Quarrie told him, 'the guy whose apartment it was, he's the dead man from Wichita Falls.' He paused for a moment then he said, 'April 28 is important to someone. Does it mean anything to you?'

De La Martin did not reply.

'What about the teletype you sent to the FBI?'

'What about it? Colback told me why you were down here. With Matthews missing what else did you expect me to do?'

Quarrie cast a glance the length of the counter where most of the stools were taken with people bellying up. 'You done with the crawdads, are you? It's kind of public talking at the bar.'

As if to humor him the detective picked up his drink and moved to a table against the wall. Resting his elbows, he knit pudgy fingers together and studied Quarrie once more.

'Let's get one thing straight,' he said. 'I don't care what Colback or anybody else said to you. The fact is I'm a fat man who eats a lot and sweats too much, but in thirty years of hitting the bricks I never took so much as a free lunch.' Sitting back he flapped a hand. 'Anyway, in case you hadn't noticed it's not me on trial in the newspapers, it's you they're hanging out to dry.'

'The cab driver,' Quarrie said. 'You asked about him the other day. What was that all about?'

De La Martin looked hard at him then. 'I've seen him driving that taxi from time to time but I only ever saw two people in the back. One was a lawyer called Tobie and the other one was you.'

*

The following morning Quarrie was strapping on his shoulder holsters when Van Hanigan called him back. 'John Q,' he said. 'There's a piece in the *Herald* about you.'

'Syndicated, huh, the one they wrote down here?'

'They're talking about the fact you're Hamer's godson and you know how that can be. Half the folks out there figure him for a sonofabitch and the other half think he's a saint.'

'Captain, I don't know what I can tell you. There ain't a whole lot I can do.'

'Well anyway, you asked about Clay Shaw,' Van Hanigan

went on. 'I've done some digging and you're aware he's got an alias, right? Nobody seems to know why, but then I'm told he likes to stem the rose so that might account for it, I suppose. As far as I can find out he's known mostly for the International Trade Mart down there in New Orleans. Got a lot of friends, John Q, arms dealers and gasoline wholesalers, they say he's buddies with Ferenc Nagy, the ex-Hungarian prime minister who's living in Dallas right now. He does a lot of charity work apparently, has some link with a foundation for underprivileged kids with offices on Baronne.'

Hanging up the phone Quarrie sat for a moment contemplating what the captain had said just now and what Nana had told him yesterday. Downstairs he went out to the car then drove the one way system to Orleans Street. As he approached the apartment, he spotted the same black Lincoln he had seen before. A couple of minutes later the small gate opened and Rosslyn Tobie appeared. Tanned in the face he sported a pair of expensive-looking sunglasses and an immaculate cream-colored suit.

Quarrie waited until the Lincoln was almost to the junction with North Rampart Street before he pulled out. Staying a couple of vehicles back he tailed them across Canal Street onto Baronne. The Lincoln stopped outside an office building where the entrance was shaded by a mauve-colored canopy and various brass name plaques were screwed to the wall. The parking bays along that section were all marked private and he had to drive a little further and swing around the block before he could find somewhere to stop. He could see the front of the building and he switched off the engine and got out. He walked half a block to the pedestrian light and was heading back towards the office when he saw Colback beckon him from an unmarked Ford.

They sat in the rear and Colback asked him to repeat what he had said yesterday. When Quarrie was finished the lieutenant stared through the windshield with his brows knit.

'I don't get it,' he said. 'Nothing's been reported. Gervais told me Moore's wife called in saying he was sick.'

'Maybe somebody did,' Quarrie said, 'but it wasn't his wife. He's dead, Lieutenant. I was there.'

Reaching over the seat Colback tapped the other cop on the shoulder and indicated for him to leave them alone. Without a word the man got out of the car and Quarrie looked on with a puzzled expression. 'What's up, Lieutenant? What gives?'

'I don't want anyone listening who doesn't need to be listening because Gervais has a history here.' Colback looked sideways at him then. 'A few years back he was picked up by the crime commission and in order to stay out of jail he gave up just about everyone he knew.' He paused for a minute then he said, 'That restaurant on Canal Street, he was having lunch with Dean Andrews, right?'

'The attorney with the sunglasses?' Quarrie nodded.

'So I figure you were about to pay him a visit.' Colback indicated the office with the mauve canopy. 'Let me tell you that after everything I've been reading in the newspaper that's not a very bright thing to do.'

Quarrie did not say anything. He had no idea this was where Andrews worked.

'Anyway,' Colback went on. 'Why I was looking for you, I spoke to the Feds and they told me if I didn't get you off the street, they would. They're asking De La Martin for everything he's got on the pharmacist and that apartment complex as well as the disturbance on Bourbon and Governor Nicholls. They want access to his files and any trace evidence he's picked up too.'

Quarrie was silent after that and Colback shifted his weight as if his pants were sticking to the seat. 'So, what do you want with Andrews?' he said. 'If it's information about Gervais you're wasting your time. I tried to flag you down just now when you left the hotel and again on Orleans Street.'

Quarrie stared across the road. 'I'm not here for Andrews. I had no idea he worked over there.'

'Are you kidding me? He's on the second floor.'

'I didn't know that,' Quarrie repeated. 'Fact is I was tailing the Lincoln. It's Rosslyn Tobie's car and once upon a time that old man had a relationship with Nana Matisse. She told me she hadn't seen him in years, not so much as a whisper, then all of a sudden he shows up not once but a bunch of times and that strikes me as a little weird.' He looked round at Colback again. 'Old family from the Garden District, I guess you must've heard of him.'

'Of course I've heard of him.' Colback pointed across the block. 'Not only does he chair that foundation over there, he owns the building and most of the street. He's an attorney and businessman. Anybody who's anybody in Louisiana knows Rosslyn F Tobie and I'm talking about the governor here.'

Quarrie studied the ornate-looking facade once more. 'Lieutenant,' he said, 'that foundation's supposed to help disadvantaged young folks but in all the years Nana Matisse lived here she can't recall anything much they squared.'

'Is that a fact?' Colback said. 'Well, I could show you dozens of good causes they've been involved with from here to the Florida Keys.'

Quarrie lifted a palm. 'The dead guy back in Texas was ex NOPD. Yesterday I had a word with a hood called Vernon who—'

'Vernon?' Colback looked round at him then. 'The guy that works for Soulja Blue?'

Quarrie nodded.

For a moment the lieutenant sat still. Then he signalled through the window for his colleague to get back in the car. 'Quarrie,' he said, indicating the station wagon on the other side of the road, 'yesterday that piece of junk you're driving was spotted on Bourbon and Governor Nicholls. Some altercation in that drugstore on the corner and this morning we get a call from a tugboat captain who found the body of a black man floating in the Outfall Canal. Small-time hood called Vernon all beaten and bloody. Half his skull was blown away.'

Twenty-seven

Hat in his hands Quarrie stared at the back of the driver's seat. 'Lieutenant,' he said. 'It might be I was the last person anyone saw with Vernon but that ain't exactly news down here. I didn't kill him. I was his best chance of staying alive.' He wrinkled the flesh at the corners of his eyes. 'So they got to him already. They sure didn't waste any time.'

'Who got to him? What're you talking about?'

'The cab driver, whoever he's working for, they've got something planned for two days' time.'

'What?'

'They're going to kill somebody, Lieutenant. I just ain't sure who it is.'

Colback stared at him. 'Here in New Orleans you mean?'

'I believe so, yes.'

'Are you telling me that's what all this is about, someone in their rifle sights?'

Quarrie nodded.

'OK, I need to get going here. I need to make some calls.' Reaching across him Colback opened the door.

Quarrie watched the Ford pull away then he walked back to the station wagon but didn't start the engine; he rested his elbow on the sill chewing over all that had been said. As he was sitting there the attorney with a penchant for black-framed Ray-Ban sunglasses emerged from the doors of the building on the other side of the road. Quarrie watched as he exchanged a few words with the concierge then set off along the sidewalk where the line of cars was parked. Thinking about that note he'd read in the DA's file, Quarrie fired up the engine and pulled out from the parking bay.

Driving slowly he passed the entrance to the building and came up alongside. Reaching across to the passenger door he told Andrews to get in. The attorney looked at him with his chin high and Quarrie opened his jacket to reveal one of his Blackhawks. Sweat working his brow Andrews got in. Quarrie drove three blocks with one hand on the wheel and the other fisted in his lap.

'Kidnap, Sergeant?' It had taken a moment but Andrews seemed to have regained his composure. 'After what I read in the papers we can add that to your list of misdemeanors. It gets more fascinating by the day.'

Quarrie pulled around the corner and stamped so hard on the brakes the attorney had to flatten a hand against the windshield to avoid cracking his head. 'Nobody kidnapped you, Counselor. I just want to know about your lunch with Pershing Gervais.'

'The one you gate-crashed you mean, what's to talk about?'

'Clay Shaw,' Quarrie said.

Andrews furrowed his brow. 'Shaw?' he said. 'Why on earth would we be discussing him?'

'He's under indictment right now.' Quarrie gestured. 'The day after President Kennedy was shot; Shaw phoned your office asking you to represent Lee Oswald. You remember taking that call?'

The attorney looked straight ahead.

'Funny thing is, before you had a chance to do anything he called again saying you weren't needed after all.'

'Sergeant, I have no idea what you're talking about.'

'Sure you do. Jim Garrison asked you about it a few weeks ago so I'm assuming that's what you were discussing with Gervais.' Quarrie shifted around in the seat. 'What I want to know is why Shaw gave you the heads up only to tell you it wasn't necessary after all.'

Andrews did not say anything. Sitting with his hands in his lap he nursed a cough.

With a sigh, Quarrie gestured over his shoulder. 'Maybe you didn't notice, but the concierge was back inside the building. No one saw you get in the car.'

Andrews remained silent. He gazed through the windshield still, but a fresh line of perspiration glistened above his sunglasses.

'Why did Shaw tell you to back off?' Quarrie asked him again.

The attorney did not reply.

Quarrie sighed. 'Counselor, on top of everything else I got going on they're looking to book me for the murder of some hood from Governor Nicholls as well.'

Still the attorney stared.

'I'll ask you one last time. Why did Shaw have you step up to the plate but not take a swing at the ball?'

*

Quarrie spent the rest of the day at the hotel on Canal Street but heard nothing from Colback and nothing from Soulja

Blue. At seven o'clock he phoned the ranch and his son picked up. 'Hey, kiddo,' Quarrie said. 'What's up?'

'I'm OK, Dad,' James said, 'but the newspapers, they're writing about you.'

Quarrie forced the air from his lips. 'It doesn't matter. Don't take any notice. There's nothing to worry about. Have you been getting a bad time at school?'

'A little maybe, the older kids, you know how they are. Miss Munro was asking as well.'

'What did you tell her?'

'Nothing really, Pious said to say that they're always writing about Rangers.'

'Is that what you did?'

'Not yet. I will if she asks me again. Dad, is everything all right?'

'Everything is fine, son. There's nothing for you to worry about. Is Pious around by the way?'

'Not right now, I think he's over at the bunkhouse playing poker with Nolo and Miss Gigi.'

'Gigi plays poker, huh? How about that? You figure you could run over there and ask Pious to come to the phone?'

'Sure,' James said. 'Dad, I like Miss Gigi and I ain't the only one does around here.'

'Pious, you talking about?'

'Uh-huh, when she's around he don't ever quit talking and he ain't ever like that.'

Quarrie smiled.

'I'll go fetch him for you. Do you want to talk to Miss Gigi as well?'

'Sure,' he said. 'See if she'll come to the phone.'

James went off to get them and a few minutes later Quarrie heard Gigi's voice. 'Hey,' she said. 'How are you?'

'I'm all right, what about you?'

'I'm OK. I've been spending time with Eunice and Mama, those girls they like to talk and they like to laugh a whole lot for sure.'

'They're good people, known them most of my life.' Quarrie paused for a moment then. 'I guess Nana told you about Earl?'

'Yes, she did.'

'I'm sorry about what happened, Gigi. I had no idea that was how it was going to turn out.'

'He warned me. He was scared when he talked to me. What's going on, John Q? What's all this about?'

Quarrie stared at the wall. 'I ain't sure yet. I need to talk to Pious, is he there?'

'Sure, I'll fetch him for you. Hold on.'

Pious came on the line and his tone was grim. 'What gives, John Q? I've seen what-all they've been saying about you and it don't look good.'

'That photo I gave you,' Quarrie said. 'I think it came from the *Fort Worth Star*. I want you to give them a call and ask for a snapper called Dixie Wells. Tell him I need him to take a look at the photo. I doubt he'll drive all the way out to the ranch. Can you meet him in Wichita Falls?'

Hanging up the phone he went downstairs to Canal Street in newly falling rain. With the onset of evening the clouds had blown in from the gulf. He drove across the Quarter and stopped a couple of blocks west of where Nana lived. It was dark on the street and few people were walking; he turned his collar to the rain. At the corner he gazed towards the river and

Cabildo, scanning the lines of parked cars. Finding no trace of the Lincoln his attention focused on the lighted windows of the apartment. He rang the bell at the gate then stepped out onto the street so Nana could see him when she came to the balcony doors. The buzzer sounded, the gate clicked open and she greeted him at the top of the stairs.

'John Q?' she said. 'I thought you told me you being here wasn't any good for me.'

'I did, didn't I.' Climbing the steps Quarrie smiled. 'I'm sorry. I should've called. I can take off again or come back to-morrow if it's too late.'

'No, it's not too late.' She ushered him into the apartment. 'All this rain, I guess you're happy to see it at least.' She took his jacket and hung it on the stand in the hall. 'Gigi called earlier and told me how there ain't been a drop over there since fall.'

She led the way into the living room and Quarrie noticed her thirty-eight lying on top of the cabinet. 'Expecting some company, were you?'

She didn't smile. 'I don't know, sometimes I have a feeling, something I used to get back in the islands when I was a child. Old as I am it still creeps up on me once in a while.'

'What kind of feeling?' Quarrie perched on the lip of the couch.

'Oh, like someone is scratching the skin between my shoulders maybe. My grandmother used to say it was the finger-nail of a witch.' She shook her head. 'It's a fact I don't believe in any of that juju stuff, but I worry when my back starts to itch.'

Picking up the handgun she slipped it into the drawer then went to the kitchen and came back with a pitcher of julep and two glasses.

'Nana,' Quarrie said, 'I need to talk to you about Ross Tobie.'

'Rosslyn,' the old woman corrected. 'It's always Rosslyn, Rosslyn F, in fact. I never once called him Ross. That was his son's name but he died of meningitis when he was nine years old.'

'On the phone you told me he'd been coming around and he was here again today.' Quarrie gestured to the road. 'This morning, I was outside when he came down and got in his vehicle. You said how he hadn't been by in a bunch of years so what's with the visits now?'

Pouring a glass of whiskey Nana took a small sip then replaced it on the coffee table. 'I don't know,' she said. 'He came around the night of the fundraiser all full of himself like he always was. Never said what it was he wanted or why he should show up out of the blue. He was here a second time and was asking about Gigi, how she was, if she was doing OK.' She looked past him then, a distance in her eyes as if she were lost in some memory she wasn't sure she wanted to recall.

'Nana?' Quarrie said.

'He told me he wanted to make sure she was all right, said he'd been meaning to look us up for a while.' She looked at him closely again. 'Today he said how he'd been reading about you in the newspaper, all about that missing pharmacist and the detective from the 3rd Precinct.'

Quarrie nodded. 'Nana,' he said, 'you told me on the phone I was messing with the kind of folks best left alone. I think Rosslyn Tobie's one of those folks, so who am I dealing with?'

She looked at him then with the light in her eyes that might have been fear. It might've been something else.

'Who is he exactly? What can you tell me?' Quarrie said.

She twisted her mouth at the corners. 'I don't know what I can say. He's a lawyer, I guess, businessman. Got him a wife and grown-up daughter. His son died right around the time we got together and all he could talk about was that boy. It seemed to me it wasn't a son he lost so much as what he symbolised.'

'I don't follow. What do you mean?'

She upturned her palms. 'I'm not sure I know myself. But he used to talk about legacy and history, his business and all, how he had to make sure there was someone to carry on after his time was done.' She broke off for a moment and then she said, 'I wasn't his only mistress and I know he had other kids. It's a fact there's probably another son out there somewhere but he wouldn't admit to it, not with the folk he mixes with.' She was silent again, her gaze fixed on the world outside where street-lights flickered through the falling rain. 'I was thirty-seven years old when I started seeing him and I doubt he was twenty-nine. I figure it was three years we were together then we broke up and it was another eight before I saw him again.' She looked back at Quarrie then. '1935, I remember exactly because Gigi turned eight years old the day they shot Huey Long.'

Her expression was no longer remote. 'John Q, do you know who Huey was?'

Quarrie nodded. 'Yes, mam, of course. He was the governor here in Louisiana, had designs on being president.'

'The Kingfish is what they called him and I remember Rosslyn really hated that.'

'On account of how he was a rich man you mean and Huey was pitching some idea for sharing the wealth?'

'Rich ain't the word for it.' Nana gestured to their surround-ings. 'To a man like Rosslyn this apartment was nothing but chump change. It's why he never so much as bat an eye when I asked him to sign it over to me.' She paused for a moment before she went on. 'I recall how we broke up around the time Lizzie Miles got sick and Lizzie was a friend of mine. She used to come over here when she hadn't had to take to her bed. Had some opinions on her did Lizzie and she'd harangue me about my soul. She kept on and on till finally I told her . . .'

The words tailed off and she dropped her gaze. 'I remember she thought the way she got sick was some kind of punishment from God on account of how she'd been lauding it all with her fans. I told her that was just a bunch of bullshit and if God gave her that voice, for sure he'd want her to use it. But when she got better, when she took to performing again she never set foot on the stage, just used to set to the side.' She drew breath through her nose. 'Before she got sick she spent a lot of time in Paris, France; and she wasn't short on telling me how over there I'd be a courtesan, though we got uglier words for it here. It didn't make no mind what she said. It didn't matter what anybody said. I had my own way of doing things and I knew who-all he was, but none of what anybody wanted to say bothered me enough to stop that man climbing into my bed.'

'Nana,' Quarrie interrupted. 'You said how Lizzie was easier on you after you told her something. What was it you said?'

The old lady did not answer. Instead she took another sip of minted whiskey. 'I ain't proud of it, the kind of life I lived, but it's a fact I ain't sorry for it either.' Her gaze had stiffened a fraction. 'You're right about what you said just now though, rich men and Huey Long. That sharing the wealth thingamajig you talked about, he wanted to pay for it by taxing men like Rosslyn Tobie, and not just their businesses but their private holdings as well. Sometimes I think that's why Rosslyn was happy to sign this apartment over. He used to joke that if I didn't get it then Huey would and if I owned it at least he could still come visit.'

Pausing for a moment, she went on. 'Rosslyn was old-school south. You know what I'm talking about, the kind of family that went back to the days of the Grand Isle auctions when folks like me sold for seventy cents on the pound. That's why Lizzie had the attitude she did. Figured I was allowing myself to be bought and sold all over again. I remember one time with Rosslyn and old Judge Pavy . . .'

'Benjamin Pavy you mean?'

'That's right; him they hounded out of office after Huey passed his election boundary bill.'

Quarrie looked closely at her then. 'Nana, Judge Pavy's son-in-law was the man that shot Huey Long. Carl Weiss, he was gunned down right after by Huey's men.'

Nana looked wary. 'Yes, he was. Right there in the Capitol Building. I remember how Rosslyn was when he finally showed up again with Huey in his grave and the boy that shot him, dead. A politician going after their money, it was un-American, Rosslyn said.'

Briefly she shook her head. 'Funny how when anybody tries to change things for the regular folks in this country up pops somebody else. Medgar Evers I'm talking about, John Kennedy; be Dr King next, God forbid.' Making the sign of the cross she kissed the tips of her fingers. 'I recall saying as much to Rosslyn but he told me that's how it's been since Lincoln and his slavery bill.

'Anyway, he came around again after all that time gone by wanting back in my life and he's a man who gets what he wants.'

237

She nodded to the spare bedroom. 'I remember when we were done with the monkey thing he'd lay back and look at those snakes in the posts of yonder bed. Pit-vipers, copperheads they were,' she said.

With a sigh she got to her feet. 'That man sure liked the sound of his voice. He'd talk about anything and everything because me being black and all, he didn't think it mattered what he said. It's been twenty years since I last saw him but the way he talks to me now is the same way he always did.'

'What d'you mean?' Quarrie said.

'I mean how that man really is. It don't matter what he's telling me, he's exercising his power all over again.'

'What power?' Quarrie said.

Lifting a hand she gestured. 'He's letting me know that it don't matter how many years gone by nothing has changed and nothing ever will. Gigi, I'm talking about, what-all happened with us. She doesn't know about any of it and as far as I'm concerned she never will.'

'Know about what?' Quarrie said.

'How she ain't my niece, she's my daughter and Rosslyn Tobie's her dad.'

Eyes half-closed she stared into space. 'That was the reason we broke up. I was pregnant and Rosslyn was real pissed off. Lot of folks knew about him and me and he didn't want anybody figuring him for having no colored kid.' She crossed to the window again. 'I guess we cut a deal. He'd sign a quit claim on the apartment, but only if I went away till the baby was born and had Gigi brought up by a couple of old mammies so nobody'd think she was his. I reckon I needed to secure our future so that's exactly what I did.' She looked at him with the hint of fear in her face. 'I remember when I first told Rosslyn I was pregnant he wanted to get rid of the baby altogether. I was almost four months gone by then though, too late for any backstreet doctor. There wasn't anything he could do short of murdering the both of us and if I gave him cause he would.'

'Gave him cause?' Quarrie said.

'Yes, sir, he made that clear right from the get-go. He was talking about me contacting him. I wasn't allowed to do that. I could never ever call his house.' A shudder rippled through her and she sat down on the couch. 'You've seen that cane he carries. It ain't for walking. It's a weapon is what it is.'

Quarrie was still trying to get his head around what she'd said about Gigi. Squatting on a Queen Anne chair he looked across the coffee table.

'A man like that there's only one way to deal with him.' Nana's gaze drifted to the cabinet where she'd stowed the gun. 'I don't mind telling you I thought about it back in the old days and just recently I been thinking about it again. If you're right about him being involved then it's down to him what happened to Gigi.' Looking at Quarrie now her gaze was thin. 'The law can't touch him. It never will.'

'He told you if you called his house he'd kill you?' Quarrie said.

'Not in so many words. But I know if I ever did he'd come up here in the dead of night and bury that walking cane in my head.'

Twenty-eight

The next morning Quarrie drove to Tulane Avenue. Stopping at a curbside phone, he slotted a dime and called the DA's office. He made a point of asking for Moore and they told him he was still sick so he asked if the DA was in. They said he wasn't taking any calls.

Back in the car he took the ramp beneath the coroner's office and parked in a bay where he could see right across the concourse. He studied the shadows from the driver's seat until he was satisfied he was unobserved. Then he got out and locked the door.

A few minutes later he opened the concertinaed gates from the elevator into the bathroom where a middle-aged man in a business suit was leaning against the wash basin with his arms folded and a pipe clamped between his jaws.

'Well,' he said, looking Quarrie up and down, 'are you going to tell me who you are and what you're doing in my private bathroom?'

'My name's Quarrie, Mr Garrison. I'm a Texas Ranger.' Quarrie showed him his badge. 'I need to talk to you, sir, without anyone knowing I'm here.'

'So you're the one they're writing about in the newspaper?'

'Yes, I am. And what I got to say you're going to want to hear.'

They went through to Garrison's office where the door was

standing open. Casting a glance the length of the corridor Quarrie closed the door and when he turned again the DA was looking a little perturbed.

'I can open it if you like,' Quarrie said. 'But what I have to tell you, you might not want anyone else to overhear.' He related what happened in Lafayette Square and from the look on Garrison's face he could see that no one had told him the story before. Garrison regarded him carefully for a moment then he sat down behind his desk and opened a drawer. Pipe in his left hand, he rested his right on his thigh just ahead of the open drawer.

'Are you sure about this?' he said.

Quarrie nodded. 'I went up on the roof of the Old Post Office right after and when I looked down the body had disappeared.'

'And who witnessed the episode exactly?'

'Nobody, that's the point, it was coming down hard with rain and that's the only lookout across the whole square. I think the shooter might be a young guy who drives a cab. He was outside the Lakefront Airport when I first got in and he's been there every time I've needed to go anywhere since. I figured he was on Lieutenant Colback's payroll at first because he was the only person who knew I was coming down here.' Pausing for a moment he added, 'Now I'm thinking there might be another leak somewhere. Mr Garrison, you're not the first person in this office I talked to. I already told Pershing Gervais.'

For what seemed an age the DA sat there. Then he told Quarrie to open the door. When he turned again he could see the way Garrison's hand was still hooked just ahead of the drawer.

'Look,' he said. 'I know how this must appear, some cop from out of state the papers are writing about showing up in your bathroom with a cockamamie story about one of your investigators, but you don't need it the piece you got back there. I'm a Texas Ranger and we're not in the habit of bull-shitting anybody. That's not the way we are.' He paused then added, 'Colback can vouch for me if you feel you need to give someone a call. Talk to him or my captain back in Amarillo. The fact is I'm not some half-ass runaround. I'm here on ac-count of a murder in Wichita Falls.'

Still the district attorney studied him. 'What happened when you spoke to Gervais?'

Quarrie sat down on the arm of the couch. 'He told me to come in through the parking garage and wait till he came down. Before he shows up, though, someone's got a gun to my head and I wake up on the wharf in Algiers.' He could see the doubt in Garrison's eyes. 'Mr Garrison, don't take my word on any of this. I know somebody called here claiming to be Earl Moore's wife. Why don't you get on the phone right now and ask if her husband is there?'

The DA seemed to ponder that for a moment then he pressed the intercom button on his phone. 'Jennifer,' he said, 'call Earl for me, will you? Ask his wife how he's doing and if we can expect him back anytime soon.'

In silence they waited and a few minutes later the phone buzzed and Garrison picked up. He listened to what he was told and his features tightened a little then he put down the phone. He looked tentatively at Quarrie for a moment before he went to close the office door.

'All right, Sergeant. You have my attention. Moore's wife says she was called by somebody from this office who said her husband had to go out of town.'

Quarrie took a second to digest that. 'Mr Garrison, I'm going to level with you, sir. This isn't the first time I've been in your office. I was here the other night trying to find out why someone would want to kill Earl Moore.'

'So it was you.' Garrison's expression was sour. 'I thought someone had been at my desk. Just who do you think you are?'

Quarrie upturned a palm. 'Breaking and entering, I know, it's a habit I need to get out of but I figure you should hear me out just the same. Trace Anderson, the dead man in Texas, he was murdered with a bottle of prescription drugs that caused a blood vessel to burst in his brain.'

Garrison's eyes tightened a little bit more.

'Proloid,' Quarrie stated. 'It's a drug you've come across before.'

For a few moments Garrison stared at him then he opened his top drawer and withdrew the files Quarrie had been looking at when he was here before. Selecting one he placed it on top of the desk then he got up and went into the bathroom. When he came out again he had an empty pill bottle in his hand. No cap; Quarrie could see that the label had been torn off as well.

'You found that in an apartment on Louisiana Avenue Parkway,' he said.

'That's right.' Garrison nodded.

'It was dispensed by the pharmacist from North Rampart and St Ann whose body was discovered at the complex where Anderson lived. The patient was Gigi Matisse. I don't know if you've heard of her, she's a blues singer who plays hereabouts. She lives in the 7th Ward and she and Moore were having an affair. I think somebody found out about that, because the way Gigi told it I figure Moore was being smacked by someone working a jackhammer.' He nodded to the empty bottle. 'Whoever that was they had him steal her meds twice in the space of a couple of months.'

'Why would they do that?' Garrison asked.

Quarrie shrugged. 'I figure Earl knew Gigi had a thyroid problem. Maybe he let it slip and they thought they could use it. Mr Garrison, if you want to fake death by natural causes you ain't going to buy drugs if you can have somebody steal them.'

'So they wanted him just to steal the drugs?' Garrison looked doubtful.

Quarrie shook his head.

'Why then?'

'You tell me. Earl was one of your investigators. What was he working on?'

'I can't disclose that, Sergeant. At least not till I know what's going on.'

'All right,' Quarrie said. 'Trace Anderson, the man murdered in Wichita Falls. Two guys went to his hotel room and found a photograph hidden in the trouser press. One of them is in the jailhouse right now and the other one is dead. I shot him on a dirt road back in Texas. His name was Wiley; he was a three-tour Vietnam Vet. Does that mean anything to you?'

Garrison shook his head. 'No,' he said. 'I've never heard of him.'

Quarrie gestured. 'The photograph I mentioned. I found what I think is a copy in Anderson's apartment. I also found a phone number for this office. I think Anderson called here and I don't know whether it was Moore or Gervais he spoke to, but sometime later he wound up in that hotel room in Wichita Falls.'

'The photograph, Sergeant: what was it?'

Quarrie told him and Garrison worked the stem of his pipe with his teeth.

'I think Anderson recognized one of the men,' Quarrie went on. 'The blond-haired cab driver I told you about. Whether Texas was Anderson's suggestion or if it came from somebody else, he had the presence of mind to check into the hotel under an alias and leave his ID behind.' He nodded to the empty drugs bottle. 'The meds were ground into powder and mixed with water and Anderson was forced to drink it. After that they burned the photograph and they were supposed to find out who he really was, only they couldn't tune him up because the murder had to look like he died in his sleep.'

'So no police officer would investigate,' Garrison said.

Quarrie nodded. 'Whatever it was they had going on they wanted it buried with the man they murdered. But that's not how it panned out. After he was done with Anderson, Wiley robbed a gun store and stole a bunch of shotguns as well as a Garand M1C. That's a military-issue rifle, the kind we used in Korea. I answered a call on the radio after he shot up a state trooper's vehicle and he threw down on me with a Winchester pump.'

Garrison blew out his cheeks. 'Sergeant, that's quite a story.'

'Ain't it though, and it's not all. After those hoods picked me up in the parking garage, I got out of the warehouse via a dousing in the river. I made my way to Esplanade and when I got there I found Detective De La Martin at the apartment complex with the pharmacist's body. I thought it was him that must've given this crew the heads up. I figured he was working for them and they were going to make damn sure I was implicated in the murder.'

'But he wasn't?'

Quarrie shook his head. 'I don't think so. I talked to him last night and I'm wondering if it didn't play out some other way.'

'What do you mean?'

Quarrie told him what Van Hanigan had said about the teletype from the coroner's office. 'Whoever sent it knew about the murder and they'd already figured Anderson for a cop. I'm guessing that had to be Moore and that's information he kept to himself. Couple that with what Gigi told me and it's obvious he wasn't working for these folks voluntarily.' Pausing for a moment he went on. 'They only discovered Anderson's address after Moore had already been there. He didn't give it to them and if it wasn't De La Martin then there has to be some other cop on the payroll somewhere.'

Garrison looked puzzled. 'Hold on a minute, I need to backtrack here for a second. You're saying that Moore sent a teletype from the coroner's office?'

Quarrie nodded.

'But why?'

'I said just now how I figure they were working him over and I think he needed an angle. He knew they'd murdered Anderson so he had to be involved in the set-up. But the murder wasn't down to him and he had to find a way out from under that jackhammer. I'm pretty sure he was in that apartment ahead of me and I think he found something that could give him what he needed. They either knew that or suspected it at least, because they shot him in the park when they could've shot me.'

246

Slowly Garrison nodded.

'Whatever it was he found – they haven't got it. I know that because they searched that apartment the night they dumped Matthews's body.'

'And you think that whatever he found might be here?'

'I don't know.' Quarrie shrugged. 'Somehow I doubt it, but why don't you have somebody search his desk?'

Garrison made no move to do that. He was silent. Sitting back in his chair he studied Quarrie with his chin high. 'Everything you've been telling me. Clearly you suspect Moore, but are you saying my chief investigator is involved as well?'

'He's the only person who knew about Lafayette Square.' Quarrie glanced towards the door. 'He asked me to come in and the blond guy was waiting in the parking garage. Is he around, Mr Garrison? I'd kindly like to talk to him.'

Garrison shook his head. 'He's not here, no. He's gone up to Baton Rouge.'

Quarrie thought about that. 'All right,' he said. 'Then I need to ask you something else. Clay Shaw, this investigation that's all over the newspapers. Is Gervais working that?'

Garrison shook his head. 'No, he's not. Sergeant, you're probably not aware but he's not well liked in New Orleans, at least not as far as law enforcement is concerned anyway. He and I go back to our days in the service, however, and he was always good on the bricks. When nobody else would give him a job, I did – and he's never let me down. That's why he's now my chief investigator. But I'm not a fool; when I found so many anomalies in the report for the Warren Commission the team I assembled did not include Gervais. I knew how things would look if it did so he has no access to any of the files.'

'But Earl Moore did?'

Garrison nodded.

'He ain't coming back, sir. Maybe you should search his desk.'

Garrison took a moment to consider that then he got to his feet. 'You stay here and I'll have somebody bring you some coffee.' He left him and Quarrie walked to the window where he looked across the road at the neon-lit windows of the bail bond companies. Nobody brought him any coffee but five minutes later Garrison was back. He closed the door and sat down again at his desk.

'Well?' Quarrie said.

'Nothing, there's no paperwork, no file or photo that I don't know about, so if he did find something then he must've taken it home or hidden it somewhere else.'

Quarrie indicated the file that Garrison had separated from the others. 'That's David Ferrie's paperwork, isn't it?'

Garrison nodded.

'The pilot Clay Shaw used to use here in New Orleans. You were talking to him because he was in Texas the day after Kennedy was shot?'

Garrison nodded.

'Ferrie was found dead in his apartment on Louisiana Avenue Parkway. I read that file, Mr Garrison, and the coroner put his death down to a naturally occurring brain aneurism.'

Again the DA nodded.

'Only when you show up you discover that empty bottle of pills right there, and when you have the residue tested you find it was Proloid. You know what that's for on account of you've taken it yourself. You also know that an overdose can cause a blood vessel to burst in the brain.'

'That's right, Sergeant. A couple of years ago I had it prescribed for an under-active thyroid.'

Quarrie looked evenly at him then. 'David Ferrie didn't kill himself and he didn't die of natural causes. He was murdered in the same way Anderson was. When you put those two deaths together you've got a direct link between your investigator and the man you indicted over the assassination of the president.'

Twenty-nine

Sitting back in his chair the district attorney pressed threads of tobacco into his pipe. 'A lot of information, Sergeant: you've given me much to think about.'

'I ain't done yet,' Quarrie said. 'Tomorrow is April 28 and I saw that date in Anderson's diary.' Again he indicated Ferrie's file. 'The president's assassination, you've made it clear you think Lee Oswald was there primarily to take the fall. Two bullets and two shooters from two different directions, it's why you're going after Shaw.'

Garrison nodded.

'I told you that Wiley robbed a gun store, right? He stole an M1C, that's a military-grade rifle, the kind a sniper might use.' Quarrie's expression was bleak. 'Whoever these people are, their business is killing people and you've re-opened a case they already closed.'

'Sergeant, what're you saying?'

'I'm saying there's a contract out on you, Mr Garrison. I think they plan to kill you, sir, and they plan to do it tomorrow.'

*

Franklin was on Canal Street when Quarrie drove back to the hotel. He saw him swing around the loop at the light and pull into a parking bay facing the way he had come. Standing in the doorway of Stein's Clothing, he wore a pair of Ray-Ban aviators and the leather pea coat, his gaze fixed as Quarrie strode under the arch into the hotel. Franklin remained where he was for a moment before stepping onto the sidewalk and considering the sky-blue station wagon. Turning again he went into the clothing store where a young man approached from the counter. 'Can I help you, sir?' he said.

'Sure.' Franklin pointed to the revolving hat stand next to the door.

*

Back in his room Quarrie was thinking about calling Pious to see if he'd been able to get hold of Dixie Wells yet, when somebody rapped on the door. He reached for his shoulder holster. 'Who is it?'

No answer from the walkway. He was on his feet with a pistol drawn. He called again and still there was no answer. He moved to the side of the door. Whoever his visitor was they knocked again, louder and more harshly this time.

Quarrie opened the door and saw Soulja Blue on the walkway. He wore gray pants over leather boots and a collarless Nehru jacket. He stared at Quarrie and Quarrie stared back at him. Neither of them spoke then Soulja glanced over his shoulder. When he turned again he worked his tongue over lips where a hint of spittle was building. 'Are you going to let me in or do I just stand here till they show up and shoot me?'

He made to come into the room but Quarrie held up his hand. 'I know you're packing,' he said. 'I want to see them, guns and knives.'

For a second Soulja stared at Quarrie then he opened his coat and slid an automatic from an inside pocket with his forefinger and thumb. Carefully he laid it on the bureau next to the door. Quarrie indicated with the barrel of his Blackhawk. 'Ankle,' he said. 'And don't be forgetting the knives.'

The big man dropped to one knee and rolled up his trouser leg where Quarrie could see the grips of a thirty-eight poking from his zippered boot. He tweaked that out and placed it on the bureau with the other gun then fetched a switchblade from his hip pocket.

'That it?' Quarrie said.

Soulja nodded.

Taking a step back Quarrie let him into the room. Holstering the Blackhawk he considered the array of weapons then he turned to Soulja. 'I find out you're holding out on me you'll know about it, I promise.'

Like a couple of fighting dogs they all but paced each other. Soulja reached for his pocket. 'Cigarettes,' he muttered and brought out a box of Sobranies. Multicolored tubes of tobacco; he selected one and placed it in the corner of his mouth. He slapped his pockets again then glanced around the room looking for a match. Quarrie tossed him his Zippo and Soulja lighted the cigarette with both hands cupped to the flame. 'They give you this in Korea?'

Quarrie nodded.

'I heard you were out there.' He blew smoke. 'Call you *John Q* back in Texas, don't they?' His lips parted in a half-smile that smacked of mockery. 'As in *John Q Public*, is it? Mean something that then, does it? Just regular folks are you?'

'I don't know. What do you think?'

Soulja rolled the cigarette between his fingers. 'Soon as they wrote your name in the newspaper the other day I knowed who-all you was. Had me a spell in Korea myself. Was over there when you wrote the president from where you were at in the hospital. Osaka, wasn't it? Japan, right? That brother they wanted to send to the firing squad. Wasn't that about how it was?'

'That's about how it was.'

'I don't remember his name.'

'Pious Noon,' Quarrie said. 'He was at your club on Governor Nicholls.'

Soulja twisted his mouth at the corners. 'That him outside with the vehicle?'

Quarrie nodded. 'Gigi told him all about you taking it to those girls you got on account of white boys stumping up gobs of cash. I get you over to Texas anytime soon, best you steer clear of him.'

Soulja sat down on the edge of the bed. 'So you know they killed Vernon,' he said. 'He talked to you and they beat him up pretty good then put a bullet in him.'

'Who did?' Quarrie said.

'The people you want to talk about.'

'So talk about them.'

The big man wagged his head. 'I ain't telling you any of what I know till we figure out what we got going on.'

'Soulja,' Quarrie said. 'What we got going on is this. Without me you're a dead man. It's why you're here. It's what you talked about with Vernon.'

Soulja inspected the end of his cigarette.

'Even if you live you're looking at kidnap and rape most

probably. That's fifteen to twenty and you won't be making parole.'

'I never raped anybody.' The big man shook his head. 'And I never kidnapped nobody neither, I just did what-all I was told.'

'Who was it told you?' Quarrie said.

'You think I'm some dumbfuck nigger going to spill my guts without cutting a deal?' He let a breath hiss between his teeth.

Quarrie sat down on the chair by the door. 'All right,' he said. 'Let's talk bottom line here. You picked up Claude Matthews from his house on Alabo Street and held him at your club. You beat him up and left him trussed like a turkey. That cab driver showed up to shoot him then you and Vernon took his body over to that apartment on Esplanade Avenue. While I was trying to figure a way out of that storeroom you were in the apartment. You were here in this room. Gigi will testify to it. You took her to your club and she saw Matthews before he was murdered.' Slowly he shook his head. 'Buddy, you're screwed everywhichway, but we both know it ain't going to come to a courthouse.' He was quiet for long enough to let his words sink in. 'I can protect you,' he said. 'I can do it here or I can ship you back to Texas, but I ain't doing anything till I know what you know, you understand? You screwed up and that blond guy's not big on forgiveness. It's why you're here and it's like I told Vernon, I'm your best chance of seeing out the day.' He looked hard at him then. 'So tell me who the blond guy is.'

Dragging on his cigarette Soulja blew smoke from the corner of his mouth. He got up off the bed and walked around to the other side where he flicked ash into the aluminum tray. 'You really think I'm going to tell you anything setting here in a hotel room?' He shook his head. 'What I know is all I got to play with and I ain't going to give it up till you get me out of town and I know they can't come get me.'

Resting forearms on his thighs Quarrie studied him. 'You've known Gigi a long time, haven't you?'

Soulja cocked one eyebrow. 'A while I guess, I knew her cousin a whole lot better.'

'Yeah, I heard what you did to him. So what did you do to Gigi?'

'I told you.' Soulja sucked again at his cigarette. 'I never did nothing to her 'cept bring her to Bourbon and Governor Nicholls.'

'And that blond sonofabitch, what about him?'

Soulja did not say anything.

'Who ordered you to come get her?'

'Mister, you don't need to ask me that. You know who it was already.'

Quarrie looked at him still. 'How did you know Colback was going to be here at the hotel? Did you talk to Pershing Gervais?'

'I don't know nothing about Colback and I ain't ever spoke to Pershing Gervais.'

'But you know who he is?'

'Sure, I know who he is. He's the DA's chief investigator.'

'What about De La Martin?'

'Homicide, 3rd Precinct.'

'All right,' Quarrie said. 'Now you're going to tell me the blond guy's name. Who is he? Where can I find him?'

Soulja shook his head. 'I ain't telling you his name. Not here, not right now. I done told you that already.'

Quarrie looked at him for a moment longer then reached

out and opened the door. He let it swing wide so the humid air filtered in. 'Have it your way,' he said. 'I got no jurisdiction in this town so I can't arrest you. Best you take your chances.'

The big man stayed where he was. The light in his eyes had hardened and sweat bubbled on his scalp.

'You want me to close the door? Figure maybe you'll talk to me?'

Soulja stared across the courtyard to the rooms on the other side.

'Do that and you might just stay alive long enough to get quit of this city.'

Soulja stared at the floor.

'The blond-haired guy – who is he?'

Lips pursed, Soulja peered at him.

'His name, Soulja, or this ain't going to work.'

'Franklin.'

'Franklin, right, now we're getting somewhere. So how long have you known him?'

Soulja lifted his shoulders. 'Couple of years I guess.'

'When was the first time you saw him?'

Soulja thought about that. ''63. Saw him driving a cab that summer and he showed up at the club.'

Taking another cigarette from his pack he rolled it against his palm. He looked at Quarrie across the room and Quarrie peered into eyes that were empty and blank. 'So who is he? Tell me who I'm dealing with.'

Soulja put the unlit cigarette back in his pack. 'First time he come to the club was with a couple of buddies and they took it to the chicks pretty good. After that Franklin started showing up on his own, then one night this older guy comes in. The way he walked, the way he carried himself, it was like he owned the joint. He showed up in the cab with Franklin driving, only Franklin he didn't come in. That old man had him a walking cane with a snake's head handle and the one chick he was with that night . . .' He let air usher from his cheeks. 'He beat up on her so bad he punched holes in her with that thing.'

'You're talking about Rosslyn Tobie.'

Soulja peered at him. 'I ain't saying any more till I'm out of here. You know what a man like that'd do if he caught me talking to you? Big as I am, big and tough and mean, he'd strip me naked and string me up with a fire to my balls just to hear me scream. It might be you're a cop and all but you don't know who you're fucking with.'

'So tell me about him, Soulja.'

'I will. I'll tell you it all when the time comes but I ain't doing it here and I ain't doing it now, you dig?' He pointed a finger at Quarrie. 'You told me you were my best chance of seeing out the day so let's see if you're as good as you think.'

Quarrie held his gaze. 'Where do I find Franklin? You can keep the rest for now, but I need to know where that cab driver lives.'

Soulja took the cigarette from his pack again and let smoke creep from his nostrils. He didn't say anything. He just stared at Quarrie and Quarrie looked back at him. 'Where do I find him?' he said. 'Tell me and I'll pick up the phone and you'll be protected. Don't and I kick you out right now and you take your chance on the street.'

Soulja took another pull at the cigarette. 'Washington Avenue,' he said. 'Mostly it's houses over that way but there's a brick-built block, he lives in one of the apartments.'

Quarrie picked up the phone and asked Yvonne for an outside line. He dialled the number with his gaze fixed on Soulja Blue.

'District Attorney's office?' a woman's voice said.

'Jim Garrison, please: tell him it's Ranger Sergeant Quarrie.'

Soulja stared. 'The district attorney, are you kidding? I thought you were getting me out of here.'

Quarrie placed his hand over the mouthpiece. 'You want protection in New Orleans? Tell me a better place.'

Garrison came on the line and Quarrie lifted an index finger to keep Soulja quiet.

'What can I do for you, Sergeant?'

'I've got somebody here you're going to want to talk to.'

'Who is it?'

'I can't tell you that on the phone but they have information and you will want to talk to them, trust me.'

'Where are you? I'll send a vehicle.'

'No, sir: we'll make our own way. Is Gervais back from Baton Rouge?'

'Yes, he is. I talked to him and he told me that when he went down to the garage you weren't there. He said he drove to Lafayette Square but could find no evidence to back up anything you said.'

'All right, Mr Garrison: I want words with him. We'll come in the same way I did before.' Quarrie hung up the phone and Soulja squinted at him.

'We're going to talk to Pershing Gervais?'

'I am. You ain't. You'll be talking to Garrison.'

Picking up the phone a second time Quarrie called Colback's office. 'Lieutenant,' he said when he came on the line.

'I got somebody with me who needs protection and I want to know where to bring them.'

'Who is it, what're you talking about?'

'I'm talking about somebody who needs protecting. Where do I bring them?'

'Right now . . .' Colback seemed to deliberate. 'Who is it?'

'Not on the phone. Take my word on this. They got information about what's going on. It has to be somewhere secure.'

'All right, you better bring them here.'

'No, sir, I'm not going to do that; your office is too close to Lafayette Square.'

Colback was silent for a moment. 'I tell you what, bring them to my house. Camp Street, Quarrie, you know where it is.'

Hanging up the phone again Quarrie crossed to the window and Soulja looked at him with a puzzled expression. 'The DA *and* Lieutenant Colback, what's up with that?'

'Don't worry about it,' Quarrie said. 'Your time working for Franklin, did you come across a cop called Anderson?'

Soulja shook his head.

'It was his apartment you searched with Vernon. The 28th, what was that about?'

'I don't know. Franklin never said.'

'But he told you to look out for anything to do with that date?'

Soulja nodded.

'Tomorrow Garrison is holding a press conference on the steps of City Hall. Did Franklin talk about that?'

Soulja shook his head.

Quarrie strapped on his shoulder holsters then slipped his

arms through the sleeves of his jacket. Placing Soulja's weapons in the nightstand drawer he locked it and took the key. Together they went down to the courtyard and he told the big man to wait while he went out to the sidewalk. He gazed across the road to the American Bank building but there was no sign of Franklin's cab. He studied the buildings beyond the Savings & Loan, the stores and shop fronts and the people clogging the sidewalk. Finally he beckoned Soulja Blue and they walked down to the pedestrian light.

*

On the other side of the road Franklin was hidden by a crowd of tourists. He had the brim of the trilby he'd bought pulled low and the pea coat secured with one button. Collar up, he had his right hand inside the coat and the sleeve tucked into the pocket.

*

'So you called the DA and Colback both. Which is it, where we going?' A film of perspiration glistened on Soulja's forehead as they waited for the light. Quarrie nodded to where the sign for the A&G diner was illuminated further up Canal Street.

'Neither,' he said. 'I figure we'll set tight and see who shows.' The WALK sign flipped and the collective throng stepped off the sidewalk from both sides of the road. The sound of traffic on St Charles was deafening. As they got halfway across a truck driver slapped a hand to his horn. Quarrie looked back the way they had come to see if anyone was following.

'Soulja,' he said. It was as far as he got because the big man was on his knees. Panic in his eyes, he was clutching his chest. Quarrie saw blood pulse from between his fingers. He spun around to face the way they had come but all he could see were the backs of a dozen people making for the sidewalk. Turning again he stared at the open windows where office blinds flapped in the breeze.

Pistol drawn, he dashed across the road keeping his eyes on those windows but he could see no hint of a gun barrel, no telltale flash of light. The people in front had not witnessed what happened and those who came behind walked around the fallen man at first. Then someone started to scream. Quarrie made it to the opposing sidewalk with people parting before him. Some were shouting, some pointing at the gun he was holding. He looked back to where a crowd had gathered and the traffic backed up the length of Canal Street. Holstering his gun he cut south to St Charles, hopped a trolley car and sat in a seat at the back where the sign for 'Coloreds' still showed.

Thirty

When he got to Camp Street the lieutenant was waiting at the front door. An unmarked Ford parked in the driveway, no sign of the Cadillac Quarrie had seen before.

'What's going on?' Colback peered up and down the street. 'You said you had somebody with you.'

Quarrie walked up the path and the lieutenant stepped aside. Crossing the hallway he went through to the living room and peered out the window.

'What is it?' Colback said. 'Who's out there? What's going on?'

Quarrie was watching the street. 'I was in my room just now when that shaven-headed fuck from Governor Nicholls shows up at my door. The cab driver's name is Franklin, Lieutenant. He's got an apartment on Washington Avenue.'

'Whoa there a minute, hold up.' Brows knit, Colback stared. 'You talked to Soulja Blue. Where is he now?'

'He's lying on Canal Street with a bullet in his chest.' Stepping away from the window Quarrie stared past Colback into the hall. 'All I got was the cab driver's name and an address. We need a warrant. We need to go search his apartment.'

'Just hold on a second. You're telling me that black guy from the club's been murdered?'

'Yes, I am. They shot him as we crossed at the light.'

'You were bringing him here?'

Quarrie nodded. 'He had it all. He knew everything about everybody.'

'What about tomorrow? Did he talk about that?'

'He didn't say anything I don't already know. He knew the date was important but he didn't know why. The target is Jim Garrison, Lieutenant. He's supposed to be talking to the press on the steps of City Hall.'

Colback wrinkled his eyes. 'Why would they want to kill Garrison?'

'On account of Clay Shaw. Back in February he's indicted for conspiracy and they're talking to David Ferrie, the pilot that flew him wherever he wanted to go. Ferrie is saying to anyone who'll listen how he's in fear for his life then he ups and dies.'

'His death was natural; I saw the DP report myself.'

'It wasn't natural,' Quarrie said. 'He died of a Proloid overdose same as Trace Anderson.'

Breaking off for a moment he stared at the floor. 'There's something else you need to know. Yesterday after you told me Dean Andrews worked in that building we had us a conversation. Something I saw in Garrison's office, a note he'd made in one of the files.' Quarrie gestured. 'Right after Kennedy was shot Clay Shaw called Andrews using the alias "Bertrand" and asked him to represent Lee Oswald. The next day Andrews took another call telling him he wouldn't be needed after all.'

'You mean another call from Shaw?'

Quarrie shook his head. 'That's what Garrison thinks, but according to Andrews it wasn't Shaw on the phone, it was Rosslyn Tobie.'

Colback sat down heavily.

'That's right, Lieutenant. Andrews told me that old man's

been trying to tie him to his law firm for a while.'

Colback was staring into space.

'We need to get hold of Pershing Gervais. We need to ask him about Earl Moore.'

'I tried talking to him this morning. If he's in New Orleans he isn't taking my calls.'

'He's here all right,' Quarrie said. 'Before I called you just now I spoke to Garrison and told him the same thing I said to you.'

'And the next thing you know that black guy's dead and you're putting it down to Gervais?'

'Who the hell else could it be? Garrison would've told him I'd called and he's the only one that knew I'd be in the parking garage.' He paused for a moment then. 'We need to talk to him and we need that warrant for Franklin's place, but there's something else I think we ought to take care of first.'

'What's that?'

'We need to pay Earl Moore's widow a visit.'

'Why would we want to do that?'

'Because her husband was in Anderson's apartment before I ever got there and all I found was the photograph. I think he found something else, notes maybe or a file, whatever Anderson had been working on. It's not in his office so I figure he must've taken it home.'

Using Colback's car they drove the causeway across Lake Pontchartrain heading for the north shore. From there it was the freeway for a few miles before they turned west on the Old Spanish Trail. They located the house in a small sub-division close to an elementary school. Two stories, it was built in a chalet style and when they pulled up outside the sprinkler system was going, though the lawn looked as if it could do with the mower rather than any more moisture right now.

Together they walked up the driveway and Mrs Moore answered the door wearing a sleeveless dress that reached just above the knees. Her hair was cut to shoulder length and fixed with a band that matched the dress.

'Mrs Moore,' Quarrie said. 'I am sorry to disturb you, mam, but my name's Quarrie and this is Lieutenant Colback. I believe Mr Garrison gave you a call.'

She hugged herself as if she was cold. 'Yes, he did, and Mr Gervais came over about an hour ago.'

'He did?' Quarrie glanced briefly at Colback.

'Uh-huh. He told me he'd been down to where my husband was supposed to have been shot but couldn't find anything at all. I told him it had to be some sick hoax because someone from the DA's office called to tell me Earl had gone out of town.'

'Someone from the DA's office,' Quarrie peered at her. 'Was it a man or a woman?'

'A man, he didn't tell me his name.'

'Mam,' he said, 'I have to tell you, it was me who called Mr Gervais about your husband in the first place. I was there when he was shot. I'm the one who saw him fall.'

Tears breaking from her eyes, she shook her head. 'But somebody phoned me. Somebody called from the DA's office and told me he had to go out of town.'

Quarrie exchanged another glance with Colback. 'When Mr Gervais was here did he say anything else? Anything about what your husband was working on maybe, any paperwork, stuff like that?'

'No, he never said anything about any paperwork. He told me what'd happened and said he was looking into it. He wanted to see Earl's study but I wouldn't let him, not without talking to Earl.'

Again Quarrie looked at Colback.

'That's his private space,' Mrs Moore went on. 'He's been studying law, night classes at Tulane. He's tired of being a cop and can't see much future in it. Mr Garrison encouraged him to try for the bar.'

Quarrie gazed beyond her the length of the hall. 'Mrs Moore,' he said. 'This is really important. I need you to let us into your husband's study.'

She shook her head. 'I can't do that. Not without speaking to Earl.'

Taking her hands in his now Colback spoke to her firmly. 'He's dead, mam. That's the truth, I'm afraid. Now, we have to catch the men who killed him and to do that we need your help.'

Fresh tears spilled onto the young woman's cheeks. Her shoulders shook with sobs but she didn't make any sound. Finally she seemed to accept what they were telling her and led them to a room at the back of the house.

A somber little space, the walls were painted a drab-colored green. Saints memorabilia adorned the walls as well as a couple of ragged-looking university pennants from Tulane. Mrs Moore left them alone and Quarrie closed the door.

'So what're we looking for?' Colback said.

'Papers; notes or files maybe, whatever it was that Moore found and Gervais wanted.' Quarrie glanced at him. 'You heard what she said, Lieutenant, no sooner is Soulja Blue shot dead than he shows up over here.'

Colback nodded. 'You said earlier that Garrison knew nothing about Moore being killed even though you spoke to Gervais?'

'That's right.'

Colback made a face. 'Maybe that's not so suspicious. Gervais is the chief investigator after all: he called me to check it out and he's not going to report everything back to his boss, at least not till he's sure.'

Quarrie had the bottom drawer of the file cabinet open where two legal text books were lying on top of each other. He lifted them out to reveal the gray metal panel that was the bottom of the drawer. For a moment he studied it, something not quite right, the color perhaps. Brushing his fingertips over the surface he discovered it wasn't metal but balsa wood. He tapped and it yielded a hollow sound. A false bottom with space underneath, it concealed a paper file similar to the ones he had seen in the DA's office. Carefully he lifted it out and inside was a large white envelope containing half a dozen photographs.

Immediately he recognized the camelback house in the 7th Ward: a photo taken on the stoop where Moore and Gigi were hooked in an embrace. The next was similar and the next again. Flicking through those he came to a couple of images taken through the window.

'Well,' he said softly, 'this ain't what Moore picked up from Anderson's apartment, it's what Gervais had on Moore.' He passed the photos to the lieutenant. 'A white police officer with a wife and kids caught on film with a black nightclub singer. That would end his marriage and screw up his career.'

'Blackmail,' Colback said. 'Why would Gervais do that? What's it matter to him if Moore is fooling around with a colored girl?'

Quarrie thought about that. 'I think it mattered a whole lot.' He turned the envelope over in his hands. 'Pershing Gervais might be Garrison's chief investigator, but because of what happened with the crime commission he's got no access to the files they're putting together on Shaw. I believe the people he's working for need that access so they made sure he got it through Moore.'

He fell silent for a moment then he said, 'I told you Anderson was ex NOPD. Did you get around to checking him out?'

Colback nodded. 'Nothing untoward in his background, he only left the job a few months back.'

'Always had a hankering to be a writer then, did he?'

'I don't know. I never spoke to him.'

'What'd he do, prowl car, plain clothes, what?'

'He was a detective working the Irish Channel: did a lot of surveillance work from what I can gather.'

Quarrie flicked through the photographs again. 'Back in Texas the ME told me he figured Anderson for thirty years old. Seven years to make detective, he does all that work then ups and quits to become a writer. Does that make any sense to you?'

Colback shrugged. 'I guess it depends on what he planned on writing.'

'You mean he came across a story while he was still in the job?' Quarrie squinted at him. 'It's what I've been thinking, how he found something that could make him a whole bunch of money only he couldn't write it if he was a serving cop?'

He returned his attention to the photographs. 'I told Garrison I think Anderson saw that photo printed in some magazine somewhere and recognized the blond-haired guy. I think he got hold of an original and figured he was onto something that could either make him a lot of money or blow sky-high.' Looking over at Colback he gestured. 'I think he used his position as a detective to do some digging then put together some kind of dossier. The way this has played out he knew if he wanted to take it further he had to quit the job. You see what I'm saying, Lieutenant? Anderson figured he was on to something big enough that he'd give up a career, but he wasn't going to go it alone. That's why he wanted to speak to the district attorney. It wasn't Moore he called or Gervais; it was Garrison he was trying to get a-hold of. He knew what they were working on and called the office, only his luck was out because it was Moore who answered the phone. Moore spoke to Gervais and Gervais told him to say nothing to Garrison then he called our blond-haired boy. By the time Anderson is back on the phone they've set things up for Wichita Falls.'

Colback was looking puzzled. 'Why there, though? All the way over in Texas, that doesn't make any sense.'

Quarrie looked squarely at him. 'Sure it does. Wiley was already there. They had him rob a gun store to get the M1C he was going to use to shoot Jim Garrison. This thing with Anderson blew up around the same time so they figure they'd kill two birds with one stone.' He paused for a moment then. 'You know what though, maybe there's more to it than that. Wichita Falls is where they were going to re-try Jack Ruby. He spent last year telling the press he wasn't alone in shooting Oswald and that trial was supposed to take place back in January.' He gestured to Colback. 'Only he died in December, didn't he. You see what I'm saying, Lieutenant? If Anderson thought he was hooking up with Garrison what would add more gravitas than a meeting in Wichita Falls?'

He slipped the pictures back inside the envelope and laid it on the desk. 'I told you what Andrews said about Rosslyn Tobie.'

Colback nodded.

'Well, that ain't all. Before he was killed, Soulja Blue got as far as telling me about this old guy who came by that club on Bourbon and Governor Nicholls. If the girl he was with didn't do exactly what he wanted he'd beat her with the handle of his walking cane.'

Colback snorted. 'And you believe him, a man like that? He was trying to stay out of jail.'

'You're forgetting Nana Matisse. Twenty years without speaking to her then this kicks off and Tobie's all over that apartment on Orleans Street.'

'That doesn't mean anything,' Colback said. 'So he likes black women, so do a lot of white men. You're talking about one of the most respected attorneys in New Orleans. If you want me to go after him I'm going to need a whole lot more than the word of some pimp from Governor Nicholls.'

'Sure you are,' Quarrie said. 'There has to be something else and that's why Moore was in Anderson's apartment. But whatever it was he found, it ain't here and it ain't in his desk so where else could he have hidden it?'

He cast an eye across the bookshelves and memorabilia, the university pennants. Opening the study door he called Mrs Moore and a moment later she appeared clutching a box of Kleenex.

'We're done here, mam,' Quarrie said. 'Thank you for letting us in, I know that was difficult for you. I got a question though, before we leave out.' He nodded to the pennants. 'Those night classes you were talking about. Did your husband have a college locker?'

Thirty-one

Back in New Orleans they drove to the Tulane University campus opposite Audubon Park. Quarrie had the locker key Moore's wife had given them and they crossed to Gibson Hall. A gothic-looking gray-stone building, they located the locker in a corridor on the second floor.

When he unlocked the door Quarrie found a pile of text books and some envelopes as well as a couple of yellow legal pads still bound with cellophane. Right at the back was a paper file and he was about to reach for it when Colback placed a hand on his arm.

'Wait up,' he said. 'This is my call now, not yours.'

Quarrie looked round and Colback indicated the file. 'If what's in there is anything like you've been saying then it could be evidence and you have no jurisdiction. Touch it and it's inadmissible. I want you to go ahead and leave this to me.'

For a moment Quarrie just looked at him. Then he stepped back and Colback plucked the file from the locker as a group of students came clattering through the fire doors.

They walked back to the car and Colback handed Quarrie the keys. 'You drive,' he said. 'I need to take a look at what we've got here, and while we're at it let's go see if Gervais is home.' They got in and Colback directed him towards the river while he flipped through the file.

'So what is it?' Quarrie looked sideways as he worked the wheel.

'Nothing I can figure.' Colback had lines cut deep in his brow. 'If you're right and Moore did have something on these guys, this can't be it. It's just a bunch of notes about copperheads and Lincoln in the civil war.' Reaching over to the backseat he grabbed his briefcase. 'History,' he muttered, stuffing the file inside. 'I guess that's how the law's written. The way things play out down the years. There's nothing in that file but historical notes, it must've been for some essay.'

Quarrie glanced over the seat. 'You're telling me there're no names back there, no phone numbers? No mention of April 28?'

Colback shook his head. 'You can look for yourself when we get back to my place; it's just notes for an essay is all.'

They drove to Pershing Gervais's single-story clapboard property a couple of blocks off Tchoupitoulas Street, but there was no car parked in the driveway and nobody answered when they knocked on the door.

When they got back to Camp Street the lieutenant told Quarrie to pour a couple of drinks while he went through to his study to put word out that Gervais was wanted for questioning. After he got off the phone he came through with his briefcase and took out the file. Quarrie considered the papers and Colback was right, it was page after page of historical notes with no apparent sequence to them. There was one thing, though, that caught his eye: the words *Adapt or Die* printed under a Xeroxed image of a crudely drawn snake that had shed its skin. Below the picture he read *The Order of the Sons of Liberty*.

'You see this?' he said, showing the page to Colback. 'I found the words *Adapt or Die* on an envelope in Anderson's apartment. Not only that, he wrote *Liberty* on a piece of notepaper I found in his room at the Roosevelt Hotel.'

'So?'

'So, if this is just something Moore was working on, that's some kind of coincidence, isn't it?'

Casting an eye across the rest of the notes he read aloud. '*The Order* was made up of a group of influential landowners out of Ohio, Missouri and Illinois; men with holdings in Kentucky and West Virginia during the civil war. Known colloquially as "Peace Democrats", they formed *The Order of the Sons of Liberty* from a group called the *Knights of the Golden Circle* who'd been outlawed a few years before. That group was banned after they tried to form a confederation of slave states south of the Mason-Dixon Line. Members of the new order swore an oath of allegiance, but the government got wind of who they were and hunted them down. A few were tried and sentenced to hang only for their sentences to be commuted to life. In the end Lincoln got involved and they were banished behind confederate lines.' Again he glanced at Colback. 'According to this the main man was some guy called James Cutler. Does that mean anything to you?'

The lieutenant shook his head.

'Disappeared in 1865 a week after the *Columbus Courier* accused him of being involved in the plot to kill Lincoln.'

'I never heard of him,' Colback said. 'Quarrie, there's nothing in those papers that tells us anything at all.'

Quarrie worked a hand through his hair. 'There has to be more than this. Anderson had the 28th marked in his diary so he had to know something was going down.' Falling silent he peered across the room at Colback.

'What?' the lieutenant said. 'Why're you looking like that? You think I'm holding out on you?' He jabbed a finger towards the door. 'You want to go search my study, it's right across the hall.'

They sat in silence after that with nothing but the sound of the clock ticking on the wall.

'So what do you want to do about tomorrow?'

Colback lifted his hands. 'I don't see there's anything we can do. If you're right about any of what you've been saying then it's Garrison they're after and you already gave him the heads up. We've got prowl cars parked outside his house tonight and he cancelled the press conference at City Hall.' A little wearily he got to his feet and Quarrie followed him through to his study. He watched as Colback locked the notes in his safe.

'A precaution,' the lieutenant said. 'You never know we might be wrong and the whole thing's in code or something. Tomorrow I'll bring it over to Loyola Avenue and have the Feds take a look just in case.'

'All right,' Quarrie said. 'What about Franklin?'

'What about him?'

'We need a warrant to search his apartment.'

Colback looked at his watch. 'It's too late now. That'll have to wait till the morning.'

Back in his hotel room Quarrie wasn't sure he could wait till morning. He remembered what Nana had said about that itch between her shoulder blades and he was conscious of it himself now. The phone rang on the nightstand beside the bed and he stared for a moment before picking up.

'Van Hanigan here, John Q.'

'Captain, what's going on?'

'After the call I just took, that's what I was going to ask you.'

'Tomorrow,' Quarrie said, 'I'm pretty sure this outfit planned to assassinate Jim Garrison.'

'The district attorney: why would they want to do that?'

Quarrie stared at the bathroom door. 'It ain't something I want to talk about on the phone, but the NOPD's got a bunch of prowl cars making sweeps and a uniform guarding his door.'

'And this is all to do with that photograph you discovered.'

'Yes, sir, it is.'

He heard Van Hanigan sigh. 'John Q, I had a phone call just now from a feller called Wells down at the *Fort Worth Star*. He was trying to get a-hold of you.'

'What did he say?'

The captain's tone was dour. 'Those two cops with the shotguns are Dallas PD. The photo was taken the day Oswald shot President Kennedy. A freight train was pulling out of the yard back of the railroad overpass at the bottom of Elm Street right where the motorcade was supposed to come through. Only it was stopped by the switchman and a bunch of hobos hauled off.'

'Those two guys were on a train?' Quarrie said. 'They don't look like hobos to me.'

'No, they don't.'

'So what happened to them?'

'As far as I've been able to find out they were taken to the Dallas County sheriff's office. But no mug shots were taken, no fingerprints or statements and nobody from Homicide showed.'

When he put down the phone Quarrie drove to Chartres

Street and the crayfish bar where he found De La Martin sitting pretty much where he'd been two nights before. 'Soulja Blue,' Quarrie said. 'Canal Street is your turf, right?'

De La Martin looked a little weary. 'Don't tell me, you were the last person to see him alive.'

'Him and his buddy Vernon, Claude Matthews and what-all else went down.'

'So what is it you want from me?'

'I've got an address for our blond-haired boy. Washington Avenue, Detective, I want you to go get a search warrant.'

'Courthouse is closed. I can't do that, not till tomorrow.'

'That's what Colback just told me.' Quarrie laid a hand on De La Martin's arm. 'But I feel like I'm getting to know you some and I'm guessing there's a district judge you can call.'

'Supposing there was – why would I want to do that?'

'Because that pimp told me stuff about Rosslyn Tobie the lieutenant doesn't want to believe.'

'So?'

'So, I remembered what you said, Detective. That cab and all, Tobie's the only other fare you've seen.'

De La Martin sipped his drink. 'This apartment, what do you figure we'll find?'

'I'm not sure. But I think Moore had information. He was at Esplanade before anybody else and I can't believe that photo was all that Anderson had.'

'And now you think Franklin's gotten hold of that information, how would he have done that?'

'They shot Moore when they thought he was meeting Gigi. It's possible he had it on him when they took his body from La-fayette Square.'

De La Martin nodded. 'All right,' he said. 'I can buy that. Supposing I *was* prepared to get a warrant, why won't it wait till morning?'

'Because tomorrow is April 28 and I got an itch between my shoulder blades I just can't seem to get quit of.'

By the time De La Martin parked his car outside the darkened building it was after midnight. On the dashboard in front of him he had the paperwork from a judge who lived in Metairie. With a little breeze in the stagnant air, they got out of the car and De La Martin opened the trunk. He took out a fire axe he'd brought from the station house and tossed it to Quarrie. Then he closed the trunk and they made their way to the entrance. De La Martin pressed a stubby finger to the buzzer of an apartment on the same floor. He held it there until they heard a crackling sound and a man's voice came over the intercom. 'All right, all right, it's late already. What do you want?'

'NOPD,' De La Martin said. 'I need for you to open the door.'

Inside, they took the elevator to the second floor and stopped outside Franklin's door. 'All what you been telling me,' De La Martin said. 'It's a fact most people in this town think the DA's just a politician on the make.'

'Maybe they'll think different when he's done with Shaw.'

The detective laughed. 'Nothing's going to happen to Shaw. I hear they're saying if it goes to trial it'll be held in Texas but that won't make any difference. It won't matter what kind of evidence Garrison shows up with or how long jury selection takes. He ain't going to get a conviction, not if we're talking old-world southern business and old world southern law.'

Quarrie rapped on the door but there was no answer so he

lifted the axe. He brought it down on the lock and the door was open. They stepped into a hallway with a living room and kitchen on their right and a bedroom at the far end. A king-size bed and nightstand stood against one wall with a chest of drawers on the other side. Switching on the lamp Quarrie opened the closet and was confronted by a rail of sport jackets, business suits and slacks. There was a rack of shoes on the floor and a set of drawers that housed a selection of leather belts and underwear as well as two brand new, unopened shirts.

Finding nothing in the bedroom they went through the living room where the windows overlooked the street. In one corner was a color TV with a remote-control box on top. A metal coffee table stood between it and four stool-like wooden chairs. Other than that there was a chrome bureau against the wall set with ice bucket and glasses, but that was all.

They searched the bedroom again and the kitchen and bathroom but didn't come up with anything. De La Martin threw a glance at Quarrie where he stood in the hallway with his hands in his pockets and his brows fixed in a frown. 'So what now?' he said. 'There isn't anything here.'

Quarrie did not reply. He went back to the bedroom for a third time and opened the closet door.

'Maybe it's been destroyed,' De La Martin said. 'Or maybe there wasn't anything other than what you already found.'

Quarrie shook his head. 'There was. There had to be. I told you what I read in that file.' He fell silent, staring at the clothes in the closet and then he closed the door.

'Maybe they don't have it,' he muttered. 'Maybe they don't know about Moore being in the apartment at all.' He turned to the bed and nightstand, the chest of drawers. He thought about the night classes Moore's wife had spoken about and the locker at Tulane. He thought about the bottle of meds, the affair with Gigi. Then all at once it dawned.

*

As they came out of the building Franklin waited in the shadows cast by the parking-lot wall. He saw Quarrie and the overweight detective make their way to the Ford. When they were gone he went inside the building and took the elevator to the second floor. In the hallway he studied the smashed lock on his door. His face expressionless he heard the neighbor step into the corridor behind him but did not look round. He waited until that door was closed again then he went into his apartment and stood in the silence of the hall. He changed his clothes and went through to the living room where he picked up the phone. 'He was here with De La Martin,' he said when the call was answered.

'All right,' Tobie replied. 'If everything is good to go, it's time you hit the road.'

*

When they got to North Rocheblave Street De La Martin parked outside Gigi's house. Quarrie got out of the car, went up the steps and opened the front door. Switching on the light he stood for a moment and considered the living room and kitchen. Then he left De La Martin to check downstairs while he went up to the bedroom. Standing in the middle of the floor he regarded the photo of Gigi and Nana on the dressing table. For a moment he thought about everything that old lady had told him then he went through the drawers. Nothing but Gigi's clothes; he checked the nightstand then turned his attention to the closet. Two hanging rails sitting crosswise, there was a space for her shoes as well as a few shallow drawers that contained underwear and nylons in unopened packages. The bottom drawer was home to a file of papers. He went through them and found nothing but bank statements and bills from the power company.

He was at the door to the landing again when he paused. The closet was built into the wall but he noticed the hint of a gap at the top where it didn't meet snugly with the ceiling.

'You find anything, Texas?' De La Martin's voice lifted from the bottom of the stairs.

Quarrie did not reply. Grabbing the dressing table stool he climbed up so his head was level with the ceiling but it was too dark to see if there was anything hidden back there. He heard the detective on the stairs then he was at the bedroom door. 'Got something, do you?' De La Martin said.

Quarrie was fumbling in a pocket for his Zippo. 'Can't see yet, the overhead light ain't bright enough.' Locating the lighter he flipped the top, rolled the wheel and held the flame to the gap between the ceiling and the top of the closet wall.

A blue paper file so thin he almost didn't see it. Scraping it clear he got down off the stool and flipped the opening page. He stared at a Xeroxed image of Wiley and Henderson getting into the Oldsmobile Super 88 he had pursued back in Texas. Beneath that was a copy of Wiley's school record, together with a commentary on his level of anti-social behavior and how his mother had run out on him and his two younger brothers before he was ten years old. His alcoholic father had been found dead in their trailer house the day Wiley turned seventeen. He had spent twelve years in the army where he had numerous run-ins with officers. There were medical reports noting what could only be described as sociopathic behavior spawned from an 'innate hatred' of black people. At the bottom of the page Quarrie spied a comment from the waitress he had spoken to at the Deacon's Mount Dairy-Ette.

As he read what she said he was aware of the hairs on the back of his neck. Catching the expression in his eyes De La Martin stared. 'You OK there? Color of your face right now I figure I should check for a pulse.'

Quarrie's mouth was dry. 'D-Lay,' he said, 'the DA told me that at least two people shot Kennedy and if Oswald was one of them he was there just to take the fall.'

'Yeah, that's what he's been shouting now for a while.'

'I told you Wiley stole an M1C back in Texas?' Tugging his wallet from his back pocket he pulled out the faded slip of paper where the word *Jacinto* was scrawled. 'Well, he never was the shooter. This ain't Dallas and it's not Garrison they're after at all.'

Downstairs in the living room he picked up the phone. When the operator came on the line he told her to connect him with the jailhouse in Wichita Falls. As he waited he glanced at De La Martin who was looking pretty confused. The connection was made and a man's voice sounded in Quarrie's ear.

'Sheriff's department,' he said.

'Who is that?' Quarrie asked.

'Deputy Olson.'

'Deputy, this is Sergeant Quarrie out of Company C. Are you in the jailhouse or is that Sam Dayton's phone?'

'No, sir, it's the jailhouse, graveyard shift till dawn.'

'Scott Henderson. Did they ship him back to Ferguson yet?'

'No, they didn't. An attorney's been in to see him but he's still not been arraigned.'

'Listen,' Quarrie said. 'I need for you to bring him to the phone.'

'I can't do that. I'm on my own here and I can't let a prisoner out of a cell, not with no one else around. It's against the rules.'

'Sure you can. He's my prisoner so tell him if he gives you any trouble I'll make certain he gets the chair.'

'I don't know. Really, I'm not sure.'

'Do as I tell you, Deputy. Go bring Henderson to the phone.'

He waited almost five minutes before he heard the scraping sound of someone picking up the receiver. 'That you, Scott?' he said.

'Yes, sir.'

'Did the jailer tell you what was going to happen if you gave him any trouble?'

'John Q, I am not going to give him any trouble.'

'So listen, the day you ran into me I want to know exactly what happened in the gun store.'

'What do you mean?'

'I mean that M1C, the rifle Wiley told you he was after. What did he do with it?'

'Do with it?' Henderson sounded confused. 'He stole it. You know he did.'

'I'm asking what he did with it after he took it down from where it was hanging on the wall.'

'He stuffed it into the duffel.'

'Is that all?'

'Sure.'

'Nothing else?'

'No, sir. No, wait a minute; I think he might've racked it. Is that what you mean? Yeah, he did that, checked the action was working and dry-fired.'

'All right,' Quarrie said. 'There's something else I need to know. The Dairy-Ette, before you robbed the store you were in there and an older waitress served you. Do you remember her?'

'Sure I do, it was her at the window. After Wiley pistol whipped the old man it was that waitress who ran for the law.'

Quarrie was staring at Wiley's file. 'After it was over with she told a reporter that she didn't like Wiley from the get-go on account of how he was cussing in front of the customers. "*Sonofabitch don't want to fight for his country then he won't be fighting at all.*" What was all that about?'

'I don't know.'

'Sure you do, Scotty. Think.'

'Jeeze, you got me now. I don't know, John Q.' Henderson was silent for a moment. 'No, hold on, wait a minute. Wiley was watching some interview on TV about the army and Cassius Clay.'

Thirty-two

By the time Quarrie got to Houston it was mid-morning and the turning onto San Jacinto was blocked by hundreds of black people carrying banners and placards. Pulling over in the 'Do Not Park' zone he climbed from the car and flashed his badge at a uniformed cop.

*

In the hotel room across the street Franklin crouched on his haunches wearing a bellhop's uniform under a dust-colored raincoat. He wore a pair of tight-fitting leather gloves and he bent to the M1C. The barrel resting against the sill of the open window, he had his finger in the trigger guard and his eye to the scope. He focused on the entrance to the building where the people were deepest, but there was no sign of the doors opening. Panning across the gathering he spotted the pale blue station wagon as it came to a stop at the junction with Capitol Street. He saw Quarrie get out and watched as he started towards the hotel.

'So much for your plans, old man,' he murmured. 'The boxer is late and the Texas Ranger early.'

*

Quarrie peered across Capitol Street to where the melee was deepest on the lawns out front of the ornate-looking building that housed the Military Entrance Processing Station. He ducked between the banks of protestors and uniformed cops and made it to the opposing sidewalk. He looked up at the hotel where a stone balustrade formed the lip of a balcony that straddled eight arches fronting the sidewalk. The balcony was wide enough to walk on; it was wide enough for someone to kneel down with a rifle if they had a mind. With the day as hot as it already was, every window was open and blood-colored drapes flapped like flamingo wings in the breeze. A clock carved into the stone facade dominated the street and Quarrie stared at the time. Then he fixed his gaze on the Processing Station where Muhammad Ali was refusing to join the army.

With no sign of any FBI agent yet, he went into the hotel and told the clerk he was the Ranger who had called in the early hours. The man confirmed that the room had been booked via a money order they received in the mail. He said it was on the second floor facing across the street and a bellhop had just gone up to check it had been cleaned.

Quarrie dashed up the stairs. Nobody in the carpeted hallway, just a soda machine and a water fountain; a cleaner's cart stacked with towels and fresh linen. Drawing a pistol he made his way down the hall and stopped outside the room. The door was un-locked and he stood there trying to pick up any sound. There was nothing at first then he heard a collective shout go up from out on the street. Throwing the door wide he was in a short corridor with a bathroom to the right and bedroom ahead where the win-dow gaped and the curtain billowed like some desperate alarm. Directly in front of the window a rifle was resting against the sill.

No sign of the shooter. Quarrie kicked open the bathroom door.

Nobody, nothing, both bathroom and bedroom were empty. He figured the bellhop must've spotted him when he got out of the car and he was pretty sure it was Franklin. He crossed to the window as another cheer erupted and he saw Ali emerge from the Processing Station. The boxer stood just outside the doors with every news hound in Texas stuffing a microphone under his chin. Tall and serene he looked utterly calm despite the mass of young black men whooping and hollering as flash-bulbs went off like firecrackers.

Holstering his pistol again Quarrie focused on this side of the street as a couple of Fords pulled up and half a dozen gray-suited men piled out. Emerging from the passenger seat of the second car he recognized Patterson, the SAC. Stepping back from the window he dropped to one knee and studied the rifle. A Garand M1C, like the one he had found in Wiley's bag, only this had a four-power scope. No muzzle flash hider, unlike Colback's, and no leather on the stock to stop any chafing.

He gazed across the street to the mass of people then a noise in the corridor made him turn. Two police officers in uniform, handguns drawn and cocked, were standing either side of the open door pointing their weapons at him. They stared at Quarrie and he stared back at them, thinking how they looked so jumpy one of them was bound to shoot.

'Mister.' The first one didn't sound too sure of his voice. 'I need you to stand up real easy and unbuckle that pistol belt.'

'It's OK.' Quarrie rose to his feet indicating his badge. 'I'm a Ranger out of Company C.'

The two cops looked at him and then briefly at each other and they did not holster their guns. 'The pistol belt,' the cop repeated. 'Use your left hand only. Do it nice and slow.'

With a shake of his head Quarrie reached across with his left hand and unfastened the buckle. The gunbelt fell to the floor and he kicked it a foot away. 'It ain't me you want,' he said. 'The shooter is dressed as a bellhop and all the time we're stood here, he's getting further away.'

The first cop stepped into the room and bent for Quarrie's weapons. He inspected the badge on his chest as if he did not believe it was real. Quarrie looked coldly at him as voices sounded from the hallway. Moments later two men in gray suits appeared followed by Patterson, the SAC.

'You took your own sweet time,' Quarrie said. 'These two boys don't seem to recognize a Ranger's star when they see one and the shooter is getting away.'

*

It was very late when finally he made it home to Wilbarger County. A long drive from Houston and all the way from New Orleans before that, he was listening to a snippet of Chuck Boyle's 'Snake Pit' talk show on KLIF where some guy from Dallas was lambasting the Boxing Commission over their stance with Muhammad Ali. Switching the radio off Quarrie got out of the car.

Judging by how the main house was in darkness he figured Mrs Feeley was away, which meant Pious was too. Lights burned in the kitchen of his place though, spilling from the window in a corn-colored glow. When he was on the road Eunice stayed over and it looked like she was yet to turn in. Opening the fly screen door Quarrie saw a woman at the table with a glass of wine at her elbow, but it wasn't Eunice, it was Gigi.

With a smile she put down her magazine. 'John Q, we weren't expecting you.'

Quarrie returned the smile. 'I wasn't expecting me either, Gigi. Where's Eunice at? I figured her for being here not you.'

'Eunice went out on a date.'

'Did she now; how about that? I always thought it was Nolo she was sweet on. You're saying that ain't so?'

'Oh, he's the one all right. I've seen the way she looks at him and whoever she's with tonight, the way she was all made-up when she crossed the yard, I think it's all part of the same show.'

Quarrie fetched a quart bottle of milk from the fridge and sat down at the table to pry off the top. 'So how'd you like Texas?' he said.

'Apart from the snakes and spiders, I guess I like it fine.'

'Have you been settling in?'

'Pretty much. Everyone's been really nice to me, including Mrs Feeley, and I'm getting on great with James.'

'Sleeping right now, is he?' Quarrie threw a glance towards the hallway door.

She nodded. 'He's a good kid, John Q: you've done a fine job with him.'

Taking a long draught of ice-cold milk Quarrie worked a pack of cigarettes from the pocket of his shirt and offered it to Gigi.

She shook her head. 'I only smoke when I'm stressed.'

'And you're not stressed anymore?'

'Not right now.'

'Is Pious about?'

'No, he's away with Mrs Feeley and the plane. Denver, I think he said.'

'On the phone James told me how when he's around you he gabbles like he ain't going to quit.'

Gigi smiled.

'That ain't like him, mam, I can tell you.'

'He's a good guy,' Gigi said.

'Yes, he is.' Quarrie sat back. 'Did him some prison time he didn't need to be doing. Did he tell you that?'

'Yes, he did.' Hunching onto her elbows she looked keenly at him then. 'So I know they murdered Earl. What else has been going on?'

Sitting back in the chair Quarrie exhaled a heavy breath. '*What ain't been going on* is the better question.' Lighting a cigarette he told her all that he'd found out. He told her about the file he had discovered in her house and what happened in Houston that morning. When he'd finished her eyes were fixed on his.

'It's all right,' he said. 'I got there before they could shoot him. He doesn't know anything about it, and unless the Feds want to tell him, he probably never will.'

'But I don't understand. Why would they go after Cassius Clay?'

Quarrie made an open-handed gesture. 'You said it right there. He ain't Cassius anymore, he's Muhammad Ali. And he's not just a boxer, he's a symbol for a lot of people in this country and he isn't going to Vietnam. Gigi, this whole deal with black power, the Nation of Islam, Ali's a rallying point.'

'What do you mean?'

'I mean for disaffected colored kids, and with the way things are right now there's a hell of a lot of them.' He upturned a palm. 'The kind of people prepared to pay an outfit like this to kill someone don't allow for folks like him.'

Reaching for his package of cigarettes Gigi pried back the foil. 'You say you found that file on top of my closet?'

'Yes, mam, I did.'

'And you figure it was Earl who hid it there?'

'That's right.'

'John Q, why would he have it in the first place?'

'I think he found it in Anderson's apartment.'

She looked at him with her brows knit.

'What is it?' he said. 'What's up?'

Gigi shook her head. 'I never gave Earl a key. He hasn't been to my house but once since he stole those meds and that was just the living room with me.'

For a moment Quarrie stared.

'You told me you figured he was in that apartment the same night you were, right?' She lifted her shoulders. 'That was long after he took those meds and he hasn't been back to the house.'

Quarrie thought about that as she got up from the table and stepped outside where the air was a little cooler. 'John Q,' she called through the screen, 'if that old man is behind all this then . . .'

Nana's admission seemed to rattle in Quarrie's head. 'I know,' he said. 'It means everything that happened to you happened on account of him.'

He followed her out and Gigi peered through the gloom. 'I asked Nana who he was and if she was scared of him.'

'And is she?'

'I don't know. I don't think so, but I'm wondering if maybe she should be.'

'That gun she keeps in the cabinet, would she use it if someone got in?'

'Sure she would,' Gigi said.

She stared across the yard to where the corral was shaped by shadow and beyond it the bluff where the big house stood. She said goodnight and he watched her cross to the Noons' cottage and then he closed up the kitchen. Pausing in the hallway he pushed open his son's door and stood watching him for a while. In his own room he shut the door and sat on the bed staring through the window at a crescent moon.

*

When he got back to New Orleans Franklin went home to take a shower and change his clothes. Wrapping the bellhop's uniform in a plastic bag he taped the top then poured himself a drink. Downstairs once more he drove to the Garden District and stopped outside a coffee bar. Grabbing the plastic bag from the back seat he tossed it into a dumpster.

It was late when he pulled up to the gates. The house was in shadow save a light that burned in an upstairs window. Franklin parked the car and made his way around back. He paused on the gravel pathway watching the old man talking on the phone. He was on his feet, a lamp lighted on the desk; he looked up as Franklin opened the doors to the patio. He spoke for a few minutes longer and then he put down the phone.

'By the look on your face I guess that was the client,' Franklin said.

Tobie still had his hand on the phone. 'I had to explain that it didn't work out because we weren't able to guarantee the timing.'

'What did they say?'

'They said exactly what I'd expect them to say. They

reminded me that their intention was to make a statement that would resonate around the world and for that there was only today.'

Sitting down in his chair he stared beyond Franklin to the yard outside. 'From father to son we've been in business for over a century and this is the first time we've not been able to fulfill a contract.'

'This is different,' Franklin said. 'Quarrie showed up before Ali came out. When we've dealt with him we can go back to the client.'

'No, we can't. I just told you. It had to be today.'

'What about Quarrie?'

The old man's gaze was thin. 'I said we'd kill him when we were sure there could be no response from the Rangers and that's exactly what we're going to do.'

*

The following morning Quarrie was in the kitchen making coffee when James came through in his pajamas. 'Dad!' he cried. 'I never knew you were coming home.' He flung himself against his father and Quarrie hoisted him off his feet.

'Never knew it either, kiddo. I was in Houston yesterday and back here late last night.'

James looked at him with a hopeful expression on his face. 'Do you have to go back again?'

'I don't know yet. Maybe, though I wasn't planning on it. Been away too long as it is.'

While Quarrie took a shower James got dressed and they ate breakfast together at the kitchen table. The boy told him how he'd been practicing making different tracks in the sand-box Quarrie had filled with dirt. Quarrie said that as soon as school was done for the day he'd show him how to figure out if a man was running or walking, looking uphill or down or about to make a turn. Outside he fired up the Riviera and let her run for a couple of minutes before driving his son to school.

As he pulled back into the yard an hour later Gigi came bust-ling out of the bunkhouse and strode across to the cottage. He could tell something was wrong by the look in her eyes and when she spoke she was a little breathless. 'John Q, your cap-tain was just on the phone.'

Quarrie peered across the roof of his car. 'What did he want?'

'He didn't say. I told him you'd taken James to school and he said for you to call him as soon as you got back.'

'OK, honey, thanks.'

'And Pious,' she added. 'Right after your captain put down the phone he called too. He's in Denver, said he'd catch up with you as soon as he can.'

In the kitchen Quarrie called the Department of Public Safety in Amarillo and Van Hanigan came on the phone.

'Captain,' he said. 'What's up?'

'Where are you?'

'I'm here at the ranch. Why?'

'I just had SAC Patterson on the phone. He's flying up from Houston with an arrest warrant.'

Quarrie stared where his gunbelt hung from a hook on the back of the door.

'That rifle in the hotel room. The only prints they found were yours, John Q.'

Thirty-three

He didn't go to Amarillo. Instead he had Gigi drive him south to Love Field and left her with a phone number for the Hotel Magnolia and another for De La Martin. Showing his badge to the attendant at the desk he jumped the queue for the shuttle and a couple of hours later he emerged from the passenger terminal at Moisant Field.

*

Franklin was outside in a year-old Mustang. Eyes bright, he stared through the windshield as Quarrie came out of the terminal building. Quarrie did not see him. He hailed a cab from the rank and the driver eased up to the curb. As they pulled away Franklin followed a few cars behind.

*

Quarrie glanced out the window as they passed an NOPD cruiser with two uniforms riding up front. The cab driver was a black man with a gold earring and a gold front tooth and he seemed to study his passenger in the rear view mirror. 'You're the Texas Ranger the newspapers been writing about.'

Quarrie caught his eye.

'Gigi Matisse and all: that pharmacist who got murdered. I

294

heard on the radio how Gigi ain't anywheres about.'

'What's your name?' Quarrie asked him.

'Amos Brown.'

'Amos, do you believe everything you read in the papers?'

With a laugh the driver shook his head. 'I know Gigi pretty good as it goes. The drummer in her band, Etienne, that's my second cousin. So where's she at then? On the radio they said how she disappeared.'

'She's in Texas right now,' Quarrie told him. 'She's fine. If I told you somebody's been hand feeding those reporters what would you say?'

'I'd say this is New Orleans.' He glanced over the back of the seat. 'So where is it you want to go?'

'I ain't sure,' Quarrie said. 'I thought about the Hotel Magnolia but there's a federal warrant out on me right now so maybe I should try somewhere else.'

'Canal Street you talking about, where-all Yvonne Pettier works?'

'That's right.'

'Well, Yvonne's a pretty good girl. She's from the 7th like me and we ain't known for being particularly blabby.'

They drove downtown and when they got to the hotel Amos told Quarrie to wait in the cab while he went inside to find out if anyone had been asking for him.

*

Franklin saw the cab pull up and the driver get out and disappear under the arch. He saw him come out to the sidewalk again then Quarrie climbed from the cab.

Yvonne greeted him with a slightly wary look and gave him the same room he'd had before. Upstairs he laid his bag on the bureau and opened the closet where the Dallas newspaper was still on the floor. He took a moment to study the piece on Muhammad Ali then tossed the paper on the bed. Unbuckling his shoulder holsters he took one of the pistols and opened the loading gate before pulling the base pin and removing the cylinder. He emptied the shells then repeated the process with the second gun, placing all twelve rounds on the bureau. Fetching a strip of oil cloth from his bag he was meticulous as he cleaned each chamber. He was reassembling the weapons when the phone rang.

'John Q.' He recognized Nana's voice. 'I just talked to Gigi and she said you were back.'

'Yes, mam, there's a warrant out for my arrest.'

'And you're down here on account of it?'

'In a manner of speaking, yes.'

She was quiet for a moment then she said, 'What we talked about in my apartment, there's something I'm going to tell you, but before I do – we never had this conversation.'

It was dark on Canal Street by the time he went out, the streetlights igniting the median like a row of massive candles. From the hotel courtyard he glanced across the road to the parking bays but there was no sign of Franklin or his taxi. Walking to the crossing at St Charles he hopped a trolley car and settled in the back.

There was no reply from the small gate at Colback's house so he rang again and finally the front door was opened by a diminutive woman with shoulder-length hair. She looked to be in her forties and seemed to hover a little uncertainly. The gate still locked, Quarrie called from where he stood in the glow of the street lamp.

'Mrs Colback? I'm a friend of your husband. Is he home?'

'Not right now, I'm afraid.'

'My name's Quarrie, mam. I'm a Texas Ranger.'

The buzzer sounded and he opened the gate. At the door he took off his hat. 'I'm sorry to trouble you. Do you know when the lieutenant will be back?'

'No, I'm afraid I don't.'

He looked beyond her to the staircase where the family portraits climbed the wall.

'There's been a mix-up in Texas and I need to fetch some papers I'm hoping might help straighten it out. We were looking at them together and he put them in the safe.'

'Well, if he did I can't help you.' Very definitely Mrs Colback shook her head. 'I have no idea what the combination is and I don't get involved in my husband's work.'

Quarrie nodded. 'That's all right, mam. I understand. Do you think I could leave him a note?'

She led him to the study where polished wooden panels scaled the walls from the floor and Colback's rifle hung on a couple of hooks. Quarrie wrote a note telling the lieutenant that he needed to talk and would come back later on. When he was done, he put his hat back on and followed Mrs Colback out to the hall. At the door his gaze drifted to the paintings once more. 'Impressive,' he said, 'all those portraits. Your husband told me they're all from your side of the family.'

'Yes, they are.' A little pride in her eyes, Mrs Colback

considered the height of the stairs. 'Louisiana since 1865, we hail from Ohio originally and might've been there yet if the Yankees hadn't chased us out.' With a smile she offered her hand. 'I'm sorry, I should've introduced myself. I'm Rosa. My maiden name was Tobie. That's my great-grandpa at the top of the stairs.'

*

Quarrie walked as far as the junction with St Charles Avenue before he stopped. Conscious of the film of sweat that laced his brow he stood staring across the trolley car tracks, thinking about what he'd been told just now and what Nana had confided earlier. Spotting a phone booth on the corner he searched his pockets for a dime. 'Hey,' he said when he heard Yvonne's voice. 'Have you had any visitors yet?'

'No, sir. Not so far.'

'OK, good. Look, I figure they must know I'm in town already so I need you to fetch my bag from my room. Hide it in the office, would you? Can you do that for me, Yvonne?'

She seemed to hesitate.

'Yvonne?'

'Sure,' she said, 'of course. If anyone shows up though, what do I say?'

'Tell them I checked in then changed my mind and checked out again right away. Show them the room if they ask. It'll be the FBI so do whatever they tell you, just don't let them see that bag.' Something else occurred to him then. 'There's a newspaper on my bed, Yvonne, a Dallas paper, get rid of it, will you? I need you to burn it.'

'All right,' she said. 'I can do that.'

298

'I need you to get me a cab,' Quarrie told her. 'Call United and ask them to have that same driver who picked me up from the airport go to Lee Circle. The Enco station, tell them he has to collect a fare.'

'Sergeant,' she said, 'you had a phone call after you left, a man called Pious, said he was a friend of yours and he needs to talk to you right away. I told him I didn't know when you'd be back so he said to tell you he was going to call the other number you left.'

'When did he call?'

'About ten minutes after you'd gone.'

'All right, Yvonne; thanks. Listen,' he said. 'I need for you to do one last thing. Call the 3rd Precinct Station House on Chartres Street. Ask for Detective De La Martin. Tell them his snitch wants to meet in the bar where they met before.'

Hanging up the phone he lifted it again and waited for the operator then asked her to connect him to the ranch, collect.

'It's me, Pious,' he said when the call was answered. 'You've been looking for me, bud. What's up?'

'Plenty.' Pious's voice was stiff. 'Gigi and Eunice been talking and there's things I think you should know.' When he was finished Quarrie stared at the streetlight across the road.

'That ain't all,' Pious said. 'I called that detective whose number you left just now, and what else I got to tell you I ain't sure I should be doing it on the phone.'

'It's too late to be worrying about that,' Quarrie said. 'What is it you want to say?'

When he put down the phone again he headed north and came out on Carondelet. From there he made his way to Howard Street and turned towards the river once more. As he approached the circle he could see the lights from the gas station and the taxi parked half a block down. He remained in the shadows watching till he was sure it wasn't under surveillance then he crossed the forecourt and got in.

'I got your message.' Amos looked round as he settled in the back. 'Is everything OK?'

Quarrie did not reply. He was thinking about what Pious had said and his mouth felt crusty and dry.

Making their way around the circle they headed towards the river and back onto Camp Street. Quarrie directed Amos to pull over a little way from Colback's house. Glancing over the seat Amos caught the expression on his face. 'So, you asked for me specially, do I need to know what this is about?'

Quarrie's attention was on the house where lights burned in the windows and he could see Colback's Ford as well as a '66 Mustang parked in the drive.

'John Q?' Amos's voice seemed to echo through the darkness.

'It's about vipers, Amos: copperhead snakes.'

They drove back to the French Quarter and rumbled along Chartres Street. 'That bar yonder.' Quarrie pointed to the seafood place across the road from the station house. 'I need you to go over there and see if there's a fat man inside wearing a grubby-looking suit. His name is De La Martin and he's a cop. If he's there I want you to fetch him out.'

Three minutes later Amos was back with the detective and De La Martin's expression was sallow as he got in the car.

'How you doing, D-Lay?' Quarrie said.

'From what I heard on the phone just now – a whole lot better than you.'

They sat side by side, Quarrie with his hat in his lap. 'I guess you know there's a warrant out, a federal ticket, so it won't be long before the boys from Loyola show.'

'Yeah, that's about what your buddy said.'

Leaning forward Quarrie rested a palm on the driver's shoulder. 'We're going back to Camp Street, bud. I want you to stop by the hotel on the way.'

A couple of minutes later they pulled over in front of the American Bank building and De La Martin got out. Crossing the road he went into the hotel and a few moments after that he came out again and signalled from the courtyard gates. When Quarrie made the sidewalk the detective told him he'd spoken to Yvonne and two FBI agents had been there fifteen minutes before.

In the lobby De La Martin chewed tobacco and watched the courtyard while Quarrie shucked off his jacket and unfastened the straps on his shoulder rig. Yvonne fetched his bag from the office and he unrolled his regular gunbelt and buckled it on. Holstering his Blackhawks he checked the leg ties and hammer clips.

Back in the cab they drove the length of St Charles with De La Martin riding up front.

'So you were right then,' he said, glancing over his shoulder, 'about Muhammad Ali, only you got there before they could take him out.'

Quarrie nodded. 'They screwed up with the timing I guess. Ali was still inside the Processing Station when I showed up and the triggerman had to take off. They knew I was coming, though. With my prints on that M1C already, the Feds were always going to haul me in.' He let a little air escape his lips.

'D-Lay, it wasn't Moore who hid that file in Gigi's house; it had to be our blond-haired boy. They knew I'd find it and figure out what was going on. It's like I told you, whoever their client is they want the case closed real quick so someone has to take the fall. Whether they're actually involved or not don't matter just as long as they go down alone.' He was silent for a moment then. 'That's the way it's always been. They did it with Oswald in Dallas, maybe Carl Weiss back in the thirties and they figured on doing it with Wiley before he ran into me.'

They drove on and Amos turned onto Camp Street where he slowed the cab to a crawl. Shifting his weight De La Martin looked over the back of the seat. 'You positive you don't want me to come in there with you? Maybe it's me that should go in first. I could make up some story about hearing how you were wanted and see how the land lies at least.'

Quarrie shook his head. 'I left Colback a note and told his wife I'd be back. I can show up and he'll let me in and we'll see what happens after that. Give me at least ten minutes before you come knocking, OK?'

De La Martin looked unsure. 'That's all well and good but you don't know who else might be in there, do you?'

'I got a hunch all right. You just show up in a piece.'

'And if it all goes to ratshit in the meantime?' The detective hooked his mouth at the corners. 'I can think of lots of reasons why they wouldn't want to kill a Ranger ahead of time but now there's a warrant out. Resisting arrest, John Q: it's better than the courthouse, right?'

Thirty-four

It was Colback who opened the door. Quarrie regarded him with an easy smile.

'Lieutenant,' he said, 'did your wife tell you I was here before?'

Looking up and down the street Colback did not return the smile. 'Yes, she did. Come in, Quarrie. There's a warrant out on you right now.' Stepping back from the door he glanced at the guns on Quarrie's hips.

'I want the paperwork,' Quarrie told him. 'What we found in that locker. I know what we said before but I need to show it to the Feds.'

Colback led him into his study. There was no sign of anyone in the living room but Quarrie noticed the door at the end of the hall was ajar.

'So this warrant, it kind of puts me in an awkward spot.' Colback spoke as Quarrie's gaze was drawn to the rifle where it hung on the wall.

'Don't worry about it. I spoke to my captain. All I need are those notes. I'm sure it was Anderson who wrote them so there has to be something there. You were with me when we found them. You were on the north shore when we discovered the photos of Moore and Gigi together and you know about the parking garage.' He spread a palm. 'We need to locate Gervais, Lieutenant; any word on where he might be?'

Colback made a face. 'I've been trying to find him but he isn't answering his phone.'

'That's too bad.' Quarrie held his eye. 'Those notes on that outfit from way back when, we can start with that and deal with him just as soon as I get the Feds squared away.'

Colback dropped to one knee and worked the combination on his safe. Again Quarrie considered the rifle where it hung on the wall. 'That the piece from Korea you showed me before?'

'That's her.'

'The one you used when Pious called the CP that time?'

'That's right.' Colback was still bent over the safe. He rummaged around for a moment then stood up. When he turned he didn't have the paperwork, he held a Colt forty-five automatic.

'I'm sorry,' he said. 'But the warrant, I got no choice.'

Quarrie held his gaze. 'The Feds said for you to arrest me, huh.'

'That's right.'

'But you'll tell them I resisted. You figure the odds are pretty good you can take me down what with Franklin out in the hall.'

He did not look round. His gaze remained on Colback, the set of his shoulders and the color of his knuckle in the trigger guard. 'This place,' Quarrie said, 'the Garden District, a house that never gets sold. That caddy in the driveway a gift from your father-in-law. Family, Lieutenant, it's such a big deal down here. I had no idea just how big till your wife told me about her great-granddaddy's portrait at the top of the stairs. Rosslyn F Tobie who changed his name from James Cutler when he quit Ohio: the last of the copperheads, right?' Hearing movement from the hall he caught a glimpse of cropped blond hair. 'That paperwork yesterday,' he said. 'I guess I should've searched your study after all. You made damn sure I never touched that file on campus, so where's the rest of it, uh?'

Colback did not reply.

'All you left was the history, nothing that could tell us anything. But it was Anderson who wrote it not Moore. A detective who specialized in surveillance, he'd done a whole heap of digging, right? He knew about you and Rosslyn Tobie, he knew about Ferrie and Clay Shaw. He knew all about Franklin and April 28. He knew what was behind that foundation on Baronne.'

Glancing above Colback's head he indicated the rifle where it hung on the wall. 'That's not the one from Korea, that's in Houston right now. Made sure I handled her, didn't you?' He saw a flicker in Colback's eyes. 'You remember over at Nana's place when you saw Pious after all this time? I had him take that photo I found at Anderson's place down to a friend of mine. The two of them looked it over with a magnifying glass and the one guy figured those cops for Dallas PD. Something about the one at the back bothered Pious but he couldn't work out what it was. Finally it came to him and he called me up asking what a New Orleans detective was doing dressed as a Dallas cop the day Jack Kennedy was shot. Funny thing is – apart from the way he was shipping his weapon – I never really looked at the cop. I was so busy spotting your buddy back there I never even noticed it was you.' He let go a breath. 'All this time I'm thinking it was Gervais blackmailing Moore and him that had Soulja shot. But it wasn't him, it was you. You told me Gervais phoned about Lafayette Square. That gave you time to have Franklin get to the parking garage and he was there when I left the hotel.'

Behind him he heard the taxi driver shift his weight and he turned to the hall. Ignoring the Beretta, he stared into the blond man's eyes. 'That photograph of the two of you in Dallas. The second shooter, was it you with the rifle or your brother-in-law back there?'

Franklin did not reply. He just looked at Quarrie and tightened his grip on the gun.

'Gigi Matisse,' Quarrie said. 'That's your sister we're talking about. I know what you did to her.'

There was no expression on Franklin's face, no hint of anything in his eyes. Quarrie turned to Colback again. 'Lieutenant,' he said, 'if this young punk thinks he's going to shoot me you better tell him to come inside. Every cop in Texas knows I ain't a runner, he's going to have to look me in the eye.'

There was no movement from the hall and Colback remained at the desk. 'I warned you,' he said. 'I tried to make it clear you'd no business being in New Orleans. I told you to go home.' Sweat trickled from his hairline to the corner of his eye. 'You should've done that. You should've gone back to Texas and left things as they were. But you couldn't do it, could you? You had to dig deeper and deeper and when you called the DA's office that time . . .'

'Come on, Lieutenant, you've been planning for this moment pretty much since I arrived. You had a contract to kill Ali and you have to have a fall guy so when I shot Wiley you figured you'd replace him with me.' He gestured. 'It's why you didn't kill me in Lafayette Square. It's a fact you needed me in Houston but you can kill me now with no comeback from anyone at all. It has to be you though, huh? Cop to cop, I mean, what with the warrant and all.'

Quietly he smiled. 'Only it ain't so easy, is it? Six feet's a whole different ballgame to six hundred yards.' He could see the sheen glistening on Colback's brow. 'Maybe you're up to it and maybe you ain't, but it don't matter that your weapon is cocked, I can put you down and still take out that piece of shit behind.'

Colback did not move. He did not say anything. Quarrie watched his face, the expression as imperceptibly it began to die. Before he could tighten his finger on the trigger, before Franklin could make the connection, Quarrie had a pistol cupped and the hammer covered with his left hand.

He didn't wait for Colback to fall. Dropping to one knee he spun around but there was nobody in the hall. He heard no footstep, no sound of any door closing but Franklin was no longer there. Gun still smoking, Quarrie glanced to where Colback sprawled then he bent to the safe. There was no sign of the paperwork, though. As he stood up movement in the hall caught his eye.

He had the pistol cocked a second time but it wasn't Franklin, it was Rosslyn Tobie at the foot of the stairs. Wearing an immaculately tailored suit he gripped his snake's head cane. Quarrie stared at him and all he could think about was what Nana had said on the phone.

'Bravo, Sergeant.' The old man's voice was rich with age. 'Very impressive, your godfather would be proud. But where does this leave you now? How're you going to explain the murder of a New Orleans police officer? There's no paperwork to back up your story. It's already been destroyed.'

'You forget I've got Wiley's file.'

'Of course you do, I left it for you to find.' The old man

smiled. 'Without it there's no way we could've gotten you to Houston. Details we'd have leaked to the press if we hadn't been compromised.'

He turned to peer at the dead man. 'I have to admit I thought Colback was better than this. I thought he'd be able to accomplish what was asked of him, but he let me down. Now there'll be a court case we didn't want and it's true your attorney can produce that file.' He looked back at Quarrie again. 'But what is it but a couple of typed pages you could've put together yourself. The file proves nothing, it's not hand-written and it's not signed.' He gestured with the walking cane. 'You've nothing in your corner, Sergeant. Not only were you the last person to see that pharmacist alive, a set of your fingerprints was recovered from the apartment where his body was found. You were the last person to see the pimp from Governor Nicholls, not to mention his driver. But most importantly you were discovered in a hotel room about to take a shot at the heavyweight champion of the world. Muhammad Ali, a Muslim who changed his name and refused to fight for his country, and you a Veteran of the war in Korea. At just nineteen you wrote a letter to President Truman that was published in *The New York Times*.'

In silence Quarrie stared.

'That makes you radical. It makes you unpredictable. And just as Wiley fought one war so you fought another. The Louisville lip, well, that *sonofabitch don't want to fight for his country then he won't be fighting at all*.'

He moved behind Colback's desk. 'You've only got yourself to blame, taking on an organization that's been around for a hundred years.' He nodded to the dead man again. 'Look at him, a highly respected police officer who tried to execute a warrant issued by the FBI. It prolongs this business a little. But we can deal with a court case and discredit whatever your attorney will tell you to say.'

'You're forgetting the photograph,' Quarrie said. 'I've got a copy. It's safe in Texas with Wiley's file.'

Again the old man smiled. 'You really believe we can't deal with that?'

'You couldn't. It's where all this started, remember?'

'That's true, it did. But we have contingencies now. Think about that photograph for a moment. Almost four years since it was taken and in all that time no one came forward until a New Orleans cop thought he saw something and called the DA. He's dead, so what does that leave except a grainy image of a police officer who might have a vague resemblance to my son-in-law? If it comes to it I can provide a dozen eminent witnesses who'll swear Lieutenant Colback was at a garden party in St Charles Parish the day Jack Kennedy died.' He gestured expansively then. 'I don't think that'll be necessary, however, because the only witness your attorney can summon is a Negro convicted of cowardice in the Korean War.'

'And your son who was here just now?'

Pacing around him Tobie furrowed his brow. 'Sergeant, I have no idea what you're talking about. There was nobody here but you and me and the brave lieutenant lying there. Everybody knows I only had two children and one of them died at the age of nine. If it's the taxi driver you're referring to then you mean the witness they'll call when it comes to trial. The decent young man on a football scholarship who picked you up from the airport and took you everywhere you wanted to go.'

309

'He's in the photograph,' Quarrie said.

'Is he?' Tobie smiled. 'I don't think so, sunglasses and all that hair. That was just some hobo they pulled off a train.'

'What about Moore?'

'What about him? A disillusioned police officer with a penchant for colored girls, a married man with young children, no wonder he disappeared. He's not dead. There's no body, remember? I imagine he's in New York or Chicago with some mulatto whore right now.'

Quarrie was aware of the beat of a pulse at his eye.

'You're done here,' the old man said. 'You were out of your depth from the moment you arrived.' As he spoke the doorbell rang and he paused. 'I imagine that'll be De La Martin come to arrest you for murder.' With that he turned for the hall.

'Nana told me about you,' Quarrie said, 'the kind of man you were.'

In the doorway Tobie looked back.

'How you were Gigi's daddy. She told me how it was with you and her, what with you being married and all.'

'Did she? Well, that woman always did like to talk. She's a lot to answer for.'

He went to get the door and Quarrie remained where he was. Seconds later De La Martin appeared with the old man holding his arm.

'Detective,' he said. 'This is the Texas Ranger the papers were writing about. He's wanted by the FBI.' Grimly he indicated the body where it lay against the blood-spattered wall. 'He murdered Lieutenant Colback as he tried to arrest him. I was upstairs and heard the commotion. I witnessed everything from the stairs.' Reaching in his pocket he brought out a business card. 'As you probably know I'm an attorney and I'll be available to make a statement, but I have a pressing engagement now.' The hint of a smile on his face, he looked Quarrie hard in the eye.

He left them then and they heard the front door open and close. De La Martin pulled a handkerchief from his pocket and mopped the sweat from his brow. 'One riot, one Ranger,' he muttered. 'We're going to need a miracle now.'

For a moment Quarrie stood where he was then he slipped his gun back into its holster.

'Is Amos outside with the cab?'

De La Martin squinted. 'I guess so. I just left him. Why?'

Quarrie went through to the hall. 'It ain't a miracle we need, it's a ride.'

Thirty-five

Outside, Tobie walked to the corner where the Lincoln was parked in the shadow of a couple of trees. The chauffeur made to get out and open the door for him but the old man waved him down. Climbing into the back he regarded Franklin where he sat with his arms folded and his chin on his chest.

'I know what you're thinking,' the old man said. 'But it is what it is and I might have to produce you as a witness later so you were never there.' Leaning forward he tapped the divider with his cane. The glass slid down and he told the chauffeur to take them to Orleans Street.

Franklin's features were set. 'You should've let me shoot him just now when I had the chance.'

'A bullet in the back of the head, I don't think so. You heard what he said. It had to be Colback only he wasn't up to it, I'm afraid.' Tobie forced away an audible breath. 'De La Martin showed up and I imagine that was prearranged. He has no choice but to arrest Quarrie for murder, though; they'll be heading downtown right now.'

Franklin stared through the glass divider into headlights coming the other way.

'I would've preferred it to go as we planned of course, and there might be some unwanted publicity for the foundation, so I want you to make sure we have a fresh initiative we can demonstrate publicly if we have to. Make it something for colored boys who might be considering leaving the bosom of Christ for their brothers in the red bow ties.'

Franklin sat up straighter in the seat. 'All this because some cop who thought he could make a buck spotted Colback in a uniform he shouldn't have been wearing in a place he shouldn't have been.' He gestured with the flat of his hand. 'What about Rosa, how's she going to be when she finds out her husband is dead?'

Tobie sat with his palms pressed to his thighs. 'She'll grieve of course, but she's family and that means she'll survive. She has me and her mother, the memory of her brother. She'll get over it. She'll be fine.'

They were silent as the chauffeur turned onto St Charles Avenue and drove to the lights at Canal. As they crossed into the Quarter Franklin glanced at the spot where he'd killed Soulja Blue. 'So why Orleans Street?' he said.

The old man pursed his lips. 'She called the house. Just as I was leaving for Rosa's place she phoned me at home.'

Franklin looked sideways at him then. 'Who did she speak to? What did she say?'

Tobie stared straight ahead. 'She spoke to my wife. She told her she needed to talk to me and I had to explain that she was a caretaker for one of our properties and I've never had to do that before.' He half closed his eyes. 'A call like that – you know it's not an option. In all the years I was seeing that woman she knew it only too well.' The walking cane across his knees, he worked the serpent's tongue with his thumb.

A few minutes later they turned onto Orleans Street. The chauffeur parked and Tobie glanced up at the darkened windows of the apartment.

'Are you sure about this?' Franklin said. 'Right now, I mean, what with De La Martin at the Camp Street house.'

'It won't take long.' Tobie got out of the car. 'I told you how it is with boundaries, if they're blurred even slightly they're no longer boundaries at all.'

He made his way across the road to the small gate and slipped his key in the lock. Inside the courtyard he crossed to the spiral staircase and looked up to where the door to the apartment was ajar. One hand on the rail he called out. 'Nana, it's Rosslyn: I'm coming up.'

No answer from above, he climbed the steps to the short landing and stepped into the hall. Nana was at the far end bathed in shadow, he could barely make out her gown. 'We need to talk.' His tone was icy now. 'The phone call, you've no business calling the house.'

Still she stood where she was, not moving from the bedroom door.

'You called the house. Why would you do that? You've never done it before.'

Nana stared at him with a light in her eyes. 'Rosslyn,' she said. 'A long time ago you made it clear that you'd kill us both if I gave you cause, do you remember what you said that day?' She stepped out of the shadows and Tobie's gaze fixed on the gun she was pointing at him. 'I've been thinking on it lately and I figure all the time you're alive then Gigi's in danger. I'm done with her living that way.'

*

In the back seat of the Lincoln Franklin heard the shot ring out and the chauffeur jumped where he sat. For a second Franklin

314

stared at the darkened windows of the apartment then he rapped on the glass. 'Go,' he yelled. 'The old fool always was too sure of himself. Get us out of here now.' The chauffeur did not move. He just looked over his shoulder with his mouth hanging open. Franklin saw the flare of headlights in the rear view mirror as another car came up the road. Again he banged on the glass. 'For God's sake, man, just drive.'

*

As the cab turned the corner Quarrie saw the Lincoln heading for North Rampart Street. Next to him De La Martin was sweating and Quarrie told Amos to pull up. Throwing open the door he got out and stared the length of the street. Half a mind to get back in the cab and give chase, his attention was diverted to the apartment as lights flooded the balcony. De La Martin came lumbering around the back of the car as Quarrie crossed to the small gate. From the courtyard he could see lights over the gantry and was halfway up the steps when Nana appeared at the door. She had a gun in her hand, the smell of cordite in the air; he could see she was trembling slightly. For a moment she looked at him and he looked at her. Then she stood aside.

Tobie was lying on his back with one palm pressed to his breast. His eyes were open and he was blinking slowly, lips moving soundlessly where blood gathered in bubbles with every broken breath. He tried to sit up but when he moved more blood pulsed from the wound in his chest. The look in his eyes was part fear and part shock; the pupils seemed to wander then they fixed on Quarrie's face. 'You knew.' The

words were no more than a whisper. 'You knew she was waiting. You...'

'Call it a contingency,' Quarrie said.

Squatting on his haunches he looked down at the old man
and for a couple of seconds they stared at each other then
Tobie's eyes were closed.

Quarrie heard De La Martin on the gantry then he filled the
open doorway with his brows drawn in a frown. 'I'll call an ambulance.' Stepping around the fallen man he reached for the
phone.

'He don't need an ambulance. Call the coroner,' Quarrie
said.

*

Nana remained in her bedroom while the crew took care of
the body and the NOPD forensics team went through the
hall. When they were gone she came into the living room and
perched on the couch. She had her hands folded in her lap, her
gaze fixed on the thirty-eight on the coffee table wrapped in a
polythene evidence bag.

'So let me make sure I've got this right.' De La Martin sat
down opposite her and glanced to where Quarrie was standing
at the balcony doors. 'He had a key to the place you knew nothing about?'

Nana nodded. 'He signed the apartment over to me back in
the twenties. I didn't know he still had a key and I never had the
locks changed. There was no need. I was asleep in bed when I
woke to the sound of someone at the front door.' She pointed
to the gun. 'This is New Orleans and I keep that piece by my

bed.' Her gaze drifted to Quarrie. 'I called out but he didn't answer. He should've answered. He should've said something. I didn't know who he was.' Her emotions seemed to get the better of her then and her shoulders were shaking again.

'Are you all right, Nana?' Quarrie said.

'I'm OK I guess. I could use a drink though, there's a pitcher of julep in the fridge.'

Quarrie went through to the kitchen while De La Martin asked her to go over it again. Fetching the pitcher together with three tumblers, Quarrie poured them each a glass.

'Quit asking the same damn questions, D-Lay. It was self-defense,' he said.

The detective regarded him briefly then turned to the old woman again. 'He gave you no warning at all?'

Quarrie's gaze was cold. 'She told you already. Give her a break. She's eighty years old.'

Reaching for a glass De La Martin sipped. 'All right, mam, I think we're done with the questions for now. If you didn't know he had a key then technically I guess it was breaking and entering. I'll be telling the district attorney you believed your life was in danger and I'll need a written statement, of course. That can wait, though.' He indicated the polythene evidence bag. 'We're going to hold onto that gun for a day or two but we'll get it back to you once this all checks out.' Swallowing another mouthful of whiskey he got to his feet. 'Is there someone you want me to call? A thing like this, I'm not sure you should be on your own.'

'I'll stay with her,' Quarrie said.

On the landing outside De La Martin rested a palm on the filigree rail. Briefly he peered across the courtyard to the street outside where a couple of prowl cars were parked.

'You knew about this,' he said.

Quarrie took a cigarette from his pack and tapped the inscribed end against the base of his thumb.

'Back on Camp Street you knew he was headed up here.' De La Martin turned to him. 'Was this planned? Did she know he was coming ahead of time?'

Quarrie did not say anything.

'You're a cop, John Q.'

'Not down here I ain't.' Quarrie held his eye. 'Nana was in bed. She woke to a sound in her hallway. When she called out he didn't reply.'

For a moment longer they looked at each other then De La Martin let go a sigh. 'All right,' he said. 'There's nobody to tell us any different I guess, so I'll be back tomorrow for a statement. Will you still be here or are you going to go get on a plane?'

'Depends how she is.'

The detective nodded. 'You know what this means, of course, don't you?'

'Sure, there's no witness to what happened on Camp Street.'

'That's right.' Again De La Martin looked him in the eye. 'It's what I'll be telling the district attorney when I talk to him and I'm pretty sure I know what his position's going to be. That just leaves what happened in Houston to deal with and you'll be in the clear.'

'Franklin's still out there,' Quarrie said. 'I need to take care of him.'

He watched the detective make his way down the stairs then went back inside the apartment. He stared at where the blood had dried on the floor and then at Nana where she hovered at the living room door. 'Are you sure you're all right?'

Nana stared into space. 'I told you, a man like him is above the law. It was that or nothing at all.'

They went through to the living room and Quarrie poured another glass of whiskey and passed it to her. Sitting on the couch she held the drink in both hands. Quarrie took a seat in the chair De La Martin had vacated and flicked ash from his cigarette.

'There's no need for you to stay, John Q,' Nana said. 'I'll be OK on my own. There's a shuttle to Dallas you can catch.'

'I think I should stick around.'

'I'm fine, really. If the truth be known after all these years I'm better than I've ever been.'

He looked at her askance. 'I've heard it said some folks are shaped by the enemies they face. I guess that old man's been bugging you for quite a while.'

'It's forty years since Gigi was born and that's half my life.' She sipped a little whiskey and cupped the glass. 'John Q,' she said. 'There's something I've been meaning to say to you. I . . .'

'Nana, there's no need.'

She shook her head. 'It's not about that. It's about those word games you told me your son was doing in school.'

Quarrie furrowed his brow.

'It got me thinking and it got me doodling too.' Picking up her glass again she took another sip. 'I told you how it was never *Ross* with him, it was always his full name?'

Quarrie nodded.

'Well, if you rearrange the letters in Rosslyn F Tobie, what is it you figure you find?'

'I don't know. I got no idea.'

'*Sons of Liberty*. I looked that up and it seems they were a group of copperheads back when Lincoln was trying to get the 13th amendment through. I never knew anything about it, not till I went to the library. Does it mean anything to you?'

'In point of fact, mam, it does.'

'All right then, I'll leave it with you. Now,' she said, getting to her feet, 'I've got a lot to think about and I want to be doing that on my own.'

'If you're sure.' Quarrie picked up his hat.

'I am. You can do one thing for me, though; when you get back to Texas tell my daughter it's safe to come home.'

Thirty-six

Two days later Quarrie was in his captain's office in Amarillo. Patterson was seated across the desk from Van Hanigan with his legs crossed at the knee. 'Well,' he said, 'for all of how this began and what I told you about old-school Rangering it turned out all right in the end.' He looked at Quarrie with a glint in his eye. 'The DA down there in New Orleans has accepted your statement and you're off the hook as far as the hotel room in Houston is concerned. We know that rifle belonged to Lieutenant Colback, though the serial number had been filed off. According to De La Martin the one on his wall in New Orleans was bought from a pawn shop in Baton Rouge.'

'He tossed it to me,' Quarrie said, 'fetched it from his study, same model as the one Wiley stole. Does Ali know yet, by the way?'

Patterson shook his head. 'No, he doesn't, and if I have my way that's how it's going to remain. He's a big enough pain in the ass as it is right now without us adding any more fuel.'

'What about Franklin? He's Tobie's illegitimate son and Gigi's half-brother. If you don't find him, I will.'

'We'll take care of it,' Patterson said. 'We have the resources. It's just a matter of time.'

Quarrie was quiet for a moment then he said, 'There's another thing you need to think on too. Somewhere out there is a cop who called the NCIC for Anderson's ID.'

Patterson looked puzzled. 'I thought you'd already gotten to the bottom of that.'

'You mean from the coroner's office? No, I'm talking about later on. The fact is any regular cop would have to send a teletype and there's no record of one other than what Moore and De La Martin sent so it might be you look closer to home.'

'One of ours you mean – an FBI agent? Now there's a pleasant thought.' Patterson got to his feet. 'OK, I'll deal with it. I'm headed back to Dallas now.'

*

Home at the ranch a little later Quarrie found Pious in the workshop working underneath an old feed truck that had a habit of leaking oil.

'So that old lady wasn't kidding then,' Pious said as he wiped his hands on a rag. 'About how she could handle herself if anyone tried to break in.'

'No, she wasn't and I guess somebody did.' Quarrie saw Gigi come out of the Noons' cottage with Eunice and Mama Sox. She was carrying the bag she had brought from New Orleans and walked to where her station wagon was gassed up and ready to go.

'So y'all can't persuade her to stay?'

'Not right now.' Pious followed his gaze. 'She's been through a whole hell of a lot and she and Nana got some talking to do.'

They crossed the yard and Quarrie said his goodbyes. Eunice and Mama went over to the bunkhouse leaving Pious with Gigi for a moment and Quarrie sat down on his stoop with James. One arm around the boy's shoulders, he saw Pious take Gigi's hand briefly before she got into the car.

'So she's taking off,' James said. 'That's a shame, Dad. I like her a lot.'

'Don't worry, kiddo: by the look of things over there I got a feeling we'll be seeing her soon.'

They watched as Gigi rolled the window down then backed up and waved before she took off. Quarrie glanced at Pious where he stood watching the dust rise with his hands in his pockets. Then he turned away. Lifting his son to his feet, Quarrie nodded to the large corral where a young horse was chewing at a pile of hay. 'All right, bud,' he said. 'That colt yonder Nolo picked out, it's time we got a saddle on him.'

*

On his way back to Dallas Special Agent Patterson pulled off the highway into the parking lot at Hank Miller's Diner where a car hop brought him coffee and a jelly donut. He ate the donut, dusting sugar from his fingers as another car turned in. It was driven by a young, blond-haired man with the window rolled down. He parked in the adjacent bay and for a moment Patterson looked at him then at the back seat where the walking cane lay.

'A word from the wise,' he said. 'A business is only as good as its weakest link and I'd appreciate it if I wasn't put in the position of having to make the kind of phone call you asked for again.'

Franklin did not say anything. Waiting till the car hop had come and gone with his order he reached in the glove box and brought out an envelope stuffed with cash. Patterson thumbed through the bills then stowed the envelope in his jacket pocket and looked through the windshield again. 'So the king is dead,' he said. 'Do we cry *long live the king*?'

Franklin did not smile. 'The Tobie name no longer exists. The foundation is closed and all donations have been transferred.' He looked sideways at Patterson then. 'As of now I'm working out of Columbus, Ohio, under the Cutler name.'

'So all goes on as before?'

'Of course.'

'What about the old man's death?'

'As it's been reported in the newspapers. She wasn't his mistress but an old colored woman who takes care of that apartment on Orleans Street. A little confused at eighty years old she mistook him for an intruder; unfortunate, but that's how it is.'

'And the future of the business, contracts, confidence, what about that?'

'All contracts remain in place.' Franklin glanced over the seat. 'I'm in charge now and your role will continue unless you figure you're through.'

With a smile Patterson stared at the empty highway beyond the parking lot. 'It never entered my head. In fact I have a couple of fresh subjects you might be interested in. One's working as a stable boy at Santa Anita race track in California right now. His name is Sirhan-Sirhan, he's anxious and irritable. I think you could make something of him.'

'And the other one?' Franklin said.

'Three-time loser who just broke out of the Missouri State Pen.' Twisting the ignition key Patterson started the engine. 'He's in Mexico. I'll let you know when he crosses the border. His name is James Earl Ray.'

Author's Note

In 1864 the United States government tried and convicted several 'Peace Democrats' from Ohio, Missouri and Illinois. Supporters of the south during the civil war, the men were members of an outlawed group called 'The Order of the Sons of Liberty' and were sentenced to hang before Abraham Lincoln commuted the sentences and banished them to the Confederacy.

One hundred years later on November 22 1963, a group of 'hobos' were taken off a freight train close to the spot where the assassination of President Kennedy took place. Marched under police guard to the Dallas County sheriff's office, no mug shots were taken and no fingerprints. No statements were recorded and no detective from the Dallas Police Department's Homicide Division interviewed any of them.

In January 1967 after claiming he was the victim of a 'conspiracy' Jack Ruby was due to be retried for shooting Lee Harvey Oswald, at the courthouse in Wichita Falls, Texas. He never made it to trial because he died in hospital a month before from cancer he swore the doctors had given him deliberately.

On February 2 1967 New Orleans pilot David Ferrie died of a brain aneurism in his grubby apartment on Louisiana Avenue Parkway. Already under investigation over the assassination of President Kennedy, Ferrie had twice been moved to a safe house as he claimed to be in fear for his life. The coroner's verdict was natural causes, but when District Attorney Garrison visited Ferrie's apartment he found an empty bottle of a drug called Proloid. On investigating further he discovered that an overdose of that drug would have caused the aneurism.

On April 4 1968 civil rights leader Martin Luther King was shot dead by 'lone gunman' James Earl Ray as he stepped outside his motel room in Memphis, Tennessee.

On June 5 of the same year presidential candidate Robert F Kennedy was shot and killed in a Los Angeles hotel kitchen by a disaffected Palestinian named Sirhan-Sirhan who used to work as a stable boy at the Santa Anita race track in California.

In February 1969 New Orleans businessman Clay Shaw was tried for conspiracy over the murder of President Kennedy. The proceedings took place in a Texas courtroom, with New Orleans District Attorney Garrison prosecuting. Less than one hour after the closing arguments had been heard Shaw was acquitted by the jury.

Acknowledgements

Special thanks to:

My editor, Angus Cargill, whose insight and assistance helped shape and enhance this narrative;

Lauren Nicoll, my publicist, who has been absolutely brilliant;

Sam Matthews, for all her help and assistance;

My great friend Charley Boorman, for all his support and encouragement.

The Long Count

A JOHN Q THRILLER

Can he uncover the truth before time runs out?

In the late 1960s, with America at war in Vietnam, John Q is an old-school Texas Ranger – a gun on each hip and quick on the draw. Called to the apparent suicide of a fellow war veteran, John Q suspects all is not as it seems, and very soon faces a desperate race across state as he starts to uncover just how dark some secrets can be . . .

'Sets the pulse a-racing . . . Highly recommended.' *Raven Crime Reads*

'Will appeal to all those who enjoyed . . . *True Detective*. John Q is an excellent and empathetic detective.' *Trip Fiction*

'I loved this book: it has such a subtle sense of place, the clear writing pulls you in right from the start, and its ingenious plot line is both shocking and inevitable.' Ann Cleeves on *The Long Count*, the first John Q thriller